FUN THINGS TO DO WITH DEAD ANIMALS

Egyptology — Ruins — My Life

FUN THINGS TO DO WITH AND DEAD ANIMALS

Egyptology —— Ruins —— My Life

Eden Unger Bowditch and Salima Ikram

The American University in Cairo Press
Cairo   New York

Copyright © 2018 by
The American University in Cairo Press
113 Sharia Kasr el Aini, Cairo, Egypt
420 Fifth Avenue, New York, NY 10018
www.aucpress.com

Dar el Kutub No. 26267/16
ISBN 978 977 416 849 9

Dar el Kutub Cataloging-in-Publication Data

Bowditch, Eden
        Fun Things to Do with Dead Animals: Egyptology Ruins My Life / Eden
Bowditch, Salima Ikram.—Cairo: The American University in Cairo Press, 2018.
        p.   cm.
        ISBN 978 977 416 849 9
        1. Egyptian Fiction
        2. Ikram, Salima (jt. auth.)
        893.13

1 2 3 4 5   22 21 20 19 18

Designed by Carolyn Gibson
Printed in the United States of America

Dedication

To Nathaniel and Nicholas, our patient and long-suffering husbands, who have dealt with mad writing, merry reveling, and mucky remains. Most of all, to the real Amun Ra, Cyrus the Great, our son (in every sense), our best-beloved muse, whose sage and silly spirit imbues every page, and to Chase and Cruz, who might follow in Amun Ra's footsteps, but probably only if trucks are involved.

Contents

Preface

Me, Amun Ra, age 3

My name is Amun Ra . . . and you have no idea.

You cannot even begin to imagine. Maybe in your wildest dreams you have imagined what life would be like with a mother who discovers hidden tombs and mummies, jets around the world exploring pyramids, and reads mystical hieroglyphs. Well, stop it. No, really, forget it. Why? Because that stuff you've imagined, that romantic rubbish you have conjured up in your innocent little head, it's all totally, utterly, without a doubt, wrong.

Has it really been a nightmare, you ask? The answer is simple: yes, it has. Life with Mummy is an endless series of embarrassing, unspeakable disasters. Endless. Disastrous. Embarrassing. Just think bones and mummified flesh in your kitchen. Jars of guts and bowls of entrails in your bathroom sink—that is my life. I am, at nearly fourteen, decidedly nearer to adulthood than Mummy will ever be. All I can say is that, yes, it is possible to die of embarrassment. I only pray to Osiris that she does not mummify me when I do.

"This is my son, Amun Raaaaaa," she'd say, rolling out the 'R' like it was a red carpet and I was a celebrity. Ugh. Yes, my name makes me sound like a mummy issuing an ancient curse. Unfortunately, I am the one cursed and must thus suffer a lifetime of being named after the head honcho of the Egyptian gods—like Zeus to the Greeks. That said, Amun Ra is nowhere near as cool. Instead of thunderbolts, he has two feathers sticking out of his head and is blue, like a Smurf. I can think of many times when thunderbolts would have come in handy. "*My son, Amun Raaaaaaa!*" Yes, that would be one of those times.

So, for what it's worth, my name is Amun Ra. This is my tragic tale of humiliation, and dirt, and the very smelly dead things that my mother enjoys bringing home.

– Amun Ra Marquis

1
A Dead Mouse in Every Bag

W hen I look back at my unfortunate childhood, there are two events that I cannot wipe from my mind. No one who was present will ever forget. Oh, people may try, but there are some things that burn a mark on your very soul. Both of these events involve Mum and mummies. And both happened in second grade.

I need to explain a few things to set the story straight. My life had always been divided into two parts, in two countries, on two continents, and often more than that. Cairo, Egypt (surprise! Egyptology, right?) and Washington, DC, mostly. But we have also lived in Cambridge, Massachusetts, Cambridge, England, South Africa and South America, and other places around the world. Depending on my mother's lecturing schedule, we could spend whole semesters flying back and forth from continent to continent. When we were in Foggy Bottom (yes, really, that's our neighborhood in DC), I would attend Haddful Arms Preparatory School on 17th Street, which was walking distance from home and the Smithsonian, where Mum spent most of her time.

Moving around was hectic. Very, very hectic, in fact. I would sometimes get shuffled around halfway through a semester if Mum decided that some piece of papyrus or statue or stone block was desperately important enough and needed to be seen immediately. Like it couldn't have waited for the end of the semester, even though whatever it was had been sitting there forgotten for thousands of years. I would get hauled out of class, thrown into a taxi, and stuffed into a seat on an airplane. Having friends was a challenge. Whenever a kid was passing out invitations in class, I would enthusiastically reach out for mine. More often than not, the teacher would suddenly ask me up to the desk or an announcement would come over the class loudspeaker and I would be heading for the principal's office. Mum would hurry out, waving a pair of tickets for a flight back to Egypt. End of that story: no party, no friends. Not easy. As you can imagine, kids in both schools always thought I was weird. It was as if I personally did everything I could to avoid a social life. I spent a lot of time wishing I could just stay in DC or Cairo and be like everybody else. Flip-flopping around is neither easy nor glamorous. It's a pain in the Tut.

But I was talking about those two horrible events of second grade. I shall now share a few details that may help to reveal their truly disturbing nature.

"I wish *I* could go to Egypt," Amy Dandridge said to me on the way to the principal's office. No, I was not in trouble. This was one of those times that Mum had to be in Cairo for the week, so she was taking me with her. Amy was helping me carry my art project to the waiting car. It was a papier-mâché carrot. At least, it looked like a carrot. It was supposed to be a pyramid, but my artistic skills were well below average. Every art teacher I have ever had has asked me to make a pyramid or a mummy. Most of my art-class mummies tend to look like long turds, except white. This papier-mâché pyramid just got taller and taller until it looked more like a carrot. I painted it orange to cover my failure. It was pretty big, but I could have carried it myself. That said, I did have all my schoolwork and other stuff I'd need on this trip to Cairo, so I guess it was good to have Amy Dandridge help me carry the carrot. She wasn't being nice, though, if that's what you thought. She was ordered to do it by the teacher. I paid for the favor with earfuls of the complaints, whining, and stupid girlie babblings that usually accompanied Amy Dandridge.

"You're only saying you wish you could go to Egypt because you didn't study for the math quiz tomorrow," I pointed out.

"That's not true," she lied. Amy Dandridge stunk at math. "I love pyramids."

"It's not all about pyramids," I said, rolling my eyes. "You hate dirt, and sand, and dead stuff."

That was totally true. Amy wore dresses and little frilly socks, even in middle school. She'd use a hanky to cover her face if it was windy so she wouldn't get dust on her cheeks. She carried a brush to keep her shoes free from dirt. She wore plastic bags on her feet on the playground all through elementary school. And, horror of horrors, she was at my seventh birthday party, where she cried for about an hour, swearing that she hated me forever. That's another story. Well, actually it's part of the same story. But we'll get to it in a minute.

"I forgot about the dead stuff," Amy admitted with a shiver. "And the dirt. And the sand."

Are you kidding me? It's a desert! It's made of sand! And dirt. And dead things. As far as I was concerned, no sane person would voluntarily go to the desert. Especially Amy Dandridge, enemy of dirt. And forgetting about the sand in the desert?

"You forgot about the sand in the desert?" I couldn't let that pass.

"Well, it all seems so romantic, with palm trees, and oases, and pyramids, and princes," said the pink and fluffy Amy Dandridge. I could see her imagination making her eyes glaze over.

"Romantic? Remember my birthday party?" And that was it. She stopped in her tracks. I don't know why I chose to remind her, but it worked. Suddenly, Amy didn't think it was very romantic any more. She retched slightly, clearly remembering that horrible event. She had obviously spent these last months trying to forget it. I'm sure she was not alone.

"I prefer to think of happy butterflies, and cheerful fairies, and unicorns, and rainbows," she said in a huff. She retched again, dropping my carrot and pulling her frilly handkerchief from her dress pocket to press to her lips.

I told her that I understood. And I guess I did understand why she'd rather think of all that lame stuff than my seventh birthday party. That birthday had not been pretty.

Back in December of second grade, my mother had made very special plans for my seventh birthday. I wished I could have buried myself in the Valley of the Kings and remained hidden there for centuries.

Like all loving mothers, she wanted everything to be perfect. She baked a special cake, organized special games, and made very special goody bags for all my friends. Sounds lovely, right? Well, there you'd be wrong. Dead wrong. Literally. It's not *that* Mum did those things, but *how* she did them, that still gives Amy Dandridge the retches and makes me queasy whenever I think of that day.

First, there was the cake. Have you ever been to a birthday party where no one wanted cake? It just doesn't happen, you say? Wrong again. My mother baked a cake with Swiss chocolate, vanilla bean, English toffee, whipped cream, and other wonderful ingredients. However, the cake was shaped like a mummified dead body. I am not suggesting she made a cute cartoon mummy covered in white icing. This looked like something dead. Really dead. Dead with attendant guts. She wrapped the legs in pressed cotton candy to represent the typical gauze bandages used to cover a real mummy's body. She placed a candy cane in the mummy's nose and made gray icing drip into a tiny bowl made of spun sugar that rested next to the head. From the center of the mummy spilled a pile of red licorice ropes. Around the cake were more tiny spun-sugar and chocolate bowls, and marzipan in the shape of jars.

"What's the stuff coming out of its nose?" asked Marybeth Fauntleroy, innocently.

"And the red stuff coming out of its belly?" asked Andy Landers with slightly less enthusiasm than the beautiful Marybeth.

Before I could stop her, my mother explained.

"It's just like a real mummy," she said, smiling at all the children (and their parents) while pointing at the candy cane. "We use this tool in mummification. We stick it way up in the nasal cavity, breaking through the bone and getting it deep inside the skull. We whip it around like this . . . and that is how we pull out the brains." Mum was all smiles and took the stunned silence in the room to be enthusiasm. "Over here," she continued, oblivious to the gulps and groans that were beginning to break through the silence, "the red licorice is the viscera, the intestines, the bowels." My mother looked at the intestines, her mind working excitedly. We were headed for a wreck. "Hmm, I could have used some chocolate to indicate the feces." She looked around, still smiling, continuing to point out the sugar-coated blood and guts (and thankfully the lack of feces) that she had made for me and my friends.

It was disgusting. Totally and utterly disgusting, even without feces. Even for me, and I was used to her. Feces? Intestines? No one wanted to eat it. No one except for Clay Koenig, who wanted to eat the whole head and attempted to steal a strand of the licorice intestine.

"Can we dip it in chocolate and make it real?" he asked, waving the red intestine around.

Clay Koenig has a lot in common with my friend Jake Räpane, in Cairo (I'll get to him later. Every school probably has at least one guy like them). Ugh. I grabbed the intestine—I mean, red licorice—and elbowed Clay away from the cake. Too late to stop him, I watched as he pointed to the marzipan canopic jars.

"What are those things that look like jars?" he asked, moving closer as everyone else inched away. After Mummy's most thorough and nauseating explanation, no one wanted to be near the cake, let alone eat it.

"Those are canopic jars," came her cheerful answer. She was still smiling. "It's where we keep the liver, lungs, and other organs we've pulled out of the bodies." She picked up one of the chocolate jars and opened it. A red jelly inside looked remarkably like a piece of liver.

Amy Dandridge's little sister started crying. "I hate liver." I heard Amy gag.

After everyone but Clay Koenig had declined helpings of the repulsive cake and disgusting gut-filled jars, there was a general edging toward the door, as if everyone suddenly had to leave the party early. I wasn't sure if that was a bad thing. I had mixed feelings: I wanted my friends to stay, but I was relieved that no one would be forced to engage in my mother's 'Pin-the-Internal-Organs-on-the-Mummy' game. I don't need to explain that, do I? The name says it all.

Obviously, my mother was disappointed. She asked if anyone wanted to learn "You Are My Sunshine" in ancient Egyptian. Out of a collective desire to get away from the cake, everyone agreed. This quickly devolved into a cacophony of mispronunciations, but Mummy didn't seem to notice. She sang the loudest, off-key and in her Agatha Christie accent. This highbrow accent was the result of a decade at Cambridge and spending much of her university years hanging around old archaeologists and historians, who were all as snooty and nutty as it gets. Given that she raised me and I learned to speak listening to her, my own accent is such that I always sound like a foreigner wherever I am. Even at my school in Cairo, where most kids have what I call an 'international school accent'—not quite American, not exactly British, not distinctly anything— mine tends to be slightly weirder, thanks to my mother. So, there she was, singing in ancient Egyptian, sounding like Queen Elizabeth. Yes, that was embarrassing, but at that point I was just glad she wasn't explaining how she had carved a red jelly into the shape of a kidney or boiled down red currant preserves to pour into the tiny licorice bowels so they would look like bloody entrails.

All the parents and kids had calmed down somewhat and everyone seemed to be in a slightly better mood. That usually happens when people are singing silly songs in a group. After the songs died down, families once again moved to depart. No one was angry or upset. No one was crying. No one was running for the door. Some parents were even thanking us for such an interesting and unique party. A few shuffled by in stunned silence. All this lulled me into a false sense of security.

But the worst part was yet to come. If I had known, I might have been able to stop it before it was too late. But I hadn't, and I didn't, and it *was* too late.

"Don't forget your party favors!" Mum called to all my innocent friends, bringing out a box of goody bags. She handed them out, beaming at each child, before I could stop to wonder what she had chosen to offer my friends.

There was a moment of silence as everyone opened their bags. Then I heard the girls scream. Blood-curdling, hair-raising, and full of horror. I rounded on Mummy, afraid of the answer. "What did you put in there?"

"It was a streak of sudden brilliance," she said, actually believing herself. She was still smiling as more screams filled the foyer.

"Cool!" said Clay Koenig, excitedly. It was then that I knew I was in real trouble.

I reached for a bag, although I didn't really want to look.

In each bag, my mother had placed sharp little wooden tools tied together with a red ribbon, miniature versions of those that were used for mummification; tiny rolls of cotton gauze; thimble-sized jars; a teeny sack of natron; and detailed instructions—with drawings—on how to mummify a dead mouse. Oh, and a dead mouse.

Yes, a real dead mouse in every bag. My seven-year-old friends were to have the pleasure of taking home dead mice that they could eviscerate and mummify themselves. Oh, yes, my mother had thought it would be jolly good fun to collect dead mice and make tiny tools to pull out tiny organs and strain the tiny brains out of tiny noses. Jolly good fun that! Marybeth Fauntleroy, the love of my life at the time, barely spoke to me again. She had pet mice at home. Mum offered to give her some extra natron if she wanted to mummify them, too, when they were dead. Marybeth declined. Andy Landers cried in the corner until his parents came and took him home. Clay Koenig thought it was all really cool and offered to eviscerate Marybeth's mouse (I will definitely remember never to invite Clay Koenig to anything ever again). I think the parents collectively decided to no longer allow their children to come to parties at my house. As a result, all future childhood birthday parties in America were rather lonely affairs. There were only three, though. The rest were spent either in Cairo or somewhere in the desert.

I tried to reason with her. "Dead mice, Mother? Really? In what world was that a good idea?" I was seven, and even I knew that it had been a disaster.

"What do you mean?" she asked. Honestly, she did.

"You can't give dead mice in bags to children at a birthday party!" I tried not to shout.

"You think I should have used dead hamsters?" she asked.

"No, I don't think that would have been any better," I cried.

"Would guinea pigs have been better? I'm sure I can find guinea pigs next time."

"Dead guinea pigs in party bags?" I wanted to die.

"You're right," she admitted. "We'd have to get bigger bags."

But that was not all. Spring had barely sprung when we lost Mr. Tickety-Boo. Mr. Tickety-Boo, the school bunny rabbit mascot, died three days before Second Grade Parents' Day at Haddful Arms Preparatory. He had been a fixture at the school as far back as any of us second-graders could remember (like, three years). He had endured the humiliation of tiny, bunny-sized witch's hats on Halloween, wee Santa caps at Christmas, and having the entire class chasing him at annual Easter-egg hunts. The school had inherited him from the British ambassador's daughter when she moved to France. The bunny had been with them for about six years, so he was rather long in the tooth, so to speak, when he arrived at Haddful Arms in our second-grade class. (I say 'long in the tooth' to mean really, really old. It's a real expression that really, really old people use. I'm not sure what it originally referred to, but if you have ever seen a mummy, with his lip curled back from a thousand years of a dry death, the connection between 'long in the tooth' and really, really old would be obvious—the gums shrink and the teeth show.) And before he was dead, Mr. Tickety-Boo was a great sport. He hopped around, let everyone pet him, did all sorts of sweet bunnyish things like rub his nose with his foot and nibble on carrots. And then, one day, he stopped mid-munch. This was two days before Parents' Day. It was sad for everyone. But while many students and teachers were filled with sadness, I was filled with dread. How could I keep this news from my mother? If she learned of this tragedy, my life would be over.

In first grade, Parents' Day had been great. I was staying with Roland Seymour's family, as my mother had to deliver a paper in Boston. My mother did not come to Parents' Day. She did not embarrass me and make me wish I had died in the Middle Kingdom, around 2000 BC. It was a wonderful year for Parents' Day, with visits from doctors, lawyers, electricians, chefs, and no Mummy. Literally. This year, no such luck.

Most people had normal parents. Arabella Paddington's father was a tax attorney and her mother was an economist and Max Elek's mothers were both bankers. Katie Bertrand's parents were bakers and brought cupcakes. It's true that Roland Seymour's mother was a neurosurgeon, and while the previous year she had brought a brain to school, it was in a jar and she wasn't playing with it so I'd still consider that somewhat normal. David Blanc's father was a lobbyist for the oil industry. His mother was a devoted volunteer for whatever cause was on TV that week. Most parents didn't do weird things that embarrassed their kids. In fact, all of these parents had something in common: they were parents who had regular jobs (regular for Washington, DC), jobs that other people could understand (at least in Washington, DC), and they did not cause endless painful embarrassment to their poor son who had been the victim of great misery watching his mother pull the guts out of small dead animals through their bellies.

I hid the Parents' Day notice in the back of my science folder and pretended it wasn't there. When I got home, though, I found that a curse had come upon me: Mummy was already packing natron salts and something dead she had stashed in the freezer. I tried to tell her that they had canceled Parents' Day. No luck. They had sent her word by email.

"It'll be fun," she said, rubbing her hands together. Her eyes twinkled and she smiled like a madwoman. "Now, what shall I bring?"

How many deaths can one die? Surely, more than nine. I was like several cats all put together, since I always seemed to be breathing, no matter how many times I wished that I could stop.

"Your mother is *not* in Egypt," said Miss Raptic. "And no, we can't change Parents' Day to a time when she is."

"Miss Raptic," I begged, "you really don't understand. It's not only better for me—it's safer for everyone if my mother doesn't come."

"I'm sure it will be a very nice addition to our visiting parents group. Your mother does *such* interesting things," gushed Miss Raptic, ever the optimist.

What she didn't know was that my mother had come to Parents' Day in Year

Miss Raptic
Haddful Arms, 2nd grade

Three when we lived in London, and Mrs. Snelbody had fallen suddenly ill, fainted, and had to be carried out by three other teachers directly to the school nurse. Mrs. Snelbody, too, had been warned. I had tried to warn everyone—teachers, the headmaster, other students, the bus driver—but no one had listened. After that, I had thought I'd made everything clear to my mother and that she understood not to bring anything dead to class. I was wrong. She never listens, and is always convinced that she knows best.

"Don't be silly, Amun!" She dismissed my pleas as if I had been asking for chocolate before dinner. No, strike that. She often offers me chocolate before dinner. I'm not complaining. Not about the chocolate.

On the morning of the dreaded visit, I tried once again to urge sanity from my teachers. I pleaded with them and every other member of the school staff. I pleaded against the smelly carcass that was surely awaiting its day in class. I pleaded against the presence of so much viscera, and blood, and yuck, not to mention the smell. The smell alone was deadly. But it was like speaking to a row of daisies. Everyone smiled, and nodded, and shook their heads, and swayed with pleasure at the thought of a real Egyptologist coming to class to speak about mummies. "How educational and unique," they cooed.

"It'll be cool," said Roland Seymour.

Good grief. He was just hoping that whatever Mum brought would stop all the talk about his mother's brain.

I thought to myself that maybe I could somehow lock the front door to the school or put up a sign that said "NO SCHOOL TODAY" or something . . . and then the smell hit me. My mother had arrived. And she had brought our furry little dead friend with her. But it was worse than I could have ever imagined.

"So, today I have your very own dead mascot, Mr. Tickety-Boo," said Mum. And there, at that moment, she brought out the dead rabbit, looking rather the worse for wear. There was a collective gasp. (This was, without a doubt, a collective gasp of horror, which she took to be awe.) And then she took out her instruments.

"It'll be fun," she said, smiling to a sea of innocent faces.

Fun? Who on this planet, other than Mum, would think there were fun things to do with dead animals? Especially Mr. Tickety-Boo, whom everyone knew and loved. This was not going to be good. On any level.

The former Mr. Tickety-Boo

With a smile, Mum raised the now-thawed body of Mr. Tickety-Boo for all to see. Ignoring the sobbing and gasping, she explained:

"Now, here we have our beloved dead, who gets to be transformed into an eternal being. If this were a human, we would stick a long, flexible tool with a hooked end up his nose so we could mush up the brain and then pull it out of his nostril. The proper term is *excerebration*." There was a squirming among those who had been at my seventh birthday party. Memories of the dead mice were still fresh in some minds. "As it is a rabbit," she continued, "the brain is too small to worry about, so we will skip this step."

Miss Raptic turned green and started to swallow hard at this point. I had warned her.

"Then we have to gut Mr. Tickety-Boo—*evisceration* is the proper term," continued my mother blithely. "If we left in all the internal organs, he would get gassy and explode—not a good look for the afterlife." With that, my mother pulled out a sharp, shiny knife and stood poised to disembowel our beloved mascot. There was nothing I could do. In went the knife and just stayed there, sticking up, while Mum continued her lecture. Dan Bladnov started retching. Ken Place and his twin sister, Kara, both turned green, but seemed to be mesmerized by the blood-covered carcass that had once been Mr. Tickety-Boo.

"After you remove the internal organs, you have to clean them—you need water for this—and maybe you should cover your noses when you deal with the intestines and stomach," Mum said, smiling. "We all know what happens down there." She alone chuckled and gave a knowing wink to a class in shock. And then she grabbed her shiny knife and sliced, opening up Mr. Tickety-Boo's stomach. There were a few muffled screams, which Mum did not seem to hear. Mr. Tickety-Boo's stomach, which was full of putrid green stuff that stank like . . . well, you can imagine . . . made an awful squelching sound as Mum sliced. She then started on the intestines, cheerfully noting what she was doing up there. "The intestines can be worse, as they are often full of highly digested material—you have to make sure to squeeze it out . . ." (and she squeezed it out) ". . . otherwise all you'll have is a big soggy mess in the afterlife, and who wants that, hmm?" I think she grinned and winked then, too, but by then I was looking away, trying to pretend I wasn't there.

As if she was milking a cow and not squeezing globs of bunny poop out of Mr. Tickety-Boo's intestines, she added, "No, indeed, we do not want that to be hanging around inside. Really not pleasant for eternity . . . and it really stops the desiccation (that is, drying, children) process."

It wasn't pleasant in the present, either—you could practically see the stench in the air. Nothing we had ever experienced in science class could match the odor. Believe me, bunny gunk in life is nothing like what it is in death. The fact that I had seen this done a thousand times did not make it any easier. I ran to the window, but it was too late. The horrid smell clung to the room (and to all of us in it) and would not budge.

"Would anyone like a squeeze?" she asked, offering intestine to the class.

I looked around wildly at my friends—would they still be my friends at the end of this? Would I have to leave the school and change my name (which would be fine with me, at this point)? No one moved. I think their brains were on overload and everyone was still in shock. Okay, I had to pat Roland Seymour on the back when I thought he was going to barf, but he insisted he was fine and found the science of it interesting. Maybe he did think it was interesting, but I know he was trying not to be sick. Only Clay Koenig stepped up to volunteer (no surprise), but Miss Raptic had the sense to hold him back.

"Once you've cleaned out the internal organs, or viscera, you wash everything with palm wine to disinfect and deodorize it, and then you pat it all dry with a linen cloth—that is the only type of cloth they had in ancient Egypt." My mother then, in front of *everyone*, popped open a bottle of palm wine and *took a swig* before pouring it into Mr. Tickety-Boo's abdomen, which was gaping open and oozing body juice. I think I heard Miss Raptic gasp, and maybe one parent mutter, "I think we could all use some of that wine," but I was too humiliated to really focus on anything other than the horror of my mother's manic impersonation of an ancient Egyptian embalmer. Oh, gods, why wasn't she an accountant?

"Now," my mother continued, oblivious as usual to the sea of green faces staring back at her, "after he has been patted dry, Mr. Tickety-Boo has to be filled with small natron bags and then buried in natron for about two weeks. Natron is a kind of natural salt compound found in Egypt. It's like a mixture of baking soda and regular salt. It helps to disinfect the body, and more importantly it sucks out the moisture like this— SHHHHLLLOOOOPPP," and she made a sucking sound and pretended to be getting the juices sucked out of her own body.

Nobody laughed. Nobody moved.

She didn't notice and grinned from ear to ear.

"It also removes the fat, so that Mr. Tickety-Boo will be preserved properly. Here, you can all help me make the natron bags," she said, and started handing around square pieces of linen cloth and the powdery white natron to be tied into bundles. Roland Seymour unsurprisingly was ready to work with the natron (he's a natural scientist). Clay Koenig had to be dragged away from the dead body. He was trying to look inside Mr. Tickety-Boo's mouth. Mum thought it was sweet that he was so interested and gave him extra natron. Even Ken and Kara got into the act despite still being slightly green. Miss Raptic seemed to shake off the nausea and shock, and tried her hand at a natron bag, too. Mother showed everyone how to fold the cloth squares, fill them with natron, and then twist one of the ends around the rest to tie it up. She sent me to collect the packets. I shot her looks of pleading, warning, anything to stop this horror. I tried to silently send her signals, begging her not to use words like 'body cavity' or tell people what would happen next. She smiled and nodded, as if I was sending her looks of joy and thanks. It was hopeless. With my head bowed in defeat, I dutifully brought her the natron bags.

"What an excellent job, children and Miss Raptic. Thanks for all these bags! Now we can stuff them into the body cavity, and then you can help to bury Mr. Tickety-Boo in natron. After two weeks, we'll pull him out, dust him off, put some oils on him, and then wrap him up in linen bandages, recite some spells . . . and Mr. Tickety-Boo will be a proper mummy!"

Just what every school wants, right? But wait, it gets worse.

"And just imagine, class," beamed my mother, "you can keep your beloved doggie or kitty cat forever, as long as you have proper ventilation during the first few months. You never have to be separated from anyone you love . . . and maybe you could be mummified, too!"

Oh, no. Please, no.

There was some stunned applause throughout the room. Two enthusiastic clappers, Roland Seymour and Clay Koenig. Ken and Kara Place both sat there silently with their mouths open. Their mother, the accountant, had stayed. She, too, was silent.

Arabella Paddington started crying. Her cat had died the week before. I felt so bad for her. Could there be anything worse for someone in mourning? I went over to her and apologized for my mother.

"What?" Arabella looked at me through her tears.

"I'm so sorry," I said, awkwardly waving my hand above her shoulder, not sure if I should actually touch her.

Arabella just shook her head and wept. Then she looked up at me, heart-wrenching misery on her face. "Why didn't I know about this before we cremated Scrambles, my cat? He could have been a mummy for all eternity instead of ashes floating on the Potomac!"

Miss Raptic could not speak. Her hands were raised and poised in front of her, a few inches apart. She seemed to be stuck between clapping and putting her face in her hands to muffle a scream. She kept shaking her head and stared off into the middle distance. What had she done? Surely, that thought was running laps through her mind. I had warned her. I had pleaded, and begged, and foretold this disaster. I had tried to stop it. But it was Too Late.

Needless to say, the whole Parents' Day event turned into utter chaos. The other parents were completely forgotten, not that they wanted to sit in that room and talk about accounting or running a boutique. The smell was so bad that other classrooms were being evacuated out of concern that there might be a chemical spill in one of the science labs. Of course, Clay Koenig was enjoying the stink, and guts, and viscera. Roland Seymour hadn't minded once he could get into the science of it. He thought the whole thing was totally fine, his mother's brain now long forgotten in the light of my mother's bunny mummification. Mr. Tickety-Boo was now Mr. Smelly-Gutless-Corpse-Wrapped-in-Gauze-and-Filled-with-Natron-So-He-Wouldn't-Explode. Clay asked if he could keep the mummified bunny over the holidays.

"Well, you'll have to ask your teacher," said my mother, pleased and smiling, wiping bunny guts from her hands.

Clay actually looked around so he could ask, but Miss Raptic was no longer in the room.

2
Letting Dead Dogs Lie...
Who Then Become the Life of the Party

Saqqara, Egypt, Dog Catacombs, Sixth Grade

E ight million mummified dogs. Need I say more? Sadly, I will. Eight million dead dogs, no exaggeration. And guess who found them. If you said "Your mother," you'd be right. Not a discovery that most parents make at work. But, like many parents, Mum often brought some of her work home with her.

"Mum, please, not in front of my friends," I begged. I often begged, but it never did any good.

"Nonsense," Mum insisted, carrying the carcass of a dead dog into the house.

That is the truth, the whole truth, and nothing but the sad, sad truth. That dog really was dead. Very, very, very dead. Okay, so it had been dead for thousands of years. And yes, it was more of a skeleton than roadkill, but it was still a dead dog. It had pathetic bits of hair dropping off it, and a scrappy ancient gauze bandage trailing off its dead tail, and I swear there were bugs in its eye sockets (even I could tell it had been poorly

Mum and her 8 million dog mummies Saqqara

mummified). Mum brought the mongrel home and plopped it down on the table where we were playing Scrabble. Everyone freaked.

"It's not going to bite," Mum said, picking up the skull and showing it around as if any of my friends actually wanted to look at it. "There's even a little fur stuck to this piece of scalp. And some embalming oils, see? It's the black goo seeping out of the rear of its—"

"Mother!"

This was not good. Not good at all.

This was a day that had begun with so much promise. Now it was crashing down around me like the Sphinx's beard.

The thing was this: after months of trying, I had finally talked some kids into coming over to my house. If all went right, I might even be able to call these kids friends. You don't understand how challenging it is, living on two continents and trying to have classmates who remember more than just your name. It's always the kids with the morbid sense of humor (or the ones who have a habit of picking their noses in public, or the ones who come to school with their trousers on backwards) who want to be my friend.

Finally, that very day, *real* people were coming over. Sadia, Tessa, Søren, and the twins, Salma and Rafiq. These were kids at Cairo International School. They were the kids who had social lives, who went to movies, and bowling, and hung out at the beach together, and had other friends— these kids were coming over to *my* house. It was an amazing challenge to get them to even consider it. And I did.

"There was a mummy head in your living room last time I was there," Tessa had to blurt out when we were walking over to my house. That had been in third grade. Thanks, Tessa.

"Cool," said Jake. Yeah, Jake Räpane was there, too. But I didn't count him as a *real* friend, as he's one of those weird kids who eats lunch alone. Okay, not alone. He's usually eating with me. "Totally cool."

"Not cool," said Sadia, shaking her head. Her long black hair was like a wave around her face, flowing over her shoulders as she pouted. "Dead things are not cool to have in your living room."

I couldn't agree with her more.

"I couldn't agree with you more," I agreed.

Of course, if Sadia had said that elephants should be given the right to vote, I probably would have agreed with that, too. I'd have agreed to almost anything she said. But she *was* right. Dead things in the living room are not cool.

Sadia's father was the ambassador from India. She regularly reminded everyone of her numerous homes around the globe and the fact that she owned an elephant.

Now and then she might lament, *"In the south of France, we rarely get to visit our Austrian neighbors."* Or *"I really miss my favorite lemon tree in our villa on Cyprus."* And, of course, *"When I first arrive at our home in Shanti Niketan, a truly lovely neighborhood in New Delhi, I'm greeted with excitement by my sweet Nikka Hathi, though he isn't a wee babe any more. Have I told you about my elephant?"*

The answer was always 'Yes'—she'd told everyone in the whole school about her very own elephant about a thousand times. I've seen photos of the elephant, of Sadia with the elephant, of Sadia taking pictures of herself in front of the elephant, and of the poor undignified elephant wearing a giant baby bonnet and holding a huge baby bottle in its trunk.

"I'm not sure," I'd lied on several occasions, and I did it again. "I'd love to hear about it."

And I did. If Sadia was saying it, I'd listen again and again. And I had. And I would, especially on this walk to my house. I was trying to control my excitement, so another story about her elephant might help. I had been trying to get Sadia to come over since she'd first moved to Cairo.

I remember thinking, when I first saw her, that she looked like someone out of a catalogue. She wore outfits. Yes, outfits. Like, matching items of clothing that all went together as a set. She'd have a shirt that matched her slacks or skirt, and shoes and socks and everything color-coordinated. Somehow, on her, it didn't look lame. It looked like the coolest clothes had just found their way onto her body and just got cooler. Cool matching clothes just belonged on Sadia. If I manage to get to school with two matching socks, or even two socks at all, it's a good day for me. Since kindergarten, Sadia had always seemed to wrinkle her nose when I walked by. It made me want to sniff my armpits in case I was smelly, but I soon realized it was my wardrobe that made her cringe. Unlike me, Sadia had *style*.

So when I heard her call something "not cool," my instincts were to agree.

"No way, not cool," I agreed, not exactly remembering what I was agreeing to as she shook her beautiful hair in the wind. By the time I realized that I was agreeing that stuff at my house was uncool, it was too late. "I mean, no way is there a mummy head at my house." I really hoped this was true. "Or any other head. I mean, that's not connected to a body. I mean, a living body. I mean, there's no dead mummy in my house. Or anything else that's dead. Recently or otherwise." I was rambling, but there was no stopping me now. "No way, nothing dead, because dead is bad. And not cool. No way. Totally uncool to be dead and in my living room. I mean, my mother is an Egyptologist, so we have artifacts and—"

"You have artifacts in your house?" Sadia said, looking intently right at me. I couldn't tell if she was asking because she was intrigued or distressed.

"Maybe," I said, not sure if the answer should be 'yes' or 'no.' "Um . . . do you like artifacts?"

"I like dogs," said Salma, interrupting Sadia. "I don't want a pet elephant or anything, just a little white fluffy dog. I really, really want a puppy."

"I told you to ask for one for our birthday," said Rafiq, her twin brother. "I want a dog, too."

"I did ask, like five times," said Salma.

"Dogs are great," I said, checking Sadia's face.

"I love dogs," agreed Sadia, much to my joy.

Yes! Nailed it!

"My mother said I could have a dog," I said, sighing with an honest, yet slightly exaggerated, sigh of the puppy-desperate youth.

"Oh, I love puppies! Let me know when you get one," said Sadia. "I definitely want to come over for a cuddle."

I almost fainted. I let myself pretend—for, like, nineteen seconds— that she meant cuddle me and not the puppy.

"You know I mean the puppy, right?" she said, in an obviously-I-don't-want-to-cuddle-you tone of voice.

"Oh yeah, totally," I said, wishing totally not.

Rafiq poked me in the arm. "Hey, Cuddles." He had the decency to whisper it out of earshot.

"What?" asked Salma, who had missed everything.

"We're almost there," I said, quickly cutting off Rafiq.

Luckily, by then we had arrived at my house. All seven of us. Me (cheeks blotchy and red from total private embarrassment), Sadia, Tessa, Søren, Jake, and the twins.

I kept pinching myself as we walked up to the front door of my building. This was so cool. I let myself bask in the glory for a moment before turning the lock. It's not like I had just met these guys or anything.

I'd known most of them since, like, forever. We had been in school together in Cairo since elementary school—that is, when I'm in school in Egypt, we're in the same class. Søren was the only new guy. He'd arrived the previous year. Like me, he was shuttled around the world by his mother. She was a regional officer with the World Health Organization, and, like us, they had moved around his whole life. The other guys, well, we had gone to each other's birthday parties and played together when we were small, before they all suddenly became cool and popular the minute we entered middle school. What I mean is that we were friendly before *they* all became cool and popular and *I* did not. Sixth grade was a challenge, to be sure. That's why this day was so amazing. Sadia, Søren, Tessa, Salma, and Rafiq were all in the group that was considered cool. In other words, they were way out of my league and I was trying not to blow it.

But then there was Jake.

I've known Jake Räpane since we were in preschool and he used to eat bugs. There's always a Jake Räpane or Clay Koenig character at every school. He's the guy who thinks weird, horrible, and disgusting things are cool. Jake would get sent to the nurse almost every day for sticking stones up his nose, eating the wrong kind of bugs, or doing something else incredibly stupid. Really.

I looked over at Jake, who was, at that moment, picking his nose with his little finger. Disgusting as it was, I hoped it was boogers and not stones that he was trying to dig out of there. Yuck, Jake Räpane. Why did I invite him? Oh yeah. I didn't. He was there because he always walks home with me, and it would have been totally douchey to ditch him. While I would have liked to hide, or lie, or do something to avoid him just to save myself embarrassment, I couldn't. Not without being a total jerk. I gulped down a big wad of terror. There were the cool kids. And there was Jake Räpane, with his finger in his nose up to the second knuckle. Really, dude? I wished I had been braver and just told him that I wasn't going to walk home or something.

Usually, it didn't matter that Jake followed me home. He always came over after school. But today was different. This was Thursday, a weekend night in Cairo since Friday and Saturday there's no school. And it was Games Night, too. Games Night was a tradition. Actually, it wasn't a tradition yet, but I wanted it to be a tradition. In my wildest dreams, this would be the first Games Night in a long line of Games Nights to come. I imagined how fun it would be and tried to spread the enthusiasm around the group. To my amazement, it was working. Everyone seemed to be psyched. At least, they were willing to come over. That was a start. Okay, so I promised pizza and maybe ice cream. I admit that the bribes helped, but everyone was still willing. And once they were playing games, they'd all realize how fun it was. Maybe they'd even tell all the other cool kids. Then it would become a tradition, for real. That was the plan. I had it all worked out.

I started by texting everyone the idea. I claimed that all the most famous movie stars and rock stars, even kings and queens, were all big fans of Games Night. Then I texted everyone all the games we could play.

"*Scrabble?*" Søren had played it, but couldn't remember how.

"Yeah, it's fun," I said. "It's old school. You know, retro."

'Retro' stuff was cool at that moment, so I thought I'd throw that adjective in.

"Yeah, I guess it might be fun," Søren agreed, sort of enthusiastically. At least, that's what I told everyone else. If one person was willing, then I could tell everyone else and then, pretty soon, they'd all know it was safe to think it was fun. To my enormous pleasure and surprise, it worked. Now, they wanted to come over.

So there we were, at my house. I was pinching myself and ordering pizza.

"Let's play something while we wait," said Rafiq.

Yes! It was really happening. I had Scrabble, and Quelf, and Hanabi, and Settlers of Catan all set out on the table. We agreed we'd start with Scrabble, since (I claimed) the whole cast of Star Wars played it on the set. It could be true, right?

We set up the board and were ready to play. Sadia was sitting next to me. Rafiq even winked at me. Salma was smiling at Tessa, who then smiled at me, I think. Jake Räpane did not have his finger in his nose. Everything was perfect.

So you can imagine that it was beyond an unpleasant surprise to have Mummy show up with the dead dog.

"Hello, children," she said, smiling and carrying the carcass.

"What *is* that?" asked Salma, looking disgusted. "Eeew."

Sadia looked at me, furious. "Is this what you meant by your mother bringing home a dog?"

I opened my mouth, but no coherent denial came to mind. Of course, it wasn't what I had meant.

"Of course, this isn't what I meant," I finally said.

"Look what I just dug up!" Mother cheerfully plopped the carcass right in the middle of the table.

Needless to say, I was mortified. Tessa gagged and I thought she was going to barf. Søren kept it together. Jake thought it was awesome, and wanted to hold the skull and touch the tiny piece of fluff still on it. Salma and Rafiq were either giggling or blushing, likely both. Sadia was staring at me like it was my fault that my mother was insane.

"Mum, really? It's on the dining room table," I said out of the corner of my mouth.

"Of course it is," Mum said. "I need to scrape out some of the particulates in the eye socket. Where else should I put it? This is a perfectly sized table for an autopsy."

Then Søren almost barfed. He jumped back from the table. Tessa had already left the room, probably the house, and Jake wanted to fondle the eye socket (I made a mental note to never, ever invite Jake Räpane to anything that included other people. Or eye sockets.) Salma and Rafiq grabbed their backpacks. They glared at me and left without saying anything.

Then the doorbell rang. It was the pizza guy. No one was hungry. I put the box on the table as far from the dead dog as I could get it.

"We eat on this table," I fumed, my face hot with embarrassment. "And I had friends here and we were trying to play Scrabble on this table, too. That is a dead dog. Now the dead dog is on the table where we eat and play Scrabble, so now we can't do either of those things!"

"Honestly," said Mum, taking a bite of a piece of pizza and sitting down in the seat that had once been Sadia's. She pulled out her magnifying glass, and little brushes and tools. "Don't be silly."

"I'm serious, Mum." I was begging.

"Of course you are," she said, looking through her magnifying glass at her new dead pet, "but that's your problem, not mine. Pass me that spray bottle. You all should be fascinated by this. After all, this shows you that there are more things to do with dead animals than just eat or wear them."

You all, by then, was only me and Jake Räpane.

"I'm fascinated," said Jake, taking a second slice of pizza. He had inhaled the first in five seconds. Everyone else was gone. They hated me. I knew it. Jake was excited to pick his nose and watch.

This was the opposite of letting dead dogs lie. And by dead dogs, I mean eight million of them. That's how it all started.

Four days earlier, we'd been in Saqqara at the site of the Step Pyramid. It isn't as famous as the Pyramids of Giza, but it is even more awesome because it was the very first pyramid ever built. That is, if you like that sort of stuff. Anyway, we were there and I was sure that Mum was going to be buried alive. Yes, I was. At the time, it was a terrible thought. Later, at the table that had once been surrounded by cool kids I was hoping to impress, the thought of Mum being buried in the sand was not so terrible.

The paintings in the tombs of Saqqara are still—after thousands of years—really amazingly well preserved. Even after years and years and years of digging, there are loads of locations in the area that have yet to be excavated. There are lots of Egyptologists in the world, but none as famous as Mum. At Saqqara, Mum was leading the crew of helpers and other archaeologists.

Saqqara is just outside of Cairo. Mum always liked to sleep out there overnight, even though there really was no reason she couldn't come home instead. It's not like most sites, which can be way out in the middle of the desert. She claimed that it was silly to go all the way home, since she always started digging at dawn. Ugh.

"It breaks my concentration to go home and come back," she'd say.

Personally, I prefer sleeping in my own comfy bed rather than on a bed of sand.

Things did not start well that morning in Saqqara. It was my spring holiday, and this was not where I wanted to be. Instead of skiing in the Alps, or scuba diving in the Red Sea, or doing something fun like other people in my school, I was helping to move dirt and sand, and passing Mum tools. I was like an assisting surgical nurse, only the patient was hidden under mountains of sand and had been dead for thousands of years. In the words of the Munchkin coroner in the Munchkinland of Oz, the patient was not only merely dead, but really most sincerely dead.

"It's a dog!" cried Mum triumphantly, holding up a skull. She had just climbed out of a hole that led to a huge underground system of galleries, which she had rediscovered. Mum had found the galleries marked on an old map from the end of the nineteenth century, which bore only the French words, 'Catacombes des chiens.' No one had actually seen the galleries in more than a hundred years, until my mother rediscovered them.

"It'll be fun," said Mum, when I asked why I had to go out there with her to help dig in the sand for the billionth time. Fun? You think? Hardly. We had been walking around and poking in the sand for days. Yes, days of nothing but poking in the sand. Nothing but sand. And poking.

On top of that, I had to study for my sixth-grade math test. Why on earth I'd need to know how to do long division by hand was beyond me. The abacus has been around since 2000 BC, so even those guys didn't need to memorize this stuff. So much of my twelve-year-old life seemed ridiculously useless. As you can imagine, poking in the sand and trying to memorize calculations was totally boring. Endless sandy ridges with little holes everywhere. Suddenly, Mum got excited about one of those small holes in the sand. Wow, another hole—I thought it looked like every other hole. I had found, like, a hundred and seven already. Mum pushed and prodded, and sand began pouring through the rocky crevice. The tiny hole suddenly started getting bigger and bigger. If the sand was cascading in, then there must have been something down there, right? Mum was sure it was *the* hole.

"This is *the* hole!" Mum shouted.

That's how Mum found the galleries, or rather that's how the galleries found Mum. After declaring it was *the* hole, she poked and poked. She poked some more. And then she fell in.

I took a flying leap and tried to grab her hand. I missed. In the blink of an eye, Mum disappeared, swallowed by the sand. Poof! Buried alive.

I did the only thing I could do: I yelled. I yelled a lot. I yelled when I dove and missed her hand. And then I yelled some more. Still yelling, I felt around in the sand, but the hole seemed to have closed up again. She was gone. And there I was, alone and in shock, with sand in my mouth from my dive.

I yelled and felt around until I saw the cascade of sand flowing into a crack in the ground. I crawled over to the crack, hoping that I might be able to dig her out before I fell in, too.

"Mummy!" I cried.

"I'm all right," she called.

My heart was pounding as I tried to spit out the sand that was crunching between my teeth. I leaned over the hole.

There was Mum, covered in sand, waving a skull, pointing around with enthusiasm! She had landed right on top of a pile of mummies. But not just any mummies. I shone the torch (or 'flashlight,' if you're an American) into the hole and saw something that had once been a dog.

More than one dog. Lots of dogs.

"There must be a hundred dogs here!" cried Mum.

But with the light, I could see more than she could.

"It looks more like a thousand dogs," I called down to her.

We were both wrong.

"Eight million dogs," Mum said with pride. "The team did a survey of the galleries, so now we know their area. Isn't it great? The samples make it easy to calculate the total number of occupants—see, there *is* some use for math."

That was the next morning. Mum had been up all night, too excited to sleep. And, starting at dawn, she had organized the survey.

"Make sure you take note of the occupants, Amun Ra."

Occupants? Hah. Guess who got to help count doggie skeletons?

"It'll be fun!" she said, way too cheery and way too awake for that early in the morning.

Several hours into counting skulls, I couldn't take it any more. "Mother, what does this all matter? Can't you just guess a big number and have that be close enough?"

Mum had been gazing lovingly at a skull that was in excellent shape for being thousands of years old. She looked up at me, shocked.

"Each one of these puppies was important to someone. A real person once requested each mummy, and teams of expert embalmers had to create each one," she said. "These sweet fellows barked, and wagged their tails, and sniffed, and licked, and chewed food, and pooped it out. Every one of these creatures was alive and was important to someone. They were reared specially, and given as offerings to the god Anubis, who safeguarded travelers and helped people go from this world to the next—after being mummified, of course. Each one of these little fellows has a story to tell, and I'm going to find out what it is!"

I opened my mouth to say something, but nothing came out. I knew she was speaking from her heart and she was going to count every dog, likely talking to and petting each one on its bony, dead little head. I knew she was right. These dogs were offerings, sort of like candles that are lit in a church. Having a mummy dog in a catacomb like this was like sending up a prayer, I guess, only they're dead dogs and not candles. I wasn't going to remind her that the sweet, furry dogs were probably killed so that whoever had bought one of those mummies could reach the dog-headed god. By offering the dogs as a sacrifice, the person was sending a message, like, "Hey, it's me! Make sure I get a good seat in the afterlife!" Anubis was supposed to help every person who had given him a dog mummy as an offering. He must have really liked dogs. So these dogs were not exactly pets. They had been specially bred for sacrifice, which meant that they were doomed from birth. Not a happy thought. But I guess they were killed out of love, religious belief, and what my mother would call 'a higher purpose.' But they had still been killed and were now all dead. Okay, so thousands of years later they would be dead, anyway, but all of these guys did not die of natural causes. But none of that mattered to Mum.

They were dead. And I had to count them. All of them.

Thanks, Anubis.

3
A Camel Ate My Homework

I believe it was Clement Attlee who served under Winston Churchill," I answered. "Here's the scale ruler."

We were in a rocky overhang somewhere in the middle of the eastern Sahara Desert. I was helping Mum on a dig near Kharga Oasis. Mum was helping me study. In two days I had a really important semester exam for my sixth-grade social studies class, and I was not prepared. I wanted to stay in Cairo and study with the twins. Salma and Rafiq had invited the whole class to come over to work as a study group. Neither of them was great at social studies. Or any other class, for that matter. This exam, and the big math, science, and language arts exams, were really important because they were placement exams for next year's seventh-grade classes. Salma and Rafiq's mother was trying to get them some help so they wouldn't fail. She had hired a fancy chef to serve pizza and pasta, made to order, for anyone who came over to study history with her kids. Yes, I know that pizza and pasta have nothing to do with history, though I have read that Thomas Jefferson brought pasta to America, long before Italian immigrants made it a big thing. And, of course, here in Egypt, I have heard that it was really the Arab traders who first brought pasta to the Italians. Apparently, the Arabs carried dried noodles through the desert and boiled up pasta dinners whenever they stopped to camp. They're given credit for linguini, and spaghetti, and cup noodles, but I've also heard that the Chinese traders who came to the Red Sea ports originally brought noodles to the Arabs. Whatever—we now have pasta, and we all love it.

Anyway, my plan was to stay out of the desert, eat huge amounts of pizza and pasta with my classmates, and memorize the US presidents and other world leaders. But Mum had other plans. She wanted me on this dig because she thought I'd enjoy some fresh air out in the desert. But I really wanted the fresh pasta and homemade pizza.

"You can have pasta in the desert," she suggested. "We can bring cup noodles."

"Like the old Arab traders?" I asked.

"Arab traders liked cup noodles?" Mother asked.

For someone who knows so much about ancient history, she sure doesn't know much about noodle history.

"Look, it doesn't matter," I pleaded. "This is really, really important and I really, really want to stay. I need to study. Really."

Just as Mum was starting to come around, Salma got chicken pox. And then Rafiq got sick, too. The study session was canceled. No pasta. No pizza. Since there were no other excuses I could think of for staying out of the desert, I had to go.

Mum promised to help me study. We had plenty of time that weekend, since there were two unexpected extra days off from school that week. Unexpected days off happen a lot at my school in Cairo. Holidays in Egypt are hard to map because they are never on exactly the same day every year. It's a lunar calendar thing. Anyway, I couldn't argue with Mum. I foolishly agreed.

So there I was, again, sitting on a pile of rocks, handing Mum tools, trying to remember who came when in British and American history, and wishing I was somewhere else doing something else. Mostly I was wishing I was somewhere else. The studying was not going well at all. What a holiday.

"Okay now, where were we . . . ?" Mum said for, like, the ninth time. "Oh, yes. Which president came after Millard Fillmore?" she said, abandoning Britain for the moment. She finished peering at a shard of pottery sticking out of the sand, and moved over to stare critically at rock engravings of giraffes. My study sheet was balanced between a piece of pharaonic pottery and a stone tool that was likely over 8,000 years old. The dead presidents seemed practically alive next to this ancient dead stuff. Still, what had she asked? Millard Fillmore? I racked my brains.

"Um . . . ." I was trying to think, but it was hard. The stone I was sitting on was poking into my bum. The wind picked up and sand was getting into everywhere. I mean, everywhere. Plus, Mum was finding some amazing stuff. It was distracting me from focusing on the old dead guys whose names I couldn't quite remember. The giraffe engravings were really cool. Some of the giraffes were on leads held by naked men. Don't ask me why so many people were naked in these old engravings. I guess clothes weren't that big a deal back then. I was glad I had trousers between me and the stone, even if my pants were filled with sand. "Um . . . he came after Zachary Taylor, right?"

"Who?" Mum was also focused on the giraffes.

"Taylor, the general," I said. I thought I was right, but I wasn't sure.

"There was a President Taylor?" she asked, clearly no help at all.

"Yes, Zachary Taylor, the giraffe," I said.

"The what?" Mum looked up. "Did you say 'giraffe'?"

"I mean, the naked general," I said, looking at the carvings. This was impossible.

"The who?" Mum was distracted, too.

"The general! Zachary Taylor was a general," I said, passing her a smaller brush. "And then he was the president."

"Okay," Mum said, looking at the paper. "Who came after Fillmore?"

"Oh, *after* Fillmore." I was stalling. Taylor, Fillmore, and someone else totally unimportant.

"Fillmore was followed by . . . ."

It was then that I saw the tiny scorpion crawling up her arm. Talk about distracted.

"Please don't move, Mother," I said very softly.

"You called me 'Mother,'" she said, frozen in place. "That means a scorpion? Or perhaps a—"

"Shhh," I begged.

"Ah, scorpion," she said softly, still motionless.

It was small, that scorpion. A baby, no longer than a knuckle. But don't let size fool you. We all know that Pokémon is short for 'pocket monster'—and they have power, no matter what size.

This was a real pocket-sized monster, though, and you wouldn't want this monster in your pocket. That little green creepy-crawler packed a painful punch. In general, contrary to popular belief, baby scorpions are not ten times more poisonous than adults. Tiny scorpions do, however, have the same amount of poison as big adult scorpions, so I suppose they must produce more venom for their size.

Scorpions are considered to be the stuff of nightmares and scary movies. Sorry, folks, what you think you know is likely fantasy and fiction. Real scorpions, I hate to tell you, are utterly unlike the massively creepy, glowing-eyed, monstrously deadly scorpions invented for thrillers. Real scorpions are not evil. True, they are creepy, but they don't intentionally sneak into the beds of unsuspecting sleepers in order to scare them to death. In real life, people don't drop dead from the mere sight of a scorpion waving its spiky tail. Well, maybe *some* people drop dead from fright, but that's just stupid. And people don't die in agony the second a scorpion stings. Honestly. The fact is . . . well, dying takes time. And not everyone dies, necessarily.

Okay, I'm not making this sound any better.

"Don't frighten it," Mum said.

As if that was my plan. Everyone knows: don't scare a scorpion. Most people are scared of scorpions, but when real scorpions attack it's because they're the ones who are scared. And, sadly for lovers of the extraordinary, *most* scorpions are actually relatively harmless. If you didn't notice, there was an emphasis on '*most*.' Most are harmless, with hardly enough mild poison to cause much of a welt . . . , but not the one that was crawling up my mother's arm.

This one was bad. Very bad. I knew immediately what kind of scorpion it was from its bright green coloring and the dark spot at the end of its tail. It was a deathstalker. If the name didn't give it away, you should know that it is the most poisonous scorpion in the region—maybe in the world. It's in the *Burthidae* family, which has nothing to do with anything except that I know that fact. But to the point, even the deathstalker won't kill you. At least, not normally. Not most people. But a sting hurts like hell and can make you pretty frickin' uncomfortable and sick. I know—I've been stung.

"Remember the time you were stung, Amun Ra," said Mum. "Let's not do that again."

"Thanks for reminding me, Mum," I said. "Like I could ever forget."

When I was eight, Mum had thought it would be fun to sleep outside at the Kharga Oasis near the fully intact tomb she had been excavating. We were there for hours and hours working, and I was exhausted. I remember that my eyelids kept drooping while I was holding the torch for Mum. I tried resting one eye, then the other. Then Mum let me go to sleep.

But that was when the cricket started chirping. It chirped and chirped, and I was getting really annoyed. As tired as I was, I couldn't sleep with the noise. The thing was making its racket somewhere by my left ear. Yeah, people get romantic about crickets singing, and everyone loves the Disney versions of crickets and all that. But this cricket was driving me nuts.

I went to hunt it down with very unfriendly thoughts in my head. But when I caught the thing, it chirped in my hand, which was surprisingly cute. It was probably trying to get me to like it. I admit, it was doing a really good job. I considered bringing it home and making it my pet. I imagined training the cricket, keeping it in a small wooden cage, and naming it Jeffrey. I was suddenly feeling much more loving toward crickets. And I wasn't the only one.

Deathstalker scorpions, as it happens, love crickets, and one had crawled up my leg, then down my arm and into my palm, while I was listening to Jeffrey. Scorpions don't have very good eyesight. Aiming for Jeffrey, the scorpion missed and stung me on my pinkie. Jeffrey jumped off my hand and got away. The pain was unbelievably bad, like someone had stuck hot pokers into my hand, and then electrified them, and lit them on fire.

What came next, I admit, was rather dramatic—a lot like what you see in films. My whole body was on fire. Fever, convulsions, eyes rolling back in my head. That's all I remember. Well, that and the sound of Jeffrey chirping loudly somewhere near my left ear again. While I have never claimed to speak cricket, as I lay there in agony I knew he was laughing at me. That was right before I passed out, and had to be rescued by a special army helicopter and taken to a hospital in Cairo. My mum always carried anti-venom in her first-aid kit. That's fine for an average scorpion sting. As we now all know, however, the deathstalker isn't your average scorpion. I did say that even deathstalkers are *normally* not deadly, but sometimes they make an exception. Small children are an exception, and, at the time, I was small.

"I remember," I said to Mum now. "And this guy is not going to get you."

There we were, at the tomb, just Mum, the scorpion, and me. And of all the scorpions Mother could have running up her arm, it had to be a deathstalker. Obviously, this being my second close encounter with one of those little green monsters, I was totally freaked out. The thought of having to administer anti-venom to Mother and call for a medevac helicopter was really making me queasy. I kept it together because running around screaming (which is what I really wanted to do) would have just freaked out the scorpion, and that would have really been bad. I had to think quickly and, I must say, that is exactly what I did.

"Be careful, Amun Ra," warned Mum. "Don't squish it."

Really? That was the worry? To be fair, I couldn't risk squishing it because it might sting. But my mother doesn't like squishing living animals, not even scorpions. She claims we're in their territory and should respect them. She loves scarab beetles, for example. You may know them as dung beetles, their less exciting name. 'Scarab' obviously sounds much cooler. The famous scarab beetle—the kind you always see in ancient Egyptian art—yep, that scarab is really a dung beetle. The ancient Egyptians had a whole thing about the dung beetle rolling giant balls of dung around, reminding them of the sun and Ra, the sun god, rolling across the sky. As for how they made the leap from dung ball to giant hot flaming ball of gas in the sky . . . ha ha, very funny—dung, gas, I get it. All I know is that I'd be a rather grumpy sun god if an entire civilization compared me to a dung beetle. Anyway, Mum loves them. She loves all creatures. I've seen her lecture kids on the importance of the 'live and let live' philosophy, how the ancient Egyptians revered the scarab beetle, and how cool it is that the scarabs roll dung balls (and they really love those dung balls. They eat the balls and lay their eggs in them, then the babies scuttle out of them. It's really all dung, all the time, for scarabs). And while I guess I can see the charm of scarabs and dung balls, I find it hard to respect a creature that wants to poison my mother with its stinger. Yes, I know I've said that scorpions don't *want* to be monsters or intend to do creepy things, but they are and they do.

"I'm being careful," I said as I carefully slid my study notes away from Mother and quickly folded the page into a funnel. I placed the big opening in front of the little green monster.

This particular scorpion was getting ready to aim and fire its stinging tail. And Mum was the nearest thing to sting.

Okay, let's process this for a moment. I'm all for the idea of live and let live, but being honest . . . I wanted to squish it. I wanted to squish it into a gooey glob. But given the circumstances, it was too dangerous. Instead, I had to find a way to coax the scorpion into the paper funnel.

And then I saw it. Right there, sitting on a piece of pottery, helplessly ignorant of its impending doom, was another cricket. Not the adorable Jeffrey, who had once laughed at my misery, but a plain old anonymous cricket who, to a certain creature on my mother's arm, looked like lunch.

Mum showing me yet another dung beetle

I hesitated for a moment. Then, remembering how Jeffery had just sat laughing at me and had left me to die from scorpion venom, I grabbed the cricket, tossed it into the funnel, and gently placed it near the scorpion. Alas, this meant certain doom for the cricket, as the scorpion took the bait. I quickly folded the open end of the paper and tossed it safely over the ledge. Or so I thought.

Unfortunately, for the scorpion (and the cricket) the adventure was far from over. The paper flew over the ledge and landed next to a resident camel. The camel noticed the strange projectile passing over his head and landing at his feet. And then he did what any camel would do: he ate it. He ate the paper funnel—scorpion, cricket, and all. Unfortunately for me, the paper funnel was made of my homework. I watched as everything I needed to know about Ulysses S. Grant, or Millard Fillmore, or Richard Nixon, or Winston Churchill was gobbled up, soon to be headed for rumination in the four different compartments (count them!) of that camel's stomach. I watched helplessly as my study notes became cud.

It was barely dawn in the Sahara, and the day was already sucking lemons. I imagined coming to class next week, and excuses ran through my head. "A camel ate my homework!" Was that what I was reduced to?

"What president came after Millard Fillmore?" Mother asked, as if nothing had happened.

The camel belched. It didn't have the answer, either.

So much for the homework!

4
A Trip Through the Museum of Death

A ll I have to say is this: Beware the Narmer Palette. Yes, a piece of stone from the end of the thirty-first century BC can still wreak havoc and bring misery thousands of years later. The Narmer Palette was, indeed, the cause of a dreadful event.

What was this dreadful event? Who allowed it to happen? Whatever you do, don't blame me. *Someone* thought this was a good idea. *Someone* wasn't thinking of the terrible consequences of allowing a crazy woman to expose the secrets of the Narmer Palette. And I mean expose. *Someone* was supposed to be a voice of reason and protect those of us who were entrusted to his care. I'll tell you now, it wasn't me. I tried to warn everyone, but no one listened.

As I explained earlier, when in Cairo, I was a student at Cairo International School. The students are from all over the globe and the teachers are brilliant, the best of the best. So, how did this happen? Don't look at me.

We got the news when we were in class that morning.

"How many of you have been to the world-famous Egyptian Museum?" asked Mr. Smithzerr, my homeroom teacher, looking around the class.

Many of the international kids had gone with their parents, but surprise of surprises, almost none of the Egyptian kids had ever been there.

"We went when we were small," said Rafiq, "but I only remember the mummies."

Not me. I knew that place, wall by wall, hall by hall. I knew every glass case and every wooden shelf. I knew where all the crazy stuff was because my mum was likely the one who found it. And so I knew the awful possibilities that awaited me there if I ever went with, say, my seventh-grade class. Fear was mounting. I knew what was coming.

"It's an amazing place," said Mr. Smithzerr. Did he wink at me? Did he think that I was going to condone the idiocy that was clearly headed my way? "You're all in for a special treat." And yes, he smiled and winked at me again. That could only mean one thing.

Mr. Smithzerr mistook the look of horror on my face for pleasant surprise. Teachers can really be blind to silent messages of alarm and signs of mortal distress.

"Madame Shoukry, your Egyptian Culture teacher, has arranged for a very special field trip next week." *Here it comes*, I thought. Mr. Smithzerr smiled at the class.

No, it couldn't be. Please, no. I could feel the sweat on my brow. No, no, no . . . Not another wink. Not another misguided attempt to bond with me over something that only promised to ruin my life. How could he be so cruel?

Let me stop here for a moment and say that Mr. Smithzerr was one of my favorite teachers ever. He won 'Favorite Teacher' in every survey. He was awarded 'Most Beloved Teacher Ever' by the school that year. He was known as an awesome listener, firm but fun in the classroom, and as an all-round great guy. He was famous for his fairness, wisdom, and ability to soothe even the saddest student. But not this time. I promised myself that I would retract my vote if he suggested the thing I feared he was about to suggest.

"We are very lucky that Amun Ra's mother is going to give us a private tour of the Egyptian Museum."

Mr. Smithzerr had clearly decided to forget the incident earlier in the semester when parents were asked to send in photos for a student collage. Mum sent photos of me assisting her with an evisceration. There I was, with a forced smile, holding the entrails of an unfortunate goat. I begged him not to include the photo. Considering the amount of blood and guts on show, he gladly agreed. Instead, he included another photograph from Mum, in which she was pretending to stick a hook up my nose and pull my brains out through my nostril. Good fun, right? And that photo greets me every time I enter the classroom. It's there next to Zein's photo on the football pitch, Gabby's photo baking cupcakes, Hoda with her cat, and everyone else doing things children are supposed to do. Thanks, Mr. Smithzerr.

"Mr. Smithzerr," I pleaded, my hand in the air, waving like a drowning man begging to be saved. Saying Mr. Smithzerr's name always made me feel like I was calling him 'sir,' since his name sounded like 'Smith, sir.' At that moment, I really wanted to add an extra 'sir' for emphasis. But 'Mr. Smithzerr, sir' felt like overkill. I was trying to save my life, not sound like an idiot in a Dr. Seuss story.

"Please, just call me Amun," I said for the umpteenth time. "And, um, maybe having my mother give the tour isn't the best idea." I could feel my unpopular, lonely life coming at me fast. It was a life of never again having any friends—except for guys like Jake and Clay—ever, as long as I lived.

Letting my mother loose in the Egyptian Museum would not be pretty. Would you let a monkey loose in a banana farm?

I then began to silently plead, aiming my silent pleas at Mr. Smithzerr: *Oh, dear Mr. Smithzerr, please demonstrate the wonderful ability to listen that you are famous for, oh, favorite teacher of mine, Mr. Smithzerr, sir!*

My fingers were crossed, but my heart fell as he replied.

"I think it's a fine idea, Amun—no one knows the museum better than Amilas Marquis," he said, using the voice that we all knew meant "That is that, end of discussion, no arguing."

I argued.

"But . . . but . . . it might be better to just go on our own," I suggested. "I can give the tour myself."

"That's a fine offer, Amun Ra—I mean, Amun," said Mr. Smithzerr, clearly feeling he could win me over by adjusting my name. "But I think your mother will have a lot to share with the class."

Wisdom? Fairness? Come on, Mr. Smithzerr, what happened to you? Have Mum share with the class? Oh yes, indeed. My mother would share things with the class . . . things that would haunt their nightmares. And all of my days.

The Egyptian Museum is, let's be honest, amazing. It has the largest collection of pharaonic artifacts on the planet. I think. It feels like it, anyway. On display, and in storage, is an incredible collection of mummies, papyri, coffins, sarcophagi, statues, reliefs, paintings, pottery jars, wooden objects, make-up holders, furniture, jewelry, and even food. Bread, cakes, and even steaks have been preserved for thousands of years. Room upon room hold incredible and unexpected treasures, as well as humble objects used by the ancient Egyptians in their daily life. There are wigs from thousands of years ago! Big black wigs that look like someone had a seriously frizzy hair day (over the years, they've expanded to a ridiculous mass from centuries of humidity). There are pots that contained food and drink, stone vessels that held precious oils and perfumes. Tables, beds (the first ever fold-up camp bed), and footstools. There are chairs that look like they come from Tiffany's art deco collection. Well, I guess all those famous designers copied the furniture from ancient Egypt. It's weird because the whole world thinks of Egypt only as pyramids and mummies. Sure, that's part of the story. But there are other really shockingly beautiful things that no one would think came from the ancient world. Not that *I'm* really into any of that, but the museum will knock your socks off, if you are. However, you would do well to beware. There are some things in that museum that I wish had remained buried or stayed locked in tombs for another millennium. I'm not talking about curses or evil spells. Not exactly. I'm referring to items that no kid should have to see, especially if his mother is the one showing it. Yep, with all that stuff in the Egyptian Museum, I could think of only one thing: the dreaded Narmer Palette.

"Mum, we really need to go through a few rules before tomorrow," I finally said, as we sat at the table.

This was the night before the field trip. After dinner, during which I plotted silently, I had claimed to be running a fever. Also, to have a toothache, to have kidney failure, to need another appendectomy, to be about to suffer spontaneous combustion, but my mother was having none of it.

"You're fine," she said, scraping the crusted sand from the teeth of yet another dog skull. We still had hundreds of them, carefully packed in boxes in our living room. She handed me a toothbrush and a dental pick, and I started brushing and scraping, as well.

As I scraped, I knew it was a lost cause. Not the scraping, but the begging. We were going to the Egyptian Museum and my mother was going to be the guide. Fine. I was resigned to Mr. Smithzerr abandoning me to my fate and letting my mother lead a tour of the museum. Even if my life was about to end in an embarrassing mess, I decided Mum and I could at least agree on some rules. I had made a list, just in case feigned illness, war, or natural disaster did not save me.

"Mummy, I need you to listen. This is serious stuff," I said firmly while she shoved a brush up the dead dog's nasal passage. "You must promise that under no circumstances will you discuss, elucidate, point out, or otherwise bring attention to the Narmer Palette or anything it contains."

"What are you talking about, Amun?" Mother really had no clue. How could a woman so clever be so utterly thick?

"Can we just avoid it?" I asked, trying to look as pathetic as possible.

"Avoid the Narmer Palette?" She looked at me as if I was insane.

I gulped. "Um . . . yes."

"No," she said, crushingly, "don't be silly—it's the most important object in the study of Egyptian art, and also a key object to understanding Egypt's early history, you know that!"

"But Mum . . . ," I tried, "can't we at least establish some ground rules about details that you might want to share?"

"Details? But one must pay attention to details." She reached for a dog pelvis that she placed next to the corresponding spine. "I don't know what you're getting all huffy about. Now, let's try to sort some of the male dogs from the females. The easiest way is by seeing if they have a baculum."

"A what?" I asked, distracted by my attempts to think of another plan of action.

"A penis bone—you know, like this." She held up a bone that was about three inches (7.5 centimeters) long, tapering at the ends, with a little groove down the middle, like a gutter or runnel. I stared at it, feeling the shattered pieces of my entire social life slipping away. She handed it to me. "Come on, Amun Ra, I want to finish Gallery 17 before bedtime!"

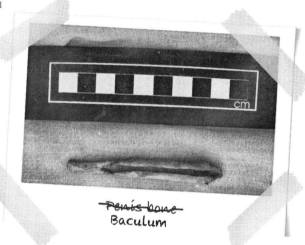

~~Penis bone~~
Baculum

I looked at the dog penis bone in my hand. I was doomed.

The next morning, I claimed to have a wicked stomachache. This was not a lie. I actually did. I was sick to my stomach as I thought of what was coming on that field trip.

"Nonsense, Amun Ra!" said Mother, pulling toast from the toaster. "You just inhaled too much dead dog dust! Blow your nose, drink some water. You'll be fine. You don't want to miss our big day at the museum!"

Oh, yes, I did.

"But . . . I may vomit," I said, looking down at the toast on my plate.

"I'll bring a bucket," said Mother.

"It's not funny," I croaked.

"What do you mean?" she asked, looking under the sink for a bucket. "I ran out of airplane sick bags."

"Never mind," I groaned.

"Eat your toast, it will help." Unable to find a bucket, she looked at me with sudden sympathy. "You're just excited about today. We all are."

I ate the toast. It did no good.

We met the class at the gate of the museum. At least I was spared a ride on the bus with Mummy. I could only imagine what fun that would have been. It would have given her an extra forty-five minutes of a captive audience, preparing them for what they would see. Thank the gods for that reprieve. One small victory for me.

Before we entered the museum, we sat in the garden outside. Mummy gave a mercifully short introduction to the history of Egypt. Everyone in my class took Intro to Ancient Egyptian Culture back in fifth grade and we were now taking Egyptian History, so my classmates were somewhat familiar with most of what she said. Mr. Smithzerr beamed with pride at his clever class. They knew so much, he thought. Oh, foolish innocence.

As we walked toward the entrance, Mummy suggested that we sniff the blue lilies in the museum's pond, as the ancient Egyptians are shown doing this in many paintings and carvings. Obediently we all lay on our bellies at the edge of the pond and bent down to sniff the sweet-smelling flowers. "Marvelous!" exclaimed Mummy. "Do you know why these flowers were so important to the ancient Egyptians, and why they sniffed them?" Alas, she did not pause for breath but went on. "They are mildly hallucinogenic, and the ancient Egyptians who were sniffing them were trying to alter their state of mind, much like people do today."

Mr. Smithzerr almost fell into the pond.

"Of course," Mum continued cheerfully, "the Egyptian lily is also linked to the sun god; the flower rises out of the water with the sunrise, and as the sun sinks the flower goes back underwater. Thus, it was a symbol of the sun, and rebirth, and resurrection. And of getting high or lit, of course, just as you all almost did!"

Mr. Smithzerr looked less cheerful.

Then we went inside.

"Maybe we want to go over here," I suggested, trying to drag Mummy off to the right. No luck.

'Well, let's start with the basis of Egyptian art," she began, heading for the dreaded glass case.

I pointed past the case. "Maybe we want to walk down to the—"

"Amun," said Mr. Smithzerr, "it's not like you to interrupt." He gave me the finger-to-the-lips shushing motion.

"But . . . ."

He did it again. Finger-to-lips, the symbol of my fate. At that moment, all hope was lost.

"This is the artifact that sets the stage for the next three thousand years—the Narmer Palette!" Mummy announced with great enthusiasm, her arms open, inviting all to come and see. I tried to block people from getting nearer, but it was no use. The class had followed Mummy straight into the central room, and now she was pointing to the very glass case that contained greater horrors than any dungeon. No ancient weapons or implements of torture could cause me more pain than this single artifact was about to inflict. Sure, from afar it seemed innocent enough. It was nothing more than a large carved piece of stone. Or was it? I knew better.

"Palettes were used by the ancient Egyptians to grind up make-up," Mum went on. So far, still safe. "There was malachite for green eye shadow, red ochre for rouge and lips, and galena as kohl."

"So ladies wore eye shadow in ancient Egypt?" That was Farah Bakri. She, Danya Sherif, Nancy Guirguis, and Dalia Dalal were the group of

Narmer Palette

Egyptian girls who sort of ran the social scene in our year. They were from the richest families in Egypt and had the most outrageous social events and parties. In fourth grade, Dalia had boat races in her indoor/outdoor pool for her tenth birthday. Danya's parents rented the Ritz Carlton for her 'Back to School' party last fall. Farah's family owned a small seaside village, where they regularly brought Farah's classmates for weekend getaways. Nancy's parents owned half of Cairo, vineyards in France and Italy, and five private jets. She and the other girls would fly to Paris for the weekend so they could shop. Wearing make-up was their area of expertise.

Mummy beamed. "Both men and women wore make-up."

"In public?" asked Mr. Smithzerr, quickly regretting the question.

"Do you mean *real* men?" asked Dalia.

Real men? Did she mean manly men? Or did she think men were different back in ancient Egypt? Men in Shakespeare's time wore make-up. The kings of France wore make-up. Men in Western countries can now wear make-up without anyone batting an eyelid. In this part of the world, at least in modern times, men were men, women were women, and there were very clear rules that went with each—and make-up was for actors or women..

"Of course, both real men and real women," said Mummy, thinking this was a joke.

The girls exchanged a derisive smirk.

"You mean, like, on Halloween?" asked Danya. Halloween in ancient Egypt? Was she serious? I'm not even going to honor that idiocy with a comment.

"And that was used for make-up?" asked Nancy, moving closer to the palette.

"Maybe we should move on to other things," I suggested. "There's so much to see. Perhaps in a different room. Or maybe on another floor. There are more make-up things upstairs."

"This particular palette is elaborately carved," said Mummy, ignoring me. "It wasn't used for everyday life, but was given as an offering in a temple. Probably King Narmer, whose name is carved on it, gave it as a gift to a temple dedicated to the god Horus, at the site of Hierakonpolis. The palette has two sides: one with the big figure of a king, and another with lots of other things going on."

It was the other things that worried me. I thought quickly and decided that if I could wedge myself in against the glass no one would be able to see it properly. I tried to move closer, but I kept getting elbowed in the stomach by Farah and her crowd. Danya stomped on my foot when I tried to get in front of her. They were being pushy because they thought this was about cosmetics, and that was their turf. There was no way I'd keep them from anything actually related to ancient lipstick and eye shadow.

I was running out of time. Panic was setting in, and I needed another solution fast. I considered falling down and foaming at the mouth, but I wasn't sure how to fake it. And the small bit of sanity left in my head noted that a foaming-at-the-mouth fit wouldn't help my social life, either. Perhaps I could have spoken to the guards, suggested my mother was an imposter—maybe a kidnapper—and insisted that they arrest her immediately. The guards, however, all knew Mum. If there was a new guard, I considered, maybe I could convince him. But then, I reasoned, if there was a new guard and I did get him to arrest Mother, I'd wind up as a ward of the state, or be sent to live abroad, or something worse. No, I had to find another way. Perhaps something magical would happen. Maybe an earthquake or another revolution. Perhaps the museum roof would fall in, and that would put me out of my misery. And then, horror of horrors, I suddenly realized that Mother was still talking. I looked around. No one had fainted. No one was staring at me as if I was to blame for something my mother had said. She clearly had not gotten to the dreaded point.

"So, the lines that divide the scenes are called registers," she continued, "and all the action happens on those lines if the person is important. See the lines? That's if the person is Egyptian, or a good person or important, like the king here." She pointed to the large figure of King Narmer. "If not, the figures are higgledy-piggledy, like the king's enemies. See, they're all placed literally under the king's feet," she said, pointing to carvings of two small men flailing about under Narmer's feet. "Remember, the king or the most important person in the scene is depicted as the biggest. This becomes standard in art dated after the Narmer Palette. Now, see this image, with the king holding his kneeling enemies by the hair and smiting them? As we go through the museum and look at the images, you'll see that this becomes a common way of showing the power of the king, and his ability to protect the country and to defeat Egypt's enemies. It's a very strong and evocative image."

Mother grabbed Danya's ponytail and pulled it up. Danya yelped. A moment of pleasure for me; Danya had spent much of first grade pulling my hair. Mother loosened her grip. "Sorry, dear, but that's what we're seeing. The king is smiting them." And mother mimed hitting Danya on the head with an imaginary weapon. Danya screamed. I shut my eyes.

Perhaps this had gone too far. "Oh, sorry, dear, I didn't mean to startle you—your hair is lovely and long and perfect for the smiting scene," said Mummy brightly. Danya smiled. She liked being the star, even if she was pretending to be murdered.

"Now, on to the other side!" Mother gestured to the class to move over to the other side.

"Is it more about make-up?" asked Omar Amin, who was interested in almost nothing that wasn't football. He was totally bored with the idea of make-up.

"Oh, no," said Mother with a twinkle in her eye. That twinkle was like a knife to my gut. "This is something you'll find *much* more interesting."

"I think I need medical attention immediately," I groaned.

No one listened. Good thing it wasn't true! I bowed my head like someone waiting for the axe. *Go ahead and chop*, I said to myself.

"Here, the center has two serpopards," Mother explained. "Mythical creatures that are lions with serpent necks. These two symbolize the unification of the north and south of Egypt by King Narmer. You remember that the north is Lower Egypt and the south is Upper Egypt, because the Nile flows south to north?"

There was a collective mumble of assent. Everyone knew that.

"And again," Mother continued, "below them are enemies being menaced by the king, who has taken the form of a bull—see, he has a register line, a line that acts as his base or ground, and divides the scenes into different registers or parts. And in the upper register, we see a marvelous scene!" She clasped her hands together and looked fondly at the palette. I started to slowly move away. Maybe I could make a run for it? I tried to step back from the rest of the class, but everyone had moved closer. I was trapped.

"See, there's a line of figures going toward a boat. Can anyone point out the king?" Mother looked at the class, smiling.

Jake pointed to the largest figure in the group.

"Well done, Jake!" gushed Mummy. "Now, if you look at these figures near the boat, what do you see?"

Once again, Jake was at the forefront. "There are a bunch of guys lying down with their heads cut off. That's cool!"

Everyone moved in closer. Even Omar.

This was it. This was the very thing I feared most in the world. As if time was standing still, I pondered the strange feeling arising within me as I met my doom. There's an odd sense of calm that comes with the end. You've done all you could do to save your own life, and now it's too late. There I was, wedged between the girlie girls and the rest of the class. I could neither move forward nor run away. My mother's voice, like an executioner's axe, rose above the crowd.

'Yes, those are the king's enemies," she said. "But that's not all. Look carefully at these figures. Do you notice something about them? Not all of them are the same."

Jake leaned forward, oblivious to my impending doom, like a jackal moving in just before the kill. "Yeah, they're wearing helmets with horns or something on them. Wait . . . that guy is different." He pointed to the one with the different helmet.

There it was.

"Absolutely! Well observed!" exclaimed my mother. "Do you notice anything else?" There was a pause. I could feel my knees giving out. As a final attempt to keep from fainting, I began to repeat these words in my head: *She is not my mother, I have nothing to do with this.*

"Well, if you look carefully, you'll see that those aren't horns on the helmets . . . ."

Please, let me die now.

"They look like horns," said Farah, moving even closer. "Why is there just one on each guy?"

"Well, they aren't horns," said Mother, gleefully. "Anyone want to guess?"

"Sausages?" suggested Jake.

"No, not sausages," said Mum.

I opened my mouth, not sure what I'd planned to say. Bananas? Magic wands? French baguettes? Anything, anything but—

"Penises!" said Mother, her voice echoing in the large hall. "Those are the penises of the prisoners that were cut off and placed over their heads." She even mimed the cutting off and placing of . . . that body part . . . on her own head.

There was a gasp from Mr. Smithzerr. There was a collective jump in the group. There was a chorus of "Yuck! Gross!" from Farah's crowd.

Some nervous giggles came from others.

Only Jake moved closer to get a better look.

There were certainly looks from other museum visitors. An adult had just used the 'P' word in front of children. It was as if the word hung in the air, echoing in the room. My ears were burning and I could feel my cheeks turning red. Perhaps the ground would open up and swallow me. I stood stock-still in hopes that everyone would forget I was there and forget this was my mother speaking.

Slowly, eyes began to turn toward me. Maybe it wasn't slow, maybe it was all at once, but it felt agonizingly slow to me.

"You see, what we have here is a general beheading!" continued Mother, unfazed by the reaction. "The king had all his enemies beheaded. And, of course, he had their penises cut off. As Jake pointed out, the only fellow who got to keep his penis . . ."

She'd said it again! Twice!

". . . was the chief. This was a charitable gesture made by King Narmer."

I quickly looked over at Mr. Smithzerr. At first, I thought he was looking intently at my mother. Then I realized that his eyes had gone all glazed and he was just staring into space.

Mr. Smithzerr hears the P-word

Jake raised his hand. "Why did the king cut off their . . . do that?"

"Good question," said Mother. "Sometimes the ancient Egyptians cut off the penises of their enemies to show that their enemies had been defeated. In fact, there's a quite fabulous depiction on a wall in the Medinet Habu temple, on the west bank of the Nile, in Luxor. On the temple wall, one can see scribes and soldiers counting penises that are in a pile in front of the king. This way, the king knew how many enemies were killed without having to count bodies. Made the job easier, don't you think?"

I'm not sure Mr. Smithzerr thought it made things easier. I don't know if Mr. Smithzerr was able to think of anything at that moment. Maybe he, too, wished for a hole to open up in the ground so that he could crawl into it. Sorry, Mr. Smithzerr, sir, I was there first!

"And now, onward!" my mother declared, as if she hadn't just exploded a bomb and we weren't all shell-shocked and in search of our body parts. No, scratch that. I didn't want to think about body parts. Any body parts.

I looked up at Mummy. Her eyes were gleaming wildly, as they always did around artifacts. "Let's whiz through the museum to see the highlights. Then you can explore on your own. Come on, spit-spot." She gestured for everyone to follow and began to walk at Mummy's pace.

Let me explain: don't let that diminutive stature of hers fool you. My mother may stand at a mere 150 centimeters (that's under five feet tall), but that's the only thing about her that anyone could ever consider small. "I'm old, and you're young, so you should be able to keep up," she said, leaving the rest of us scrambling to follow at top speed as she flew through the halls. Even tall and athletic Mr. Smithzerr, who led the running club and was assistant coach of track and field, was having to jog at a fast pace just to keep up. I was prepared, having spent a lifetime of moving fast behind her. I was taller than her by the age of nine and learned to move my legs at a high-speed pace. The class was struggling but I managed to keep up. That didn't keep a stitch from pinching my side. Mother's tiny legs were a blur. She moved like a cyclone.

Without warning, she turned abruptly. There was a minor pile-up as we all tried to change direction. Some kids just didn't make that turn at all and ran into one another at the next archway. Completely oblivious to the tangle of arms and legs behind her, Mother was chatting away to no one as she whirled off down a corridor of statues. The entire class managed to get back on its feet and hurried to catch up.

And then she stopped, causing another catastrophe, with students piled on the museum floor and Mr. Smithzerr narrowly avoiding a collision with an ancient spear. Farah yelped as I accidentally tripped her with my fallen body (after Jake had knocked me over with his). Mother eventually turned around. She jumped back.

"There's no time for messing about, children," she scolded after finally noticing the disaster she had left in her wake. "Now, pay attention. See this crumbly bit of stone?" she asked, pointing to a sad-looking chunk among the other statues. "This is actually part of the beard of the Great Sphinx of Giza—the rest of it is in London, where the excavators took it. Maybe they'll give it back someday, and we'll be able to restore the Sphinx." She gazed at it longingly, as if to apologize for the stolen beard. With a sigh, she pointed at the ceiling. "Now we're going upstairs—follow me!" And with that, she dashed up a flight of stairs.

"But shouldn't we . . . break for lunch?" I suggested. I feared what was upstairs, too. It was as if Mother had mapped out the most embarrassing displays to introduce to the class.

"It's only 10:45," said Mr. Smithzerr, though I could see something in his eyes that wished it was later.

Mum was too far ahead to hear us, anyway, even if it was lunchtime. Mr. Smithzerr and I raced after the stumbling class. It really is amazing how fast Mum can move.

"I want to show you," she was saying when we caught up with the others, "the first monumental sculpture that we have from ancient Egypt. It's of the god Min, who was the god of fertility—very important, as you needed to have fertility if the crops were to grow and animals were to breed." She beamed at us, seemingly oblivious to the fact that we were all sweaty and panting, holding our sides and wiping our brows. "See, he looks pretty much like a column. But something's missing. Anyone?"

For a moment, we were all just catching our breath. But I knew where this was going, and nervous sweat ran down my furrowed brow.

"See the gap between those legs?" she said, pointing to the crotch of the headless statue. "There used to be something else there. What do you think that was? Mr. Smithzerr?"

"It . . . I, um, I . . . ." But Mr. Smithzerr knew exactly what it was. That was the problem. The statue was headless in more ways than one.

Everyone moved in to see where she was pointing.

I fled into the Animal Mummy Room and wished for death.

Sadly, death didn't come. Mummy did.

"Amun Ra, you knew I was going to come here next!" she said, standing on her tiptoes and kissing my forehead as she passed. "In this room, we'll see incredible examples of mummified animals, from baboons, to fish, to a giant crocodile from the Nile, to a furry dog that looks like he might walk right out of the display case, though he's been dead for thousands of years." Again with the dead dogs. But that wasn't the worst.

She stopped in front of a large display case in which a rather messy clump of mummified cow parts was sort of glued together with blackish dried guts. She turned to the group. "Here, we're going to learn about enemas."

I think it was at that moment that Mr. Smithzerr finally understood. He put his hand on my shoulder and gave it a little squeeze. I think this was his way of letting me know that I was not alone.

Some of my fellow students looked confused. Some seemed to contemplate what she meant. Others turned to me in fear of what was to come. I tried to look off into the middle distance as if there was a more interesting dead animal in the room than the poorly mummified cow.

"Remember how I told you about mummification when I visited your class? The standard process was to remove the lungs, liver, intestines, and stomach—basically, all the things that putrefy. For a human, the brain is removed by breaking through the bone behind the nose. Brains get wonderfully gooey when you squish them around using the special hooked tool. It's like brain soup!" Mum smiled, whirling her hand around as if she was scrambling brains, not noticing the green faces looking back. She continued:

"After that, there's the washing with palm wine, the drying with natron, then the oiling and wrapping . . . and all this was done within seventy days for humans. For animals, it could take either more or fewer days, depending on the size of the animal. Well, as you can imagine, this complicated process was not cheap. It's costly having your insides removed, prepared, and repotted. Naturally, some people went looking for a deal. The historian Herodotus described a cheaper and faster way of mummification. In fact, there's evidence of this other method being used for cows and bulls."

She waved grandly at the glass display that contained the rather flattened cow mummy. It was lying on a wooden board that had metal loops along its edges. The cow's head was slightly propped up. Mother explained that the loops on the board were to help the cow retain its shape. From the look of the cow, those loops had not done a very good job. The cow looked like it had melted.

To be honest, this was nothing surprising. I knew this cow. I knew the story of it well—too well. I'd been to this museum and heard the gruesome tale more times than I could count. Now my schoolmates would also learn the unfortunate truth about the puddle of cow in the glass case before us. My mother loved the story. No surprise there, either.

"It's really interesting how the process worked," she began as my poor innocent classmates leaned closer to the glass, the only thing between

Mum and the poorly mummified cow
~~due to the cedar oil enema~~

them and the cow. She was thrilled that they all seemed so interested. I was less thrilled.

"The Buchis bulls and Buchis mothers were made using enemas of cedar oil," she explained.

Rafiq's hand went up before I could stop it. I tried to attract his attention, shaking my head, pleading with him to put his arm down. No such luck. I looked at Mr. Smithzerr, who narrowly stopped himself from lunging at Rafiq. I thought Mr. Smithzerr might try a tackle, but he just hung his head and gave up. Mr. Smithzerr knew what an enema was.

"What is a . . . ?" Rafiq's question faded as he looked from Mr. Smithzerr to me and back. Rafiq suddenly looked fearful, his hand slowly descending. But it was too late.

"An enema," Mum took it upon herself to answer with great alacrity, her voice booming in the hall, "is the procedure by which a tube is inserted into the rectum—that's your bum. Then liquid is poured through the tube and up into your anus. People do it all the time, even today. It's a way of flushing out your bowels—it's very good for solving issues of constipation, you know. Has anyone here had an enema?" She beamed around; I shuddered. Mr. Smithzerr squeezed my shoulder again.

As expected, no one raised his or her hand. Had she really thought that anyone would volunteer that information?

"Well, the next time you—"

"Mother!" I had to stop her. I couldn't let her go any further.

"It's a common—"

"Mother!!" I implored.

Mr. Smithzerr looked like he could use an enema, but I didn't want to even go there.

"Well, it's something to consider," she added, miffed that I was being so peevish.

She turned back to the unfortunate cow.

"In this case, however, we're not talking constipation. Evacuating the bowels for mummification purposes is different, since the cow was already dead." She pointed to these funny things that looked like oil cans. "See these funny things that look like oil cans? These are actually the enemas that were used to introduce cedar oil into the body of the animal through its anal hole." Oh gods, she actually said 'anal hole.' She was miming the action of the enema, and I had nowhere to run.

"The cedar oil is like turpentine. You know how turpentine is so powerful that it's used to remove or dissolve paint? Well, the cedar oil was pumped into the body of the animal through its anal hole or bum," she went on, pointing at Jake's bum, as if anyone needed help locating one. There were a few anxious giggles, but mostly unbearable silence from my classmates. Mum took this for awe instead of horror.

"So they squirted a load of oil up the anus, and then shoved a plug made of linen into the anal hole." She held up a finger, as if it was the plug. "Then the bull or cow was desiccated using natron. Then, after enough time had passed—probably forty days or so—the plug was removed, and teams of priests had to press on either side of the animal to squirt out the liquefied guts from the now unplugged anal hole." I'd now counted three times she'd said that in less than forty-five seconds! She continued:

"Standing behind the animal would have been most unpleasant, as you can imagine. The dissolved guts and feces are rather smelly, and they do rather shoot out of the hole at top speed."

And then she looked at me. I froze. I could feel my heart pounding in my ears. She smiled as if we both must be remembering the same thing. I wasn't remembering anything. My mind was trying desperately to go utterly blank, but a memory was seeping in like cedar oil, threatening to dissolve my guts. Mum was smiling at me, nodding and winking.

It took me a moment . . . and then I remembered. Like a rush of horrid smelly fluids shooting out of an anal hole, the memory rushed back into my brain. My mouth fell open and my throat went tight. I remembered. And I panicked. Oh no, not *that* story. I closed my mouth and then opened it again, trying to remember how to say something—anything—to stop her, but my tongue had gone numb after the second 'anal hole' in her story.

"Amun Ra and I should know—we experimented with this method on a goat. Remember, dear? Of course you do. You must have been about seven. Well, we were in my lab, and I was pushing on the bloated goat belly, and suddenly everything came gushing out at once in one massive squirt! And we can tell you, that squirt gave off one noxious stink! It took six washes to get the smell out of his favorite T-shirt. Now, *that* was a mess!"

She laughed like it was all great fun. Thanks, Mum. Thanks for sharing that disgusting and humiliating moment of my life with my entire class. I'm sure every boy wishes he could share such a special, unforgettable moment when his mother accidentally squirted him with poo-covered goat guts. The kids standing next to me inched away like I was still covered in stench. Surely, that vision would linger among my classmates forever. Thanks, Mum.

"As you can see," continued Mother, "although in its initial stages the method is effective, in the long term the cedar oil continues to contribute to the breakdown of the body, which is why it was not a favored method of mummification. Instead of a mummy, we get something like mummy soup." She chuckled. No one else did.

Thankfully, she turned toward the next display. "And now, let's go in and look at the amazing crocodile mummy, a manifestation of the god Sobek. This fellow is over 5.6 meters long—about eighteen feet or so— really quite charming!" She swept on, ignoring the fact that most of the class was still recovering from the cow display, and that the rest of them were looking at me like I was still covered in goat crap. Mr. Smithzerr looked thankful that we were moving on to our last display and that we had survived Mum's lecture on enemas and anal holes. There were only a few minutes left before the museum trip was over. I watched the hands of the clock, which did not seem to be moving nearly fast enough.

"These little things were pulled from the mouth of the crocodile," Mum said, pointing at what looked like sticks. "We thought they were sticks. But if you look closely, you can see that they're tiny baby crocodiles! They were being carried in the crocodile's mouth for safety! Isn't that sweet? Now, who's ready for lunch?"

5
Elvis Is (Unfortunately) in the House

D id I mention that, in most countries, stealing from ancient ruins is a serious crime? There are international laws about antiquities. And in some of these countries, unlike in the US, no one would bat an eye at arresting a thirteen-year-old boy. Just saying.

Mother is a big supporter of preserving artifacts and keeping them in their home countries. Of course, when artifacts are in danger, Mum has been known to hurry them to safety—whatever the cost. She has single-handedly been responsible for risking her life and sneaking out ancient pieces of history to keep them from being destroyed by various extremists and zealots, or stolen by creepy collectors. This is not the reason she was arrested in Sudan, nor why I had to break in to bust her out of jail (that's another story entirely). This *is*, however, why we had to flee A Country That Shall Not Be Named, and why I'll never be able to face the former Serbian deputy ambassador as long as I live.

As you already know, Mother is the world's most famous Egyptologist. At least, in some circles. She's certainly the world's foremost authority on the mummification of animals, among other, more Egyptologically conventional subjects. She's taught graduate classes on mummification.

So it was no surprise that the Society for Cultural Repatriation and Antiquities Preservation (SCRAAP) asked Mother to head an excavation in Sudan near the ancient site of Gebel Barkal (the Mountain of Barkal—whatever Barkal was). This part of Sudan was called Nubia in ancient times, and Gebel Barkal was a big religious site, with tons of temples clustered around a massive rocky hill that looked like a rearing cobra. Ancient folks there identified the cobra with the sun god, which is probably why there were so many temples around this particular rock. And that was also supposed to be where some of the gods were born—most particularly, as Mum pointed out, Amun Ra, which according to her made it *my* special site. Mum was supposed to look for temples dedicated to sacred animals and see if the Nubians had been into animal mummification like the Egyptians. So far, there was no evidence of this, but hey, it was worth looking, and we got to work in Sudan, which was pretty cool. I mean, if you're into that stuff. SCRAAP was prepared to fund Mum's dig. But there was one catch.

The head of SCRAAP was Mr. Fadeaushka Floosbaganov, a ridiculously rich businessman from, well, let's say The Country That Shall Not Be Named (I don't want to either offend anyone or cause anyone to feel they need to exact revenge for speaking ill of that country), and he was a big fan of Mum. He wanted his whole region to know about the dig, and how great he was for funding it. So, before heading to Sudan, the world's foremost authority on mummified animals and her son (that's Mum and me, FYI) went to Hungary. And Montenegro. And Croatia. And Serbia. And Moldova, and finally to The Country That Shall Not Be Named—south of Ukraine, like Moldova, and with a similar temperament. Mr. Fadeaushka Floosbaganov planned a gala event there at the end of the regional tour. It was going to be held at his castle, overlooking the river Bảc, in honor of the SCRAAP dig and, of course, in honor of Mum.

The tour was over the winter break so I went with her. For two weeks we flew together all over the region to speak with various smarmy ambassadors and cultural diplomats. The best part of the trip? Flying to Europe first class from DC. Usually, sitting on a plane for hours, stuck in uncomfortable seats, eating yucky food, sucks lemons. Flying first class is different. I got to watch movies, play games, sleep, and eat whenever and whatever I wanted. Flight attendants brought me fizzy drinks, sweets, sandwiches, and snacks whenever I pressed the tiny button or waved, looking hungry and pathetic. I know it's weird (what isn't weird in my life?), but I enjoyed the long flight. I entertained myself since Mother was boring. She spent most of the flight reading, writing, and resting.

I must have been asleep when we landed. I had a headphone in my mouth and my stomach ached from the many chocolates and mini cheesecakes I had been eating all night. The headphone was stuck to my tongue and left an awful taste.

We were the last passengers to leave the plane, because Mum was bringing back samples and objects to be taken to the Smithsonian Institution (legally, I should say!) from Sudan for analysis. The artifacts were now on their way back home with Mum and me. First, however, the artifacts would be making stops in all the countries where Mum would be presenting her findings and giving lectures to her adoring fans. Among the artifacts was some papyrus, which was flat and had to be kept in the galley (that's the kitchen on a plane or boat) in one of those metal cupboards where they put those weird airplane food trays. In addition to the papyrus, Mum was escorting bits of ancient coprolites (ancient poop) that had been analyzed to see what ancient people ate. She had the flight attendants store those, too. If anyone on that plane had known what was being stored right next to their food trays, they would all have brought their own dinners and rejected the chicken in airplane sauce. Somehow, my mother always managed to get the flight attendants to do whatever she wanted, no matter how inconvenient or absurd. I don't know if she charmed or terrified them. Mother had to periodically go check on the ancient paper and poo throughout the flight. It was weird, I know, you don't have to say it.

As we were entering the airport, I wondered if people were waiting for us at the Chişinău International Airport in Moldova.

"I wonder if people are waiting for us at the Chişinău International Airport in Moldova," I said to Mum. "Are they going to know we're here?"

Mum pointed to a pair of tough-looking men holding a sign that said "The Esteemed Amilas Marquis and Son."

"I guess they know," I said, now wondering if they were the ones who had diverted the plane in the first place. Maybe it was more convenient to fetch us from here. Mr. Fadeaushka Floosbaganov's associates led us through The Airport That Shall Not Be Named. They glowered at people and shoved other travelers aside. Honestly, those two had clearly watched too many gangster films and looked like they were dressed for a 1930s Chicago shoot-out with the notorious Samoots Amatuna (yes, real name!) and his machine gun-wielding, fedora-wearing crew of Mafioso villains. If you've ever seen photos or films showing old gangsters carrying violin cases that secretly held machine guns, it's thanks to Samoots Amatuna. It was a thing back then: hide the gun in a violin case and people will never know. Smooth move, Samoots. At least Samoots actually played the violin, unlike the copycat gangsters. I know this because I had to do a report on American Prohibition for Ms. Featherstone's social studies class at Haddful Arms, and learned about Al Capone, Samoots Amatuna, and the crazy, violent history of Chicago gangsters.

It was the class unit on the dark side of history. I also had to do a report on an outlaw for the pre–World War One part of the unit. I was assigned Elmer McCurdy. With a name like that, I thought that maybe the guy was famous for milking other people's cows or stealing sheep. Wrong. He was a train robber and was killed in a shoot-out. After that, his body was embalmed and shown in public, like a freak show of the dead. It was a popular thing to do before there was the internet. Wondering why I'm babbling on about this? No reason except that I think it's interesting because, at some point, about fifty years later, Elmer McCurdy's mummy was discovered in a haunted house at a carnival. I guess television came along and old Elmer was forgotten. What everyone thought was a wax dummy was Elmer's real mummy. Yes, my teacher had picked him for me because clearly I didn't have enough mummies in my life. Really? Ugh.

Anyway, I digress. Back to the freak show in Eastern Europe. Or rather, back to *Central* Europe—these guys all feel that it's a put-down to be called Eastern Europe (and that that title should be saved for the Ukrainians).

We arrived at our hotel in a stretch limo. Mother thought it was silly and ostentatious, but I thought it was cool. Lots of food and candy in the nifty mini-bar. At the hotel, we were greeted like royalty. At first, I thought someone had died. All the hotel staff were lined up outside, looking down at their feet. But they were there to greet us. They led us into the ridiculously fancy dining room and sat us at a table with more forks and spoons at each plate than I knew what to do with. A massive tea was laid out, with tiers of cakes and scones (and, for some reason, pork rinds) waiting for us, as well as eleven businessmen from SCRAAP and, I think, the mayor of Chișinău. There were photographers snapping photos and lots of pushing. When we were in our seats, I quietly asked Mother if I could put a couple pieces of chocolate cake in my pocket for later. She mouthed 'no,' but she did pass me a couple miniature scones under the table.

I managed to eat all the chocolate cake, anyway. There was a lot of chatting and fussing over Mum from the crowd around the table, which I ignored. A few stragglers came in and greeted us. Nearly knocking the cucumber sandwich from my mouth, a heavy, clammy hand patted me on the head as a stout, sweaty man reached over me for Mum's hand.

"Forgive my tardiness. We are so very pleased at having you here, esteemed doctor," he said, using a kerchief to wipe his brow. "I am the number one assistant to Mr. Fadeaushka Floosbaganov. Mr. Fadeaushka Floosbaganov is having enthusiasm to show you his own Egyptian treasures, brought from the tombs of Luxor."

Mother, who knew her artifacts and where they came from, turned red—although the man had said "brought from the tombs of Luxor," she had understood the underlying meaning: "stolen from the tombs of Luxor." The theft of antiquities, any antiquities, made her so angry that steam began shooting out of her ears. Okay, steam didn't actually shoot out of her ears, but I always imagine that happening when she hears about some creepy people stealing artifacts. I grabbed her arm in case she was going to go for his throat. She was still holding a scone and it looked like she was going to throw it at him. I managed to get it out of her hand and into my mouth, just to be safe.

"We have many treasures rescued from Egypt," said someone else at the table, making room for the short, stout guy to take a seat. Neither was aware of the danger they were in, admitting their heinous crimes to my mother.

"So interesting," I said, cutting Mother off before she could sputter something rude. "We'll go and . . . um, freshen up before the evening."

I stood up and lost a scone. Drat.

Mother stood up, too. Several of the businessmen stood out of politeness as we inched away from the table. I smiled. Mum scowled. I tugged until we were out of earshot.

"The nerve of that . . . man, boasting of his treachery!" Mother muttered under her breath, as I steered her toward the door. She was spitting mad.

"Mum, I don't think it was *his* treachery, personally," I said, smiling at the people coming over for a handshake, who luckily didn't understand English or hadn't heard my mother's accusations. "I think these artifacts were stolen, um, I mean, purchased or discovered ages ago. Maybe given to local royalty from Egyptian kings, who knows?"

"Still." Mother was now attempting to contain her anger as other people came between us and the door. "These are precious antiquities that belong to Egypt! And if they *have* been removed from Egypt after the law of 1979 forbidding the export of antiquities, then they're here illegally."

I managed to get us through the door, but a small crowd moved into our way, speaking to us with incomprehensible words in what they thought was English. We were more or less being ushered back toward the tea settings. I took Mum's hand and forged ahead, smiling and nodding, until we broke through the crowd.

"It's plain theft!" Mother whispered loudly, ignoring the noisy chatter behind us. "Egypt has been robbed long enough."

I didn't want to say it, but Egypt has not had a great history of caring for its own antiquities—but then, who has?—not Greece or Rome or even other places in Europe. Ancient tomb robbers were, for the most part, Egyptian. Black-market sellers were, and often are, Egyptian. Sure, people have always bought artifacts to take back to their own countries, but lots of those artifacts were first stolen from tombs by locals. I can't say that I blame the locals, although I certainly couldn't say anything remotely like this to Mum. Imagine you live in the desert and suddenly some idiot from some foreign country comes along with buckets of cash. He says he's willing to pay enough to feed your entire village for five years. For what? For some little trinkets that come from the tomb of a long-dead pharaoh, or even some poxy nobleman's mausoleum that your family's been using to shelter your goats for generations. Or someone offers lots of money for the rotting mummy of some unknown guy who's been moldering in an underground room for thousands of years. Or, most often, for chunks of carved stone that were obviously valueless (at least gold has a value!) and had been lying around for centuries. No one ever cared about the mummy, or the tomb, or the trinkets, or the stones, or the goats. Can you blame the people who sold their heritage? What do those things matter if you're trying to feed your family? More problematic are the ones who buy the stuff—or just take it away. They don't have an excuse.

After tea, we went back to our room. I took a bubble bath in a giant tub. I looked something like a mummy when I got out. I was very wrinkled and prunish. The plan was to get all dressed up in our fancy clothes for the gala, but there was a big problem. Or rather, a way too small problem. Mum had packed the suit that I'd worn to every important event since last summer. Unfortunately, I hadn't tried it on again before we left. It was way too small. The trousers came halfway up my calves and the jacket halfway up my forearms. It looked ridiculous. We had to rush to a shop and get new clothes. Ugh. I hate shopping for clothes.

"You could just wear this suit," Mother offered when I grumbled about having to go. "We can say they're capri trousers and three-quarter sleeves. Maybe you can start a new trend."

"Maybe I can kill myself," I offered back, rolling my eyes at her. Next to the alternative, going shopping suddenly didn't seem so bad.

The doorman at the hotel gave us directions to a shop for men, which we actually found, and Mum made me try on, like, a hundred different suits. She wouldn't let me get the slim-fit, trendy, light purple herringbone suit that the very pretty salesgirl showed me. Mother wanted me to get the most boring brown suit, because it would be less likely to show dirt. I hated it. We finally agreed on a reasonably trendy dark blue suit. They tailored it right there so I wouldn't trip over the trouser bottoms. Mum let me get a bright blue tie with a picture of R2-D2 on it. I let her get me a light gray shirt. I looked awesome. At least, the tie looked awesome. I looked pretty lame, as usual.

The embassy sent an assistant to bring us to the gala that evening. Mum has always insisted that we learn a few words of whatever language is spoken in the country we're visiting, as guests need to be gracious. I can say 'Hello' and 'No mushrooms, please' anywhere in South America, Western Europe, and most places in the Middle East. Since there were going to be businessmen, officials, and diplomats from around the region, Mum had made me look up how to say a few things in several Eastern ('Central') European languages before we left on the trip. Since I had some down time, I decided it would be fun to expand my word knowledge beyond the usual greetings and rejection of fungi, but my language-learning skills (besides ancient Egyptian) were weak. I used Google Translate and tried to memorize a few of the more interesting words and phrases.

Mum and I met lots of SCRAAP and embassy people, and shook a bunch of sweaty hands. I had managed to successfully learn 'Hello' and 'Thank you' in Serbian. Unfortunately, I learned how to say a few other things, thanks to Google Translate. Of course, I've since forgotten everything I had learned in Serbian. Okay, not everything, sadly. I still remember 'Ваш банана не лако увући,' and likely will never forget it after the humiliating experience with the deputy ambassador of Serbia and his assistant.

I smiled at him and said, "Ваш банана не лако увући."

Everyone gasped.

'Ваш банана не лако увући," I said again. Unfortunately, this means "Your banana does not easily retract."

Everyone gasped again, especially the deputy ambassador from Serbia, whose hand I was shaking when I inadvertently made the comment about his poorly retractable banana. No, he didn't actually have a banana. Can we move on? Mother just giggled when the ambassador's assistant told her what I'd said. Let's just say it was unpleasant for all involved. They thought I was being smart (and slightly forward) until they realized I was being stupid.

We were escorted out of Floosbaganov's main ballroom into what he called his Hall of Egypt. This little viewing was something that Mr. Fadeaushka Floosbaganov and the Ukrainian ambassador had organized with the officials of The Country That Shall Not Be Named. They thought Mum would be impressed; I thought she was going to explode.

There were glass cases filled with papyrus, statues, and canopic jars, even the hand of a mummy. Mum stopped at a case with five small painted limestone statues of the same character in different poses. He was sitting, standing, stepping forward, kneeling, and crossing his legs with his head turned to the side.

"We are particularly proud of these," said the minister of finance. "Mr. Fadeaushka Floosbaganov had to buy these on the black market."

Mother leaned over, her nose pressed against the glass. I thought she was going to break the case with her forehead. I didn't think the night could get any worse.

And then I met Elvis.

Elvis Aaron Presley Floosbaganov. His father was apparently not just a fan of my mother! Elvis was the son of the head of SCRAAP, and Elvis was a douche. He was the typical posh boarding school–educated rich kid. His hair was strategically unkempt—every hair placed perfectly to look like it hadn't been. He was wearing the most expensive retro 'distressed' sneakers and a much cooler and more expensive version of the suit I wished Mum had bought me. We were supposed to 'hang out,' even though the

Elvis Aaron Presley
(NOT Floosbaganov)

guy was old. I mean really old. He was, like, almost seventeen.

All of the diplomats were acting like they worked for Mr. Floosbaganov, like he owned the place. He probably did. Mother was dressed in her flowing gown and jewelry made for her by Ikram Nakhla, the famous jewelry designer from Egypt. When my tiny mother enters a room, she seems ten feet tall—every head turns. And Mr. Floosbaganov bowed so low and for so long that I thought he must have knocked his head on his own knee and passed out. He was holding Mother's hand, and there was a hush while he was bent double. I tried not to lean, but I swear, if you looked closely, you could see his toupée starting to unstick itself from his bald head. I was worried he was totally nuts and was going to cling to mother's hand forever, but he finally came up for air.

"My dearest, esteemed, brilliant, beautiful . . ."—I was gagging as Mr. Floosbaganov went on, and on, and on, and on—". . . talented, capable, amazing woman. Oh, the wonder of you."

My mother stifled a yawn. I tried not to giggle. I couldn't look my mother in the eye. We would both have lost it.

"It is lovely to meet you in person, dearest, lovely, remarkable . . . ," he went on, ". . . breathtakingly, staggeringly sage, Amilas Marquis." He then slobbered all over her hand. Yuck.

"Well," said Mother, trying unsuccessfully to pull her moistened hand out from his, "thank you for the . . . very warm greeting."

"Madame, you are truly—"

"And . . . ," Mother quickly cut him off, but she clearly had no idea what to say next. A rare moment. So she turned to me. I had nowhere to run. "This is my son, Amun Raaaaaaa."

I knew it. Everyone turned. Everyone except Elvis, who was busy playing Candy Crush on his phone. I could hear the tip-tap of his finger on his touchscreen.

"Um . . . ." I quickly tried to think of something to say, something in Serbian. Before I could stop myself, I said the only thing that came into my head, "Ваш банана не лако увући."

As people started to laugh, I could feel the blood draining from my face.

"And your banana does not easily retract, either," said Mr. Fadeaushka Floosbaganov, shaking my hand.

Thanks, Google Translate.

After some damage control, we continued to mingle. Luckily only about a third of the guests understood Serbian. A few of those who did thought I was being silly. A couple of women were offended and thought I was being rude. I would have preferred to crawl into a very small space and hide, but I plastered a smile on my face that did not go farther than my lips. If anyone could read faces, they'd know I was wishing I was invisible or in another country far, far away.

Attention was soon drawn to the reason for this gala affair in the first place.

"Ladies and gentlemen," said the minister for the arts, who seemed like a jolly man, slightly too large for his waistcoat and jacket. "Thank you for coming. We are not only honoring the ancient wonders we have in our possession . . . ."

I had to hold Mother's hand to keep it from rising up to stop the speech or throttle anyone.

"We are honoring," he continued, "a brilliant Egyptologist who will head the excavation in Sudan, funded by the generosity of the Society for Cultural Repatriation and Antiquities Preservation and, in particular, Mr. Fadeaushka Floosbaganov."

There was a round of applause. The minister of the arts was handed a giant cardboard check for €500,000. The giant check was for show, but the money was real.

"We are pleased to give this check to Amilas Marquis to help initiate the excavation in Sudan. Tomorrow, she will be heading there with her son, Amun Ra."

And, of course, there was a murmur of giggling in the crowd, along with applause. An Egyptologist with a son named Amun Ra? Very funny indeed.

Suddenly, there was a clinking of glass. Someone was demanding attention. It was Fadeaushka Floosbaganov.

"Thank you, esteemed Minister of the Arts," he said. "I want to add that it is my deepest, most sincere, lifelong, heart-filling . . . ."

Oh no, he was at it again. It was like he had a thesaurus and was sucking up all the adjectives. There weren't going to be any left for anyone else!

"It's like he has a thesaurus, Mum, and he's about to . . . Mum?" But my mother was suddenly not by my side. I looked around in a panic.

"I'm right here," she said, suddenly reappearing with a smile.

"Where did you go?" I asked. For some reason, I was anxious.

"Never mind," she said. There was something smug in her twinkling eyes. "I'm back and feeling much better."

Maybe she'd just had to use the toilet. I took a deep breath.

". . . prevailing, steadfast, deep-rooted dream—one might say a 'Burnin' Love' (and here he winked) to be part of an Egyptological excavation. It is such a fabulous, tremendous, remarkable, amazing . . . ."

"What was that wink for?" I asked Mother, whispering during the Floosbaganov long list of whatever. "Is he sending secret messages?"

"No, he does that whenever he sneaks in the name of some Elvis Presley song when he's talking," Mum explained. "But that's not what worries me."

"As I react badly to sand," continued Mr. Floosbaganov, "and chafe in the heat, and am terribly allergic to those smelly camels, I cannot join the most esteemed, exciting, remarkable (blah blah) expedition. But 'It's Now or Never' (wink), so it is with my greatest pleasure, enthusiasm, eagerness (blah blah) that my son will join the lovely, talented (blah blah blah— Whoa! What?) Amilas Marquis as an assistant. (What???) I am, one might say, 'All Shook Up'!" (wink).

There was general applause. My mother and I were not part of it.

"He's doing *what*?" Mother and I both said aloud, unheard over the clapping hands. No way was the Candy Crush–playing jerk going to be joining us anywhere. Elvis Aaron Presley Floosbaganov didn't even look up from his phone for this announcement. I grabbed Mum's arm. She wriggled out of my grasp.

"Excuse me, Mr. Floosbaganov," she called, waving.

The smitten billionaire was quickly shoving his way through the crowd, heading straight for Mother.

Fadeaushka Floosbaganov reached for her hand and I quickly grabbed it before he could, pretending I needed her hand to scratch my ear. I know that was a lame move, but at least he couldn't slobber all over Mum's hand again. I did, however, have to then actually use Mother's hand to scratch my ear to keep up appearances, silly as those appearances may be. Mum pulled her hand back and wagged it at Mr. Fadeaushka Floosbaganov.

"I'm sorry, but your son isn't trained for this work. It isn't easy, nor is it particularly fun, unless you're an Egyptologist." Mother was firm.

"It really is true, sir," I said, speaking honestly. Very honestly. "It isn't all that fun."

Fadeaushka Floosbaganov smiled like the simpering, smarmy fanboy that he was. "That is so kind, considerate, thoughtful . . . (blah blah blah for like fifteen minutes) . . . solicitous, unselfish and gracious of you, Professor Madame Marquis. But it is already done, so have no fear. You have an assistant who is very excited to take part in this adventure."

We all looked over at Elvis Aaron Presley Floosbaganov, who was either texting or playing on his phone. Our burning stares didn't even graze his thick skull.

"Aren't you excited, Elvis?" his dad asked loudly. Elvis continued to ignore him. "Elvis!" Mr. Floosbaganov yelled.

Elvis Aaron Presley Floosbaganov looked around like he was just waking up. His eyes seemed to come into focus and lock onto his father.

"What?" he asked.

"I was telling the esteemed doctor how excited you are for this exciting, brilliant, amazing . . . adventure in Egyptology," said Mr. Floosbaganov, his ears turning slightly red (I left out about a hundred adjectives, but you get the drift).

Elvis looked blank-faced from his father, to my mother, to me, and back to his father. "Uh, yeah, I guess," he said, turning back to his phone.

Mr. Fadeaushka Floosbaganov went all splotchy. He took a couple of deep breaths, managed to stick another smile on his face like a fake moustache, and nodded, fake-smiling at my mother.

"There, you see? Thrilled."

Back at the hotel, things were grim. Mother was in a fury. As we were packing that night for an early departure the next morning, she was throwing things in the suitcase and pulling them back out, grumbling to herself and to me.

"You know what he's doing, don't you?" she said, again.

"Yes, by now I do," I answered. Since we got back from the reception, it was all she could think of.

"He's funding this dig so he can say that his son actually did something worthwhile," she said again as I mouthed the familiar words to myself. "Floosbaganov is paying a fortune for me to babysit his son. No doubt this excavation will look good on that lazy boy's indubitably puny college application. I doubt he's ever done anything."

"Yes, that does seem like what Mr. Floosbaganov is doing," I agreed, again, like I had all evening. Though, to be honest, I did wonder who was really going to do the babysitting. Yours truly, no doubt. Since everyone under, like, nineteen is the same age to grown-ups, I would get stuck with Elvis. Like we'd have anything to talk about, even if he could be bothered.

"He's blackmailing me into taking that . . . that . . . I don't know what he is, but it isn't good." Mother plopped herself on the bed. Her feet didn't quite reach the ground, so she couldn't stomp. She wanted to, though, I could see it. How dare this billionaire buy his douchey son a spot on her excavation?

"How dare this billionaire buy his douchey son a spot on your excavation?" I said. And I meant it, too.

And then, I saw it.

What the . . . .

"Mum, you stole it!" My throat seized up as I tried to shout and whisper at the same time. I was shocked. I stood there, pointing, and gaping, and suddenly having to pee.

"I wouldn't call it stealing exactly," Mum said, clearly not believing her own words.

Right there, about to be wrapped in Mum's pink flannel nightgown, was one of the five limestone statues that had been in the case in the Hall of Egypt. This small statue was of the man in a forward stride, holding a long staff in one hand and a baton in the other.

"It was stolen by these horrid thieves!" said Mother, defensively. "I'm only stealing it back. Rather, I'm retrieving and repatriating it. Not stealing."

"Uh, yes, it is stealing. Notice the word 'stealing' in the phrase 'stealing it back,'" I said, feeling my legs go numb and imagining life in an Eastern European—sorry, Central European—prison, starving on a diet of sauerkraut and tongue.

"I'm taking it, Amun Ra, because it doesn't belong to these thieves," she said. "It's coming home, and will be returned to the Antiquities Ministry. It was stolen from a storeroom, I'm sure of it. In fact, I believe I was there back when it was being excavated!"

"Fine. Um . . . Mum, where are the other statues?" I asked, searching through her suitcase. There had been five, but I could only find one. Now curiosity was creeping up on my panic. "Why did you just steal—I mean, steal back—this one?"

"The others were fake," she said, winking.

She actually winked, my international criminal mother! She was loving the fact that these tomb raiders were boasting of the artifacts they had procured and secreted away . . . and that those artifacts were fakes. Except the one that she'd stolen—stolen back—from right under their noses.

". . ." was all I said. I opened my mouth, but nothing came out.

"Oh, come on, you must have spotted all those ridiculous errors," said Mother, amused. "The crossed legs, the turned head—never! I saw the statues and immediately recognized inconsistencies in the four others. Pink cheeks on the one sitting, and blue eyes on the one kneeling. And the standing one had women's clothes—not that there's anything wrong with that, but that tunic with a long fringe all over every edge certainly wasn't one used by the ancient Egyptians."

I still didn't know what to say.

". . ." was all I could say, or not say, again.

Mum took a deep breath and placed a gentle hand on my shoulder. "Let's get some sleep, Amun. The car will be here to take us and Elvis Presley, Jr. to the airport." She shuddered as she said his name.

She would be sleeping like a baby in a matter of minutes. I, on the other hand, would be up worrying until it was time to escape the country before we got caught.

6
All Shook Up and a Devil in Disguise

I previously explained that the events in The Country That Shall Not Be Named were not why Mum was arrested.

Well, this is the part where she was arrested and where I had to throw myself on the mercy of the Sudanese government to get her out of jail.

Morning in The Country That Shall Not Be Named snuck up on us in the form of a screaming alarm.

"Five more minutes," I said automatically. I didn't want to go to school.

Then in came the flood of memories: the flight, high tea, Elvis, Eastern Europe, retractable bananas, Elvis, (re)stolen artifacts, Elvis . . . .

"Argh, we're in The Country That Shall Not Be Named and you stole priceless artifacts!" I cried, jumping out of bed. "We're going to jail!"

"No," said Mother, with a kind of scary calm, "I *re-stole* a single artifact and we *aren't* going to jail. We're getting on a plane."

Who are *you?* I thought to myself. Without a doubt, I was going to hell in a handbasket full of stolen artifacts with an insane woman and Elvis Presley.

When I came out of the bathroom, Mum was already standing by the door. She was wearing a black turtleneck, black trousers, and boots. Stealth mode?

"Mum, you look like a spy," I said. "But it's not like you're invisible. They can still see you."

She glared at me over her sunglasses.

"Let's go." She threw her backpack over her shoulder, stood on her tiptoes to reach the chain on the door, and marched down the hall to the elevators.

I was still in my pajamas. I just threw on a hoodie and my sneakers. We were getting on a plane, hopefully, and I didn't care if I was in my pajamas. But I did wear sunglasses in hopes that no one would recognize me as the son of an international antiquities thief.

The limo was waiting for us in front of the hotel. All of the hotel staff were running around, bringing Mum cappuccinos and espressos—like, five people brought coffee, each vying to be the one she picked. She swallowed one espresso down in a gulp, then grabbed one in each hand and indicated that the other two cappuccinos were to be left on the table. She wasn't messing around. She drank all five while we were waiting for the bags. I kept my eyes peeled for police in case Floosbaganov discovered his missing statue, but none appeared.

I looked around. No sign of Elvis. Maybe he'd forgotten to come. Maybe Floosbaganov had changed his mind. Maybe . . . but no. The chauffeur opened the back door of the ridiculously stretched limo. There, sitting sprawled out, taking up most of the big comfy back seat, was Elvis Aaron Presley Floosbaganov. Guess what he was doing? If you guessed that he was texting and/or playing on his phone, you'd be wrong! Just kidding. Of course that's what he was doing.

"Ahem." Mother cleared her throat in hopes that Elvis would realize he needed to move out of his man-spread position. He didn't.

"Excuse me!" Mother said loudly.

Elvis tried to pry one of his eyes away from his screen, but failed. He grunted some acknowledgment of our presence.

"Young man, move your lazy ass so we can get into the limo!" Mum said. Well, no, Mum didn't say that, though I wish she had. So did she.

"Young man, do you see that we're standing here?" That's what she did say.

Elvis looked up. "Oh yeah," he said.

And then she grabbed his phone and threw it into the middle of the street, where it was smashed by a giant truck carrying huge blocks of marble. Then a huge crane on the back of the truck picked up Elvis and threw him over the building. Then Mother laughed and said, "Serves you right, you douche." No, she didn't really, but I wish she had.

In real life, she just said, "Elvis Aaron Presley Floosbaganov, please move over so we can get into the car. Now."

I was sorely disappointed, still thinking about Elvis, *sans* phone, flying through the air. Instead, he edged his bum about three inches over, still man-spreading across the seat. I could see Mother flushing red with anger, but then she simply gave up. She took my hand and we walked around, getting into the limo on the other side.

After telling Elvis Aaron Presley Floosbaganov three times to close the door, to which he responded with a grunt but no action, the chauffeur got out and walked around to close the door. Mum hated that as much as anything else. Treating everyone with respect is important. Elvis Aaron Presley Floosbaganov was not winning points. And it got worse.

"Master Elvis, could you please move your foot?" the chauffeur asked, politely, since Elvis Presley's foot was now sprawled out of the car.

Elvis shifted his foot slightly, but was still blocking the door. The chauffeur looked very anxious so I leaned all the way over and picked up the foot. It was heavier than I'd expected. He didn't even move it after I was basically lying across his lap. Would we have to carry him? Luckily, there were baggage handlers at the airport who might be able to help with Elvis Aaron Presley Floosbaganov, who seemed unable to move himself. I was suddenly worried about toilet duty, so to speak. I just hoped he could wipe himself.

On the way to the airport, Mum told us (me and Elvis Aaron Presley Floosbaganov's left shoulder) about the dig we were headed to excavate. Elvis would grunt periodically, though we came to understand that this was his way of pretending to listen.

"And then we'll reanimate the mummies, and turn them into cannibal zombies who will eat your brain, if you have one," I said. Yes, I did say this. However, the zombie comment received the same grunt as "There will be tents set up when we arrive."

But when Mum said, "And, of course, there will be no internet or electrical outlets," Elvis Aaron Presley Floosbaganov nearly jumped out of his seat.

"*What?* What do you mean?" His inertia had turned to panic.

"Simple," said Mum, clearly pleased that something had drawn him out of his torpor. "We'll be in the middle of the desert. There will be no lights, other than gas lamps, solar-powered lights, and battery-operated lamps. There will be no electricity, other than a minimal amount from the emergency generator. And, most obviously, there will be no internet. What did you think I meant?"

"Wait." Elvis seemed flustered. He looked around as if suddenly aware that he was in a car on the way to the airport, heading to what he clearly considered his doom. "You mean I'm going to be somewhere without internet?"

"Do you even know where you're going?" I asked. The guy was seventeen going on five.

"Like, yeah," he clearly lied. It was obvious he had no idea where he was going.

"Great," I said with false enthusiasm. "Where are you going?"

"Like . . . ." I could almost hear the minuscule wheels in his brain trying to move. "Like . . . doing Egyptology stuff."

"And where does one do this 'Egyptology stuff'?" Mother asked.

"Like, with mummies and, like . . . I don't know, mummy stuff." Elvis was now on edge. Having to use his brain was really not in his comfort zone.

"My dear Elvis Aaron Presley Floosbaganov. We are going to be out in the desert. I'm sure you've heard of the desert. Maybe it's popped up on the Facebook in one of your games? The desert is where we often find mummies and other artifacts of archaeological interest. Your father seems to think that this is an endeavor you'll find compelling and has therefore thrust your presence upon us. If you feel he's wrong and you are not so compelled, I suggest you speak now, before we board a plane that will take us to Sudan. Abstinence from clarifying your preferences will be to the detriment of all involved."

Elvis Aaron Presley Floosbaganov stared at my mother, his mouth hanging open. His eyes didn't quite seem in focus, but he was looking at Mum as if she had just spoken to him in ancient Egyptian.

"Huh?" he finally managed.

"Dude, if you don't want to go, you'd better tell us now," I translated.

"Huh?" he asked.

I didn't think I could be any clearer, so I repeated what I'd just said, only slower:

"If . . . you . . . don't . . . want . . . to . . . go . . . , tell . . . us . . . now."

"What do you mean?" Elvis was looking at us, blinking. Maybe blinking was his way of trying to suck thoughts into his head from the air. If so, it didn't seem to be helping.

Mum and I were nonplussed, and just blinked back.

"Go where?" Elvis managed to say, many blinks later.

Again, Mum and I were stunned into silence.

Finally, I managed, "We're going to the airport."

"Who?" he blinked.

"You," I said. "And me. And my mother. All three of us. We're in a limo, and we're going to the airport. At the airport, we'll get on a plane. The plane will take off and fly. We'll be in the plane. It will fly to Sudan via Egypt"—where we would be leaving the stolen statue in the hands of her colleagues. "Then it will land. We'll be in the plane when it lands, and then we'll get out of the plane. We'll then be in Sudan. You, me, and my mother."

It took a while, but he seemed to understand. Each small section of my explanation seemed to burrow through his ear into his brain and find a home in the tiny spaces that were available. He seemed to struggle when one sentence came too quickly after another. But, after several moments of silence and blinking, his eyebrows rose up and a look of shock passed quickly across his face.

"Where?"

By the time we boarded the plane, Elvis was not a happy camper. The fact that we boarded the plane had a lot to do with it.

"Nobody said anything about no internet," he argued as Mother handed the flight attendant our tickets.

"Dude, we'll be in the desert, digging up carved stones, and dead bodies, and artifacts, and stuff. Plus, you'll be too busy tumbling down sand dunes and trying to get scorpions out of your sleeping bag to worry about your phone." I smiled at him. It was funny, I thought. Elvis Aaron Presley on a dig gave new meaning to 'rock and roll.'

After fighting with the flight attendant about turning off his phone, Elvis began to sulk. Unfortunately, this wasn't a silent affair. He sat (next to me, of course) grumbling, swearing, and punching his fist into the seat in front of him. Mother wasn't happy at all; it was her seat.

"Elvis, man, what did you think was going on?" I asked, really wondering.

"When?" he asked.

"When your father told you about this trip."

"I was like, whatever," he said, predictably.

"Well, 'whatever' got you here," I said. "If you'd paid attention for two minutes, maybe you'd have figured out what was happening before it was too late. Now you're headed to Sudan. You're going to be digging in the sand and dirt. No more games on your phone."

"But I'm almost done with level 732, and I'm about to run out of lives," he whined.

"Complaining won't make Wi-Fi magically appear in the desert, Elvis, however compelling your plight may be." I had a feeling that Elvis spent his life doing just that—complaining and then getting his way.

"Huh?" Elvis grunted.

"Why didn't you tell your father you didn't want to come?" I asked.

"Because he said if I didn't, he'd take away my Porsche," whined Elvis. "And my Jag. And my wall-to-wall plasma screen."

"He threatened to take away your cars and TV?" I tried to sound sympathetic for the guy, but it was hard.

"Yeah," Elvis sneered, "I'd have to use the Mercedes. Totally sucks. It's yellow."

He used hand gestures for emphasis on this last point, shaking them, palms up, as if he was showing me how cruel and unusual such a punishment was. I think the "yellow" bit was supposed to be my cue to offer sympathy for his plight.

"You spoiled jerk of a douche," I didn't say, but wished I had.

"Bummer," I did say, but wished I hadn't.

"Tell me about it." Elvis rolled his eyes at me, knowingly, as if I really did think it was a bummer he'd be left with a yellow Mercedes.

We landed at a tiny airport near Khartoum where we could walk right from the plane into the arrival hall. Mother gathered her papers before we exited the plane. And she retrieved the papyrus and poop from the airplane kitchen. Yes, once again, the airplane crew had conveniently stored her crap. Literally.

As we disembarked past soldiers with guns, I heard a whiny voice call out from the crowd. A tall, thin man with a very unflattering hairdo edged his way toward us. He was wearing some kind of uniform that looked official.

"My dear Amilas," he simpered.

"Shaker Babek! You? Here?" Mother roared. "I thought you'd been banned from the region! If you think you're going to worm your way onto this excavation, then—"

"Mother!" I squeezed her arm. Who was this guy? Mum did not care for fools and thieves, even if they worked for the government. If she made this guy mad, could he arrest us? Did he have the power to do that? Shaker Babek was in a uniform, and that had to mean something. Mum obviously hated this guy and wasn't in the mood to be restrained. She pulled her arm away. I was worried. Elvis didn't notice.

"No, my dearest Amilas," Shaker Babek said, trying get hold of her hand, which she pulled away, nearly giving me a black eye with her elbow. "I'm not going to join you, I'm afraid. You'll have to get along without me, unfortunately. You see, I have become very busy since I was presented with the post of Chief Inspector of Antiquities for the Karima region. Yes, thank you for your congratulations." He smiled triumphantly at her. It was like he was in communication with some other person, because she hadn't congratulated him, nor did she intend to. Strangle him was more likely what she intended to do. But this information caught her in a stranglehold.

Her mouth fell open. She was utterly nonplussed. It was as if the words (likely swear words and certainly no words remotely flattering to Mr. Shaker Babek) died inside her before they could come out.

Mr. Babek seemed to think she hadn't heard. "As I have had the pleasure to share with you, I'm the Chief Inspector of—"

"Yes, I heard you, Babek. What extraordinary news," Mother managed to say through clenched teeth, her eyes still goggling slightly. "That is infinitely better than being jailed for theft and fraud, as some might have anticipated given your history. I'm sure you're both relieved and likely as surprised as everyone else in the region."

"Thank you for your congratulations, Amilas," he said, smiling. "It is such a pleasure to see you again. And your generous wishes mean so much to me." Whatever he was hearing was certainly not the same conversation Mum was having. She couldn't get the shock off her face or stop a hissing sound coming from her lips. He seemed to think that the sneer was a smile and the sigh was a cheerful greeting.

"It is little Amun Ra, yes? Not so little now, yes?" Shaker Babek rounded on me.

"Nice to meet you, Chief Inspector Babek," I said. "Or to see you again, if we ever met before."

"Indeed, young Amun Ra," said Shaker Babek. "I am so pleased you can join your mother. And that you will have a top quality crew. I'm very happy to provide—"

"*Provide?*" Mother turned a frosty glance on him. "I sent my list of workers, as per usual. The request was clear and within my—"

"Not available," said Shaker Babek, wagging his finger. "Oh, there are two of your men we accept, but we have provided you with my personal choices for the other helpers to . . . assist." He grinned broadly in a slightly menacing way, and I swear his yellow teeth were not made of teeth.

Mother's face was turning red. I took her arm and steered her away from Shaker Babek. We were still standing in the middle of the moving crowd of other travelers descending from the plane.

"All righty, Mr. Babek, thanks, and congrats on your new uniform," I said quickly over my shoulder, trying to get Mum away before she said something that he would actually hear. She was still spluttering like a cat faced with a slobbering dog. I suspected Shaker Babek was not as big an idiot as he seemed. His personal choice of workers? This didn't bode well. But there was nothing we could do without causing a scene. I was still trying to squeeze through the crowd of other passengers, but wasn't getting far. I grabbed Elvis by the sleeve since he wasn't moving on his own.

"Why, thank you, *habibi*," Mr. Babek said, as if we were best friends. Everyone in Egypt calls each other 'my love' in the form of '*habibi*' for men and '*habibti*' for women. In this case, it was yucky. "As always, my dearest Amilas, such a pleasure. Amun Ra is as if my own son."

Now I gagged. "I . . . not . . . you . . . ."

"It is no bother," said Shaker Babek, still simpering and smiling.

"No, I mean, yes," I said, not sure which word was the right response. "Yes, well, off we go. I . . . that is, *we* are very happy for you in your new position." I was still trying to get Mum and Elvis to move away from Shaker Babek. It wasn't easy: I had to keep Mum from throttling the man and keep Elvis from bumping into anything else. Shaker Babek was grinning and waving as we inched away from him. I kept smiling and nodding. Luckily, he accidentally knocked a guy's hat off while waving his arm. That distracted him for a moment, so I shuttled the three of us away through a gap in the crowd.

I really had my hands full with Mother and Elvis. Mother was still in shock and spluttering about Shaker Babek. Apparently, the jerk had once worked with her on a dig and had been both incompetent and corrupt—both inexcusable offenses to Mum. Most people in Sudanese archaeology are great, but corruption and incompetence happen. She explained, through sputters and invectives, that Shaker Babek had been in charge of getting tools and laborers for an excavation she had led a few years back. He had tried to charge Mum's team rent for equipment that didn't exist and for workers who never arrived, as well as skimming off pay from the workers who *were* there. And, most unforgivable, he had tried to make off with artifacts as well.

Mum simply would not move unless I pulled her along. Getting her through the crowd was a challenge, because she kept wanting to stop and stomp her feet in fury and frustration. Elvis, who was "just a second" from "finishing this level" on his phone and was totally unaware of anything else, also wanted to stop every few seconds. He would just wander off in a random direction if I let go of his arm. I'd grab him, and then she'd get shuffled off in a mob of families on holiday. I'd grab her, and he'd disappear in a sea of German tourists. Both of them were somewhat zombified.

When Mum explained that she had once called Shaker Babek "the son of a donkey" and "a hopelessly ignorant buffoon" and had threatened to report him to the authorities, I began to suspect that it was possible he had not personally selected the best-qualified and most honest workers he could find to help Mum. Passive aggression seemed to be his thing. Apparently, he had not been pleased about the donkey comment, though he hadn't been sure what a buffoon was. Now that buffoon had the power to shut down her dig. Or to make it a wholly unpleasant, impossible misadventure. In that region, it tends to be culturally expected to forgive and forget almost anything. Two guys can literally beat each other up and then, maybe just hours later, will be found sitting and having tea together.

But Mum had never forgiven Shaker Babek, and was certainly never going to have tea with the guy. While he pretended otherwise, he clearly felt the same way.

I recognized the driver who met us at the airport. It was Hamid. He had helped out on lots of previous digs in the region. Mum seemed to shake off the whole Shaker Babek thing as we jostled and loaded our stuff into the car. Meanwhile, Elvis was trying to get his phone to work. Once we had stepped out of the airport, the Wi-Fi was gone. Gone. And there wasn't going to be any where we were going. This still didn't seem to sink in. He didn't help unload luggage from the baggage belt. He didn't help load the bags into the waiting van. He was much too busy, his hands full of his non-working phone that he was repeatedly tapping at, like a woodpecker. He climbed into the car and sat there, pressing at the phone screen as if the harder he tapped, the better the chance it would work.

Once we'd loaded everything, we were off. For a while, anyway. Elvis grumbled in the corner, only coming to life once when we passed the Khartoum Happy Time Hotel.

"Look, they have Wi-Fi!" he cried. Aha, he could read.

"And?" Mum and I waited for a reply.

"Why don't we stay there, instead?"

Mum and I ignored him. He went back to tapping his phone screen, which he did for most of the ride, and had to stop to pee every half hour. And every time he got back in the car, he would whine about sand getting on his blue suede Vans and ask for the seven-hundredth time, "Are we there yet?"

Setting up camp in Sudan

We finally arrived at the site late that evening.

"No way," said Elvis, like it was a shock to him to find tents set up at a campsite.

And that was the beginning. I'd like to say that Elvis turned over a new leaf and came to love Egyptology and all of the wonders it held . . . but I won't, because it would be a lie. Elvis kept his phone in his pocket and checked it, like, every fifteen minutes, until it finally ran out of juice. That took about eleven hours. After that, he kind of fell apart. For the next two days, he looked like someone had emptied out the last few tiny pieces of shriveled brain from his head. I caught Mum looking at him, presumably wondering what she'd find if she stuck a hook up his nose.

She did try to engage him in conversation. We were stuck with him, after all, and he with us.

"Look, there's a piece of pottery," Mother said, pointing to a piece of pottery.

Elvis just stared off into the distance, his shirt unbuttoned, wearing one shoe. Mother handed him a brush. He took it, looked down at it. He seemed disappointed that it wasn't a phone. Then he went back to staring.

"Look, it's a piece of pottery," I said, handing him his other shoe.

He looked down at it, hoping it was a phone, then went back to staring. Crap. This was bad.

"Hey, there might be dead people over here," I said, pointing to some lumps of sand. I hoped that might interest Elvis. I tried another tactic.

"It'll be just like playing Candy Crush, only in real life." Bingo. I was pretty sure that made no sense whatsoever, but it seemed to do the trick.

Elvis was shaken out of his torpor by the promise of something close to a phone game.

Even if Elvis wasn't much interested, it was a pretty cool site. The next morning, as we were unpacking gear, we saw a familiar face.

"Ahmed!" Mum called out, her smile wiping away the frown she had carried with her from The Country That Shall Not Be Named.

Ahmed Almusaeid Abu Nadir came hustling forward to greet us. He was a core helper, taking charge of diggers and workers at excavations. Mother had worked with Ahmed many times. He didn't seem very happy.

"Madame Doctor Amilas," he said, almost apologetically. "Our people, they are not allowed here. Now we have a group who . . . who is not the most helpful."

"That isn't a surprise," she said. "Shaker Babek?"

Ahmed nodded. He had been on the dig back when Shaker Babek had tried to swindle them—Ahmed knew Shaker Babek as a lowly worm, oozing his way through the system.

"Is there *any* of our crew here, besides you, my friend?" Mother asked quietly.

Ahmed looked around, then nodded quickly. "I was able to have Mustafa and Abdu join us. Their salary may have to be arranged separately, if this suits, Madame Doctor." He looked anxious.

"Of course, Ahmed," Mother said reassuringly. She would trust these three men and only these three men.

The site at Gebel Barkal was huge. The small mountain dominated the area, with the peak looking like a rearing snake. At its base, in almost all directions, spread a series of temples. According to Mum, thirteen temples and three palaces had been found here. And there were probably more to be found. Mum had plans—her goal was to find the temple of the cult that was connected to sacred animals, if it existed. Some of the temples were actually cut into the mountain itself. They were pretty amazing and probably the most sacred of all, as they were in the heart of this holy site. There had been a lot of action here, back in the day. Not that I really cared all that much, but this was a major site for Amun Ra, my namesake. There were tons of statues of Amun's sacred ram, that were, I have to say, kind of cool, as well as images of kings worshiping Amun and bringing him offerings (I could have used some offerings myself—chocolate, perhaps a swimming pool). Besides the temples, there were some pyramids. Mummy called them "Toblerone Pyramids," because they were steeper and smaller than the Egyptian ones and looked as if someone had broken up a Toblerone bar and scattered the triangular pieces over the site.

I had to share a tent with Elvis. The first night was rough. Elvis kept grumbling and trying to get a signal for his dying phone. I'm still amazed at how utterly thick he was. It was weird, but the phone was like a part of him and he seemed lost without it. He seemed lost with it, too, but he clung to it like he'd die if he let go, carrying it around like a toddler would carry a blankie.

That night, he freaked out when he heard the howling of jackals.

"Holy crap!" he cried, shaking me awake. "There are werewolves out there!"

"No, werewolves aren't real," I tried to explain. "You're hearing jackals, who are hunting small mammals. They're far away."

"Yeah, but they can come closer, right?" Elvis was peeking out of the tent flap.

"Jackals are not going to come and sneak into the tent," I said, dismissively. "That just doesn't happen."

I decided not to tell him about the time a pack of jackals did sneak into our tent and stole all of our sandwiches and *basbousa*, a delicious, and very traditional, semolina cake soaked in sugary syrup, which we were stashing for an early-morning snack. We woke up and they had already gone, leaving a turd as their calling card.

"It doesn't happen," I lied. "Now go to sleep."

I was used to Mum's wake-up call, but the morning after the werewolf incident, Elvis fell out of his camp bed when she started banging on a tin cooking pot. That was her way of getting the camp up and running. Elvis was still clutching his phone when he climbed out of the tent. I was glad to see he was wearing shoes, but he was tapping on the dark screen of his phone. His hair was a mess—not a stylish, curated one, but a real mess—and you could almost feel sorry for him.

"You'll have to put that down when we get to work," Mum warned, pointing at his phone.

"Work?" Elvis, again, looked confused at the suggestion. "What work?"

"Work, Elvis," said Mum, containing her frustration. "You're here to work, and you'll be digging like the rest of us."

"Digging what?" Elvis asked.

"Treasure," I blurted out, thinking it might engage him.

"You mean like points?"

"What?" Mother looked at me to translate.

"No," I said. Then I rethought my answer. "Yes, just like points. It's a treasure hunt."

"Is there a way to get extra lives?" Elvis asked.

I looked carefully at his face, hoping to find some tiny element of humor or something. He could not possibly be serious.

"Um, no, Elvis," I said. "This is the real world. There are no extra lives. Try to use the one you have."

"Huh?" He must have tuned out.

I handed him a bowl for his breakfast.

"What's that?" he asked.

"What's what?" I asked. "This is a bowl and that's cereal. This is a spoon."

"Duh," he said. "What the hell is that cereal?"

"It's corn flakes, like it says on the front of the box." I pointed to the English words 'Corn Flakes.' It was written in Arabic on the other side, but the English side was facing him.

"I want Captain Crunch," he said. He was serious.

"We don't have Captain Crunch, Elvis," I said, trying to be pleasant. "This is what we have."

"Well, send someone to get Captain Crunch," said Elvis. "I don't want this stuff."

"Elvis . . . ." I tried to take a deep breath. It came out in a groan. "We're in the desert. No one is going to drive into town for a box of cereal that they won't find because it isn't available in this country. You're welcome to have any kind of cold cereal you'd like, as long as it's corn flakes."

"I want Captain Crunch," Elvis said, as if he was speaking to his silent phone.

"If you don't want corn flakes, you can have porridge or toast," I said. "There might be eggs. And there's lentil soup or *fuul*, both very traditional. That's what most of the workers have. *Fuul*. You know fava beans?"

"Yeah, I know," he said.

There were a few seconds of silence.

"All righty," I said. "Have whatever you want from the choices we have. I'm going to get a trowel."

"For what?" he asked.

"To dig," I said.

"Dig what?" asked Elvis.

I had a few answers on the tip of my tongue, but I let it go with a smile.

"Exactly."

Just after lunch, Mum let out a yelp. I immediately thought, *Scorpion? Snake?* But her second yelp made it clear that this was a yelp of excitement, not a yelp for help.

I ran over to her spot. I yelped. Mum had uncovered part of a statuette. It was of sandstone and was small enough to fit in my hand. It had painted bits and some gilded bits, gilded with real gold. Mum kept digging and the carved image of King Amenhotep III emerged. She carefully removed the king and placed him on a soft cotton sheet. Right beneath him was a statuette of Horus as a falcon.

"Mum, this is awesome," I whispered. I don't know why I whispered, but I did.

"Look," said Mum, "there, on the other side of Horus." She pointed to a section of sand next to the Horus statuette. She handed me a brush.

I leaned in and brushed away the sand. I had to look carefully, but I could see a tiny statuette of a creature rearing up on its hind legs.

"It . . . ." I looked closely. "It's a . . . shrew."

Yup, it was a shrew. A shrew is a small rodent-like creature

Shrew statuette, Sudan

with a pointy nose, sharp teeth, and the ability to see in the dark. It's smaller than a mouse, but is closely related to the elephant. Strange but true. But I digress.

"Can you read the inscription?" asked Mum, pointing to symbols on the side of the tiny thing.

I could read a lot of hieroglyphs and some hieratic, the cursive handwriting form of the language of ancient Egypt. Most people think the Egyptians always wrote in hieroglyphs, but that's yet another common misconception. Hieroglyphs were special, even in ancient Egypt. The word 'hieroglyph' is from the Greek and basically means 'sacred image.' Hieroglyphs were generally used in sacred places, like on the walls of temples and tombs. They can be found carved into statues and stone slabs (called stelae) that were given as offerings to the gods. Most of the everyday stuff was written in hieratic, though—less beautiful, less special, and much faster to write. Still, it was nicer to look at and easier to read than demotic, the last incarnation (it would be too weird to call it 'the most modern') of everyday ancient Egyptian writing, which looks as if a bunch of insects have dipped their legs in ink and raced all over a papyrus or wall.

"It says: 'The king, who is like Horus and Ra, who sees . . . everything . . . from the heavens like the hawk, and everything in the . . . night, like the shrew.'"

"Excellent job, Amun Ra," said Mum, kissing me on the forehead. "Isn't that such a lovely word for shrew? It's *amam*, in ancient Egyptian. We could have named you—"

"Mum, Amun Ra is bad enough. Please don't regret that you didn't name me Shrew!"

Shrews aside, this was a really incredible find. Not that I'm all into artifacts or anything, but come on—anyone would freak out for this.

"How rare and wonderful!" Mum said as we stared at this beautiful piece of art emerging from the sand. "Amenhotep was certainly keen on the animal manifestations of the gods—look at his gifts to the cult of the Apis bull and the crocodiles of Sobek. I believe we have every chance of finding traces of animal cults here, Amun Ra!" Mum was hopping up and down with excitement by now.

The statuette wasn't too far from the *gebel* (remember, that means 'mountain' in Arabic).

"This would be the perfect place for an animal catacomb," I agreed. "And how cool to find one made by Amenhotep III." From what Mum was mumbling to herself, I knew there might be mummies here, as well as some cool animal statues. I'll admit, it was exciting.

It was hours later that I remembered Elvis. Worried that he might wander off and get lost and we'd get in trouble for losing him in the desert, I went to look for him. I found him leaning on a rock, looking at his dead phone. I suppose he was imagining the game he could have been playing. From the look of his clothes and hands, he had done zero digging. At least he was consistent.

"Dude, we found some cool artifacts," I said.

"Uh-huh," he said, not looking up.

"Dude, there's a porcupine in your sock drawer and a potato ate your tablecloth," I said.

"Uh-huh," he said, not looking up.

Mum walked over and gave me a funny look. "A potato ate your what?"

"Just testing," I said, heading back to the dig with Mum.

Over the next few days, it was pretty much the same thing. Elvis wanted Captain Crunch for breakfast. Elvis wanted his phone, but it didn't work. Elvis did nothing to help. Nothing got better. Nothing changed.

And then something changed.

On the sixth day, I woke up, as usual, and threw the first pillow of the morning at him, as usual.

"Get up, Elvis," I said, as usual. But, unlike usual, there was no stream of swear words coming from the other camp bed.

Elvis was already up! I mean, he was already out of the tent! Before me!

I scrambled to get dressed, and hurried out to find him. Maybe he walked in his sleep and fell in a hole. Wishful thinking. Nope. He was at the breakfast table, looking at the corn flakes.

"Wow, Elvis, you got out of bed and I didn't have to dump your mattress or borrow a foghorn," I said, finding him pondering the one cereal option.

"What's a foghorn?"

"It's a loud horn that . . . never mind," I caught myself. Why bother explaining? "What have you been doing?"

I really wondered. Without his phone, he'd been sleeping as much as he could and moping the rest of the time.

"Stuff," he said.

"Ah, well, that's good," I said, pouring a bowl of corn flakes. "Always good to do, stuff. What kind of stuff?"

"Digging stuff, you know," said Elvis. "And other sandy, dirty stuff. Like we do here."

"Well, that's . . . possibly a good thing," I said. "You were digging?"

"Yeah," said Elvis, sniffing the corn flakes, "That's what we're doing, right?" 'We' was a bit of a stretch. Elvis had yet to do anything and I was worried that Elvis had suddenly kicked his habit of doing nothing and now might be causing damage to ancient artifacts, or maybe he was digging holes at our campsite and people might trip and fall into them in the dark.

"Where did you dig?" I asked.

Elvis looked a bit confused. "In the sand."

"That's very clever of you," I said. "Whereabouts in the sand?"

Elvis waved his hand around. His hand was flappy and didn't point in any particular direction. I only hoped that he hadn't dug under our tent or where we had chosen to make our latrine (that's the toilet).

"Got it," I said, though I didn't get it. "Are you starting to like it?"

"Like what?" asked Elvis.

"I thought you might . . . never mind," I caught myself again.

"I'm hungry," he said. "Is there Captain Crunch yet?"

"I think that's a very good sign," said Mother. "Perhaps he's coming out of his phone game stupor and using his brain."

"Maybe," I said. It did seem as if Elvis had undergone a shift in his enthusiasm. I was skeptical until he came over to our table.

"I want to dig," he said.

"Excellent." Mother stood up so quickly that she almost knocked over our glasses of tea. I think she wanted to encourage him before he reverted back to his coma-like regular state. "Go ask Mustafa—the fellow I introduce you to every morning, over there—no, the other gentleman—no, that's a camel. Mustafa is that human there. He'll get you tools, show you where to work, and help teach you how to go about it. And don't forget your notebook to record information in."

"Well, now that is something," she said, watching Elvis go to the wrong guy, then another, who was kind enough to turn the seventeen-year-old dingus around to face Mustafa. "He seems enthusiastic, more or less."

"Hmm," I said, wondering if Elvis just thought digging would get him out of here. Maybe he did suddenly change. Who knows? Stranger things have happened. Maybe he really was starting to find excavating ancient artifacts almost as interesting as playing Candy Crush or Robot Unicorn Attack.

"Madame!" Ahmed, who was in charge of packing artifacts, came running up in a panic. "Three of the small pots have gone missing."

"I'm sure they're around, Ahmed, don't worry." Mother didn't look worried. I think she was still in pleasant shock over Elvis's change of heart. Or maybe she was distracted by Mustafa running after Elvis, who was trying to dig next to the campfire.

"But last night I placed all of the pots together for packing," said Ahmed. "Today, there are only eight. Last night, eleven."

"I have one in my tent—it had a faint inscription on it that I was trying to make out," Mother said. "Let's check with Mustafa; maybe he packed the other two. Don't worry, we'll find them."

Poor Ahmed looked only slightly relieved. Being responsible for the artifacts was a nerve-racking job. Thefts at Mum's dig sites aren't that common since she knows her crew. But this wasn't her crew. Thefts are creepy when they do happen. Often, it's a new hire who steals items to sell on the black market. But a few pots, that's nothing. They were probably misplaced. There are hundreds and hundreds of pieces of pottery at almost every big dig. I'd prefer to think they were just misplaced rather than stolen. When pots get stolen, they are usually from the earliest period of Egyptian (or Nubian—though they made beautiful pots for longer) history, when very delicate and fine-walled vessels were made, or when some of the pots were decorated with images of animals or people. These were not so fancy. I wasn't worried and neither was Mum.

But the next day, Ahmed came bursting into Mother's tent in a panic. Mum and I were looking at part of a stela dedicated to Amun Ra that had been uncovered late the day before when Ahmed arrived.

"Madame, please forgive my incoming," he said. "The statuettes and the stelae we found yesterday are missing. This cannot be anything but theft, unless you came to get them. Perhaps this is so?" He looked hopeful, but his hope died as Mother jumped up.

"All of the statuettes? *All* of them?" Mother cried. This was no small thing. "Those statues are extremely rare, and key to understanding the site. They're also worth a lot of money. It's impossible that they're missing!"

"As I, too, believed," said Ahmed, sweat pouring from his brow (that says a lot, since it was freezing in the desert that early in the morning). "I was careful to put them in a box next to the crate from the same location. I left the lid off so you could check them before we put them in the crate. But this morning, may God help me, they were gone!"

Ahmed and Mother left the tent. I quickly followed them out. I stopped at my tent to check on Elvis. He wasn't there. I ran from tent to tent, checking for him. Not there. I yelled his name, in case he had wandered off somewhere. No answer. Then I went to the dining area. I found him at the table, having tea.

"Elvis," I said, rather breathlessly, "what are you doing? Didn't you hear me yelling?"

"What?" he said.

"You didn't hear me?"

"I'm having tea." He pointed at his cup.

"Look, I've been calling out . . . fine, never mind. Have you seen the statuettes we found yesterday of people praising the gods? Or the stelae dedicated to Amun Ra or the goddess Hathor?"

Elvis looked up, taking a moment to recognize me. "What's a stela?"

"It's a carved piece of stone that acts like a tomb marker, or a gift to a god," I began for some stupid reason. "You know, like a . . . never mind. What about the statuettes? Have you seen them?"

"What's a statuette?"

"It's a small . . . never mind."

If we really had a thief among us, we were in serious trouble. While thieves were punished harshly in the region, the threat did little to actually prevent theft. It wasn't uncommon for artifacts to be sold on the black market to wealthy people like . . . hmm, Elvis's father.

Mother was already gathering the workers together. Someone might have seen something. Someone was responsible. I looked at all of these unfamiliar faces. Originally, we had planned to have six workers from Mustafa's village—Mustafa, Mustafa's two helpers (Abdu and another Mustafa), Ahmed, and Ahmed's assistant, Ahmed—who had all worked with us before. Instead, we had Shaker Babek's questionable crew, which consisted of four other Ahmeds, another Mustafa, and a Hamdy, none of whom we knew and who weren't from any village our Ahmed had ever heard of. Then there were three big guys—*another* Ahmed, a Muhammad, and a Habib—who were responsible for meals, clean-up, site management, and other things. Again, strangers.

Mother was getting suspicious.

"Is anyone here related to Shaker Babek?" she blurted out. All hands went up, except Mustafa, Ahmed, Abdu, and one other fellow. That one fellow looked down when Mother walked up to him. "Is that true? You are not related to Shaker Babek?" she asked in Arabic.

"Well, my cousin Habiba is married to Ahmed, Shaker Babek's sister's brother-in-law," the fellow explained.

"Right," Mum fumed.

So these guys were all related to Shaker Babek? Wow. Good thing we had an honest workforce, uninfluenced by crooked relatives. Mother would put nothing past that slimy official, including hiring his whole family to undermine her excavation. If Amilas Marquis was in charge of a dig and a lot of artifacts went missing, Shaker Babek would have just the ammunition he needed to discredit her. He would use this catastrophe to either blackmail her or get her banned from digging.

Mother gave the one guy a stare that would have had Dracula shaking in his boots. The guy was shaking, though he was not wearing boots. Then she turned to the crowd. "Some things have been . . . misfiled and misplaced. We'll need to check everywhere for them." She dismissed the workers, but called Mustafa aside. "These men are never to be left alone with anything from the site. I'd like to check everyone's tent to see if the missing pieces are there, though I doubt anyone would be that stupid— Shaker would know that I'd check his people."

The next day, Mum and Ahmed began to search around and quietly investigate without making a big deal. They were still stumped as to who exactly might have taken the artifacts. Maybe they were all working together? There were so many shady characters to choose from, it was a serious possibility. While we were discussing the many shady characters thrust upon this dig, we received a surprise (and wholly unwelcome) visit from none other than Shaker Babek himself.

"Well, good morning, Amilas, *habibti*," he said in his smarmy, sticky voice, picking his way carefully around the stones that littered the site in an effort to preserve his highly polished and utterly inappropriate purple shoes. "It is lovely to see you! How are things going on the dig?"

"I'm very well," said Mother, flustered and clearly not happy. She collected herself, though her cheeks were flushed. "Given the limitations of your choice of workers, it's been an excellent excavation. Excellent."

"How wonderful," he answered, though I doubt he was listening. "May I see your finds? I am particularly interested in the statuette of the king. It is rather unusual, no, the animals with him?"

"The statuette?" My mother's eyebrows could not have risen any higher. She quickly contained herself. "Remarkable that you have already—"

"My position is very important." Shaker Babek took off his hat and wiped his forehead with a handkerchief. "Indeed, Amilas. I know a great many things."

"Do you, now?" Mum actually sounded amused.

"Well, yes." Shaker Babek smiled at Mum and, for some reason, Mum smiled back.

"Ah, Mr. Babek, honorable Shaker," she said in her smoothest, deepest, I-am-going-to-bust-you voice, and focused her stare on him. "I find it interesting that you know about a statuette that we only just discovered the other day. Indeed, only my team and I knew about it, since we located it and my team uncovered it—yet you seem to have seen it, too, yes? How could that be, Shaker? Goodness, how on *Earth* could that be?"

Where he had wiped moments ago, tiny beads of sweat reappeared on Shaker Babek's forehead before he could even stutter out a syllable. "My dearest, *habibti*, Amilas," he smarmed, "I-I . . . I'm the Director, and must know everything." Unable to ignore the sweat, he had to take out his handkerchief again and wipe his forehead. It was like *he* was being interrogated, not the other way around as he had clearly intended.

"Of course you should," said Mother. "But it's miraculous that you'd know so quickly and accurately about our discovery, considering you've surely been back in your office all this time, and couldn't have known unless . . . oh, I don't know, could it be . . . you had someone spying on me? As we all know, that isn't good form. Spies? Very low-class, Shaker."

"Never, Amilas, *habibti*," Shaker Babek groveled. Then he composed himself. "I would simply like to see the statuette of Amenhotep so I can report back on your . . . your remarkable find."

"Remarkable?" Mother's eyebrows climbed her forehead again. "We have yet to even establish how remarkable."

Now she scanned the workers, who were standing around and not working. There were seven as she counted from left to right. There were six going from right to left.

"Where's Ahmed?" she demanded.

The other workers looked around. There were several Ahmeds, but everyone seemed to know she meant the one who had been there a moment before.

"And where's Elvis?" I asked. He had been right behind me.

"Goodness, the son of the important and venerable Mr. Floosbaganov is missing?" Babek seemed to grow in height, which wasn't saying much, but is saying something. "Are we having trouble holding on to precious things and people? Tsk, tsk, *that's* not good form, my lovely Amilas."

"*Yalla!* Come!" cried another Ahmed, and the workers began looking for the missing Ahmed and Elvis.

Mother was in a fury, but Shaker Babek was doing his best not to smirk. He wasn't succeeding.

"Well, Amilas, we seem to have a problem here," he said, folding his arms across his chest. Then he went into the artifact tent and began walking, inspector-like, along the rows, stopping at several empty spaces.

Daggers. There were daggers in my mother's eyes.

"You think?" she spat out.

"Tsk, tsk, you are perhaps losing your control." Shaker Babek shook his head as if he was really concerned.

"As you can see, we have a thief," she said with restrained contempt. "Perhaps more than one. Perhaps a whole family of thieves."

"Indeed," said Shaker Babek, not realizing he had agreed that this was *his* family of thieves. And then an evil smile spread across his face. "As you can imagine, this simply will not do. You know that I must detain you for legal purposes, *habibti*. It is the correct thing to do." He could not help folding his hands into one another, then tenting his fingers into a pyramid, as if in deep contemplation. "It saddens me to think that Amilas Marquis is now a thief of antiquities."

Leaving Mother and me standing open-mouthed in shades of fury and shock, Shaker Babek called his guards (who were looking around furtively and seemed rather ashamed) to handcuff mother and take her to his waiting jeep.

Nothing else was said. They arrested Mother, and left the rest of us standing in their dust. Of course, by then 'the rest of us' consisted of Ahmed, Mustafa, Abdu, and me. The others had scattered. And Elvis was still nowhere in sight.

7
Breaking Mummy out of Jail

L et's take a step back here and consider the situation. Let's see if I can wrap it up in a short description. Yes, this about sums it up:
ARRGGH!

Does that make things clear? Because that was pretty much my take on it. Shaker Babek had planned this whole thing. Mum was set up, and Ahmed, Mustafa, Abdu, and I all knew it.

"Amun Ra." Abdu looked at me. "What are we to do?"

I had to think. I had a few things on my side. I was not quite fourteen, but I could drive the desert jeep. Still, probably not a good idea to do something else questionably legal. But I had to get into town. I had a sinking feeling that the disappearance of Elvis and the artifacts had something in common. I couldn't help but think that one had followed the other.

I decided to do what would be most helpful at that moment.

"Let's have tea," I said.

Within moments, we were sitting with sweet tea and a developing plan. Ahmed would drive me into town. I knew where I could find Elvis,

Ancient Egyptian handcuffs

if he hadn't gotten lost or run off to join a band of dervishes, the holy men who wandered around Sudan.. My guess was that the jerk was somewhere with his phone. Could he be more predictable? The guy was so lame and so totally, unquestionably, obviously guilty of *something*. Exactly what, I wasn't sure. But I knew he would sell out the whole excavation for a Wi-Fi connection and a bowl of Captain Crunch.

"Mustafa, you and Abdu guard the camp. Ahmed, take me to the only place in town where there's working internet."

"The Karima Happy Time Hotel?" he asked.

Indeed.

Driving way beyond the speed limit, had there been one in the desert, we got to the town of Karima in a matter of minutes. I left Ahmed in the jeep and ran into the lobby of the hotel. Scanning the room, I found him. Elvis Aaron Presley Floosbaganov was sitting with his bag, staring into his phone, using his opposable thumbs to do the only thing they seemed capable of doing—playing Candy Crush. The thought that millions of years of evolution had brought us to this flashed through my mind. Ouch. I considered being stealthy, but I doubted he'd even notice me. I walked over and stood right next to him. He didn't even look up. I glanced at the backpack that sat open next to him. Right there, on top, was one of the missing stelae. What a jerk. I picked up the bag.

"Is my plane ready?" he asked, finally sensing that there was someone standing an inch away from him.

I knew he would realize it was me, and that he was in deep doo-doo, as soon as I responded. I thought he might try to make an escape. So I did the only thing I could do to keep him from fleeing: I grabbed his phone.

Still looking into his hands and moving his thumbs, he took a moment to realize that it was gone. Only then did he look up.

"You, wait here," I said, as menacingly as I could, which was fairly menacing considering my utter fury. "Or . . . or you'll never see your phone again!"

I took the stolen stuff and the phone and ran out, jumped into the jeep with Ahmed, and we sped off to the jailhouse. On the way, I saw a single-engine plane land on a dirt road that doubled as a private landing strip. I had to hurry. As we pulled up in front of the jail, I wrote down instructions for Ahmed to contact the head of all antiquities in Sudan—Shaker Babek's immediate boss.

"I demand to see my mother," I said, stomping into the jailhouse. Obviously, I would have liked to burst through the doors for effect, but they were standing open. Slightly disappointing.

The desk clerk nearly fell off his seat. He didn't know what to do, but allowing me to see Mother didn't seem high on his list.

"See this?" I asked, waving the phone, trying to think up something quick. "I have the president on the phone and he is NOT happy!"

The clerk suddenly jumped into action and used his walkie-talkie to call someone. He kept looking anxiously over at a door on his right. A bit of a giveaway. I pushed past him and threw open the office door. Shaker Babek was sitting at his desk with, literally, egg on his face, dripping from the end of his bushy moustache. He was eating his breakfast, but next to his plate of eggs, fuul, and some kind of meat swimming in oil was the statuette that he had claimed was missing. He looked at me, looked at it, then back at me. He could see that I could see the thing, too. Now he had egg on his face literally *and* figuratively. He was busted.

"You release my mother NOW," I said. I waved the phone again. "We've contacted the authorities, and you're in big trouble, Babek. They're on their way right now."

"But my dear Amun Ra," Babek said as he jumped up, "such a miraculous thing, *alhamdulillah*. We have found the thief, and—"

"Oh, I found the thief, too, Babek. You got your guys to bribe Elvis Presley to steal artifacts in exchange for Captain Crunch and the internet."

"Captain who? I do not know this Captain Crunch, I only—"

Suddenly, a rather pudgy man in a Hawaiian shirt came waddling into the room. His timing could not have been more perfect, since this guy was Habib El Batal, the Head of Antiquities for Sudan! *Wow, that was fast!* I thought. *Ahmed is amazing.*

"What's this?" roared Habib El Batal. "I'm on my holiday, and I hear *you* have been the one at the center of these thefts? And I hear you've engaged a young European to steal for you from our beloved Amilas Marquis? Shaker Babek, you are in trouble!"

"*La-a, habibi,*" said Babek, shaking and bobbing. "The beloved Amilas Marquis has been helping herself—"

"You're a liar, Shaker Babek," said Habib El Batal. "You were only given this position because you're the brother of my wife's cousin's husband. I have long suspected . . . ."

I didn't wait to hear more. I ran from the room to get the guard.

"Open the jail and release my mother!" I cried.

The guard looked panicked, but clung to a big key chain, trying to get his walkie-talkie to work. But it was the television control in his hand, and instead of getting an answer from the other room he only managed to change the channels on the old TV next to his desk. I grabbed the keys from him and ran to a big metal door at the far end of the jailhouse, which I assumed was where they were keeping my mother. There were fifty keys to choose from. No way! I tried the first one, which did not fit but got stuck in the lock. When I tried to get it out, the door just opened. Somehow, I was not surprised.

"Mother!" I yelled, hoping she'd be able to wave her arm from one of the cells.

"I'm right here," Mother said, who was indeed right there.

As it turned out, there was only one cell and she was in it, right there by the door. It took me a couple of minutes to find the key to the cell, which did need a key to open (why did they have so many keys if there was only one cell?), but I got her out soon enough. We hurried back to Shaker Babek's soon-to-be-former office.

"Habib, *habibi*," said Mother, entering the office, looking disheveled but determined.

"Amilas," said Habib El Batal. "What is this terrible thing that has been thrust upon you? Are you hurt, *habibti*?"

"I'm holding my own, Habib," she said, brushing the dust from her trousers. "How are Amira and the children?"

"Amira is very well," said Habib, smiling. "Little Noor has learned to sew with the machine and to translate hieroglyphs. Tarek is starting classes at the international academy."

"Tarek, *da mish mumkin* (that is not possible)!," she said in mock disbelief. "Such a clever boy. And Noor, already learning to translate—and sew, too? How lovely." Mother looked at Shaker Babek, who was now mortified and gulping nervously. "I'm so glad the sewing machine I gave her is helping. And the hieroglyphs—she's enjoying the books I sent?"

"Oh, indeed, indeed," said Habib, beaming.

"I'm so happy to hear this, my friend," said Mother, smiling at Habib, then turning a triumphant smile toward Shaker Babek.

"Now, as for this *mushkela kibiir* . . . ," said Habib. Whether he meant that the 'big (*kibiir*) problem (*mushkela*)' was the thefts or the thief was not clear, but now Shaker Babek certainly had a *lot* of egg on his face.

"Yes, a very big *mushkela*," agreed Mother. "It seems there's been a ring of thieves stealing from your precious sites." She eyed Babek. "Not only is there a plot to remove artifacts from Egypt and Sudan, but there has been theft of important antiquities for the personal gain of corrupt individuals."

Here Shaker Babek jumped up and began to splutter. He tried to sit back down in his chair; he missed. After a rather cartoonish attempt not to fall on his ass, he did. Habib El Batal now looked both angry and worried. No matter what he felt about the slimy Shaker Babek, the creepy man was still his relative. Habib's honor was, vicariously, at stake. But he was also clear that Mother had been wronged, and the antiquities compromised, and there had to be action.

"And we are lucky that Shaker Babek was able to help us uncover the problem." Mother smiled knowingly and with a gleam of power in her eye. At first, I was going to protest, but I realized she was using this to her advantage. I smiled, too, as did Habib. He sighed and looked relieved. This would mean that no charges would be filed and he would not have to deal with arresting a relative. The man on the floor was his cousin by marriage, after all. But that didn't mean that Habib El Batal necessarily had to play nice. He glowered when he looked at the cowering creep. Shaker Babek's balding combover hairdo was suddenly visible from behind his desk as he lifted his head.

"This fool of a man was actually helpful?" Habib asked, pointing at Shaker Babek like he was something smelly that the cat had dragged in.

"Well, I think he would have liked to be helpful," said Mother, graciously. "The position of Chief Inspector is such a tiresome job, perhaps not a job equal to Mr. Babek's talents. I'll debrief you on all of the secret dealings that have occurred, though surely we won't find the man at the center of this misadventure, since, as we know, such a man cannot be Sudanese. No Sudanese official would ever stoop so low as to steal from his own country. It must have been foreign smugglers. I do have a recommendation for a new Chief Inspector, though, who would be happy to allow Mr. Babek to retain his uniform and work under supervision."

She smiled, knowing she had won.

An hour later, Mother and I waved at the plane that carried Elvis back home.

Before he left, Mother made me give him his phone. And she handed him an envelope that contained a note for his father.

Dear Mr. Floosbaganov,

We are returning your son, who was indeed at our excavation. He learned to use a trowel, and to survive breakfast without his Captain Crunch cereal.

He was instrumental in the decision to elect the new Chief Inspector of Antiquities for Khartoum, Ahmed Almusaeid Abu Nadir.

Sincerely,

Professor of Distinction, The American University in Egypt
Newly Appointed Head of Bioarchaeology

He took it from her, head bowed, no doubt wondering if he would from now on be driving a yellow Mercedes. And so, Elvis Aaron Presley Floosbaganov went home with little more than shame to show for his trip to Sudan. Just shame, and his phone.

8
Toilet Trouble

I thought my life was falling into a groove. This was a big improvement. Mum was teaching, and we were in Cairo. I was actually doing normal things, like going over to friends' houses and playing board games or video games, swimming and playing sports. Badly, but still playing. It felt like normal. I had a life without the constant imposition of mummy bandages, bits of pottery, or fragments of coffins for most of August and September. All that, and my mother had promised me a dog. No, I mean a *live* dog, as opposed to the mummified or skeletonized dogs that Mum kept piling up on our dining room table.

Okay, maybe things weren't totally normal, but they were generally looking good.

Then came Eid al-Adha and the mission to the Nile Delta in Egypt. After the fiasco in Khartoum, two things had happened. Mr. Floosbaganov decided it was in his best interests to give another massive amount of money to fund any future excavation in Egypt, as long as Mum was leading the project. To be honest, this gift was likely Floosbaganov's way of showing his appreciation to Mum for putting up with Elvis. Word must have gotten back to him that his son had been up to some naughtiness: in addition to being the world's biggest douche, Elvis had managed to (almost) become an international antiquities thief. But you didn't hear it from me. Or Mum. As a result of his donation, Mum was able to get the most advanced satellite access and GPS, the best scanners, and even phones that had GPS tracking and 3D imaging capabilities. She was able to pay the best wages to get the best workers, and everyone loved her.

The other thing was the big news of Mum's new position as Head of Bioarchaeology in Egypt. As an official, she had to agree to dig in some places she didn't particularly love. The Nile Delta was one of Mummy's least favorite places to work ("Too wet, too humid, and it turns the mummies to mush!"). I wasn't too bothered, as it meant we'd be there for as few days as possible and I'd be back in Cairo in time for the Teen Dance. I was never super keen on dancing, but the girls all wanted to go. Not that I cared about the girls, but . . . oh, never mind.

The drive to the Delta was long, boring, and bumpy. We finally stopped for water and a stretch after more hours than I could count. Mum and the driver were looking at some castor plants that she claimed the ancient Egyptians had used to make oil that could be used as a laxative, make hair grow, and treat acne, warts, and fungal infections.

"Look, the very same castor plants that ancient Egyptians used as a laxative, or to make hair grow, and to treat acne, or warts, and fungal infections," Mum said, cheerfully.

Yuck, yuck, and yuck again. I could feel her looking at my face to see if I had any spots she could rub with her smelly castor plant. No thanks. I was about to get back in the jeep to hide when I heard a sad little whimper from near the wheel of the car. I bent down.

Ouch. Can cuteness hurt? Like an arrow to the heart. That's what it felt like, seeing the small sandy nose sticking out from behind the wheel. It was a tiny puppy. She could fit into my hand. I've seen *baladi* dogs, and this one looked about half the size of the smallest puppy I'd ever seen. *Baladi* dogs are what Egyptians call their street dogs. The word *'baladi'* literally means 'my country' or 'of my country'; when they say *'baladi* dog', they mean a local dog or a dog of the country. Many of them are descendants of the pharaonic hounds, which were domesticated thousands of years ago by ancient Egyptians. Then, when the pharaohs and their descendants faded from power, the hounds were left to wander. They're like the opposite of pet wolves. There's always something of the wolf still there, even if the animal was hand-fed by a human from the time it was a puppy. It might wag its tail at you, but you can never really turn your back on it. On the flip side, pharaonic hounds were left to roam for thousands of years, but there's still something of the pet in these wild dogs. If you approach them, you know what they usually do? They lower their front legs so their bums are in the air, then they roll over on their backs and wag their tails. It's hilarious! Wild dog? Yeah, right. This is an act of submission, like begging to be given a cuddle. Great attack plan! They must have been bred for companionship and not for guard duty, because even the mothers—wild dog mothers, mind you—will let you play with their puppies! Their trust in humans is so deeply bred that they trust even strange humans to come and cuddle their pups.

This little puppy hiding behind the wheel must have wandered off from the rest of its litter. I looked around. I listened. No dog sounds or waddling mother dogs coming over and rolling over on their backs. No other puppies. Nothing.

"Mum, we have a visitor," I called as I sat down next to the tiny dog and let it sniff around.

Mum looked up from her leaves. She was waving them around behind her behind, embarrassingly miming their laxative properties to the red-faced driver. I picked up the puppy to show her. The puppy decided, at that moment, to empty its bladder.

"Watering the plants, are we?" Mum said, laughing.

I held the little dog away from my feet and managed to avoid getting peed upon.

"I don't see a mother or other pups, do you?" I asked.

Mum came over. "A pharaoh hound? But so tiny?" She ruffled the tiny creature's head. It yawned. "She may sadly be the runt, the littlest. It's possible she was abandoned."

"Poor thing," I said. "Who'd abandon her?"

I put her down and she chased her tail for a few seconds, then waddled over to me, crawled into my lap, and fell asleep in two seconds flat.

Uh-oh.

"Mum?"

"Absolutely not," she said with absolutely no conviction whatsoever.

Once she was done with the plants, we checked at the nearby village to see if they had any missing pups. No one did. But most laughed when they saw the tiny puppy.

"Too small, no mama want," said most of the people in various ways.

"It's true, like I said. A runt might get left behind," said Mum, her eyes falling on the tiny snoozing fluffball.

I put on my saddest face, sticking out my bottom lip and fluttering my eyes.

"Put that lip away," warned Mother. "Don't use that or your batting lashes as a weapon."

I pointed at the puppy and stuck my lip out farther. I know how to fight the good fight.

After collecting eggs, onions, dates, and firewood, we were on the road again. ALL of us—Mum, the driver, me, and my dog! Yes, it's true! I really truly had my very own dog with us in the car as we drove, bouncing and bumping, deeper into the Delta. The puppy buried her nose under my arm and quickly fell asleep. She was so cute . . . I couldn't wait to tell Sadia.

So there we were, on our way to the Eastern Delta. Because of Mum's new position, she was now also responsible for overseeing all human and animal remains found on excavations in Egypt. She might have been able to get out of driving out to this excavation, except that she was helping a friend who had found a temple dating from the early years of ancient Egyptian history, about 2800 BC. Mum had promised to examine some bones he'd found, as well as some statues that were made of bone or ivory.

She was not looking forward to it. "Apparently, those artifacts are completely encrusted with Delta mud. They have to be carefully cleaned by dissolving or gently chipping off the mud and salts." Delta mud is the most fertile soil in Egypt. Things grow in it, lots of things. Unlike sand, it isn't easy to remove, and apparently this had made it quite difficult to tell what these statues were. She sighed, "That said, because these artifacts are from such an early period in Egyptian history, they are sure to be important." I could see excitement barely hidden under the resigned look on her face. "Still, it's the Delta. Yuck."

After driving through endless fields separated by a complicated system of canals, and having to stop every seven minutes to let the dog (okay, and me) out to pee, we were getting close. By late afternoon, we made it to the dig house. This was a big house made of red brick that was plastered and painted yellow. There were a few other red brick and concrete houses around, but most of the houses in the area were still made of traditional mud brick. I know that Mum would rather have been in a mud-brick house, as they're cooler in summer and warmer in winter, but I figured that the house we were in would have a better bathroom—I was tired of having to go to an outhouse in the dark of night to do my business. I'm not too fond of running into snakes, or scorpions, or the-gods-know-what-else in the dark, ready to slither up a leg and climb down a neck!

We went in and were welcomed by the gigantic dig director, Willem van Delft, who made my tiny mother look even smaller when he rushed up to greet us. To him, on the other hand, she was a tiny giantess. Big Willem seemed to shrink in her presence and literally looked up to her, though he had to stoop. He nodded to me and bowed deeply to Mum. He continued to bow several times after we'd returned the greetings. He kept mumbling about how delighted he was, but I was used to people fawning all over Mum. No big deal.

So Willem blushed and smiled. And then there came a squeaky little snuffling yap from somewhere inside my hoodie. Willem jumped. He looked around. I pulled out the puppy. She wagged her tail and yawned while she dangled there by her scruff. I quickly ducked out of the room so she could have a toilet break. She immediately tinkled when I let her down. Such a good girl. I came back in, and Willem smiled and opened his arms. I handed him the puppy, who instantly disappeared into his embrace. Willem laughed as the puppy tried to lick the chin rolls that made up most of his neck. He held out the dog, who looked like a tiny spot in his hand.

"Vat is the name of this *hond?*" Willem asked.

"I'd hardly call her a hound," I joked, knowing full well that *'hond'* means 'dog' in Dutch. "She's just a plain d-o-g."

"Dee-o-gee," laughed Willem. "Excellent name for such a creature."

I thought about it for a moment.

"Yes, her name is D-O-G. DOG is the perfect name."

After dinner, we got settled into our bedroom. The housekeeper wanted me to put DOG outside, but finally agreed to give me a small basket for her that I placed next to my bed. Needless to say, DOG whined in the basket, wondering why I had suddenly abandoned her. I waited until the housekeeper's bustling around the room came to an end, and then smuggled the puppy onto my bed.

That night, I got up with DOG every hour, so that she would learn to pee outside. It was exhausting, but I'd been preparing for this my whole life, and had read countless books and visited countless websites on dog training. By 4 a.m., DOG would whine when she needed to go. Miracle of miracles, she was nearly trained.

"Up, up, up!" cried Mother. "Things to do, objects to see, and a dog to walk!"

That was at 6 a.m. Oh, gods. Even DOG yawned and crawled deeper under the covers.

"It's not even light," I complained, knowing full well that it was hopeless to argue. Digs with Mum start at daybreak. This meant we generally got dressed when it was dark so we could be on the site at first light. But today I had a dog to walk, and, judging from the pitiful whining from deep under the covers, it was not a moment too soon. I leapt out of bed and shoved my feet into my *shib-shib*. *Shib-shib*, slippers, are the preferred morning footwear, since no scorpion or snake can hide inside them at night. I took DOG with me for a quick walk around the dig house, or rather *she* took *me* for a walk. I had fashioned a little leash out of rope, and she pulled me around, to dig, or chase a leaf, or sniff a poo. She ran around for about five minutes and then fell asleep in her tracks. I carried her back to our room and I got properly dressed to join Mum and the others.

They were a small team of specialists: Willem, the director (huge); Mum (small only in stature); two site supervisors (of moderate sizes), who oversaw different parts of the excavations; an artist (tall and thin) to draw pictures of the finds; a conservator (taller than Mum, but who isn't?), who would clean and mend the finds; and a pottery specialist (okay, she *wasn't* taller than Mum—we're talking tiny). Just as we had finished the last of boiled eggs, tea, and toast, a man burst into the room, shouting.

"*Ya, doktor, doktor*, there has been a remarkable find! There is a statue, maybe of a king!"

"What? Where? Who's been at the site?" bellowed Willem.

"No, no, not at the site, but in the small village not far from where you're digging. Come, all of you, at once!" Gesturing at us all, he turned and ran out. We followed, grabbing our bags full of tools and cameras, and, last but not least, DOG, who I carried since she was still asleep.

It was only a short walk to the clump of houses they were calling a village. But I had no idea what was going on or why we were following that man.

"Who is that guy, Mum?" I panted as we hurried after the fellow running in front of us.

"That's the local antiquities inspector, Abdel Raouf. I remember him from last year," said Mum, not the least bit out of breath. "How terribly exciting—a royal statue in a village! If it's in its original location, it means that part of the village was built over a temple." We continued speed-walking on through the collection of small houses. To call this a village was *definitely* an exaggeration. And it might not have been far from the dighouse, but it was far enough. I was out of breath, and DOG, still sleeping, was getting heavier and heavier with each step.

Finally, Abdel Raouf stopped abruptly. We were at the edge of the village where new houses were being built.

"Here! It's in here! In the house of Mustafa, the house that he is illegally building—the land belongs to the Ministry of Antiquities." Abdel Raouf pointed to a partly finished building. A man stood in front, arms crossed, glaring at us.

"I'm telling you, it's nothing. There's nothing here," he insisted, nervously, speaking Arabic in a strong country accent. "It's just the toilet that I am making in my new house."

"Ooh, how lovely, Mr. Mustafa. I'm terribly interested in the construction of contemporary toilets. Can we come and see?" Mum bestowed one of her charming smiles on the surly man, and then she headed straight into his half-built house without waiting for a reply.

I stood my ground. "Mum, do I have to go?"

"Of course, you have to go to the toilet," she yelled, already inside the house.

I know my cheeks turned red—I could feel them burn. I hung my head and followed. I was headed into a stranger's house to look at his unfinished toilet. Lovely. DOG was now awake but unbothered, happily chewing on my shirt. I reluctantly entered, stalling at the threshold, but Abdel Raouf and Willem were following behind, so I had no choice but to move forward. The owner followed us, I suppose to make sure no one pooped without permission.

"Here, it's here," the man said, shoving ahead, pointing to a door on our left. The whole house was rather a tight fit with all of us in there at once. Especially Willem, who could barely stand up beneath the low ceiling.

Mustafa nodded emphatically. "You can go in to see it." He flung the door open.

I closed my eyes. Did I really want to see this guy's toilet? I've seen country toilets, and they aren't pretty. I was expecting the worst, but to be fair, it wasn't as disgusting as some of the hole-in-the-floor stink piles I've seen (and been forced to use) over the years. It had these purple and black tiles with green circles that seemed to swim around, hurting my eyes and making me queasy. There was something very wrong about the whole thing. It was like an underworld version of a bathroom designed to scare anyone wanting to use it. Abdel Raouf and Willem seemed a bit queasy, too, and mumbled something to each other, both nodding and shading their eyes.

"Hmm, really?" said Mum, her head to tilting to one side as she looked at the guy. When my tiny Mum looks up at someone like that, it feels like she's a goddess looking down at a lowly mortal. What was up? It was as if she somehow didn't believe this was his bathroom.

"I would have thought that the toilet we're after would be back there." Mum pointed down the hall. I couldn't believe it—she didn't believe him! Weren't we in the bathroom? How could she doubt the guy's toilet was where we just saw it? I just wanted to leave. It was getting really stuffy in there, all of us standing in the guy's startling bathroom.

She leaned closer to the man, who was now cowering.

"Most house plans put another toilet at the back. I'll just check there, shall I? The others can admire your beautifully tiled front toilet while I take a gander in the back." And with that, she darted out before the man had a chance to stop her. He did reach out to grab her, but Abdel Raouf blocked him. What was going on?

"Aha!" I heard Mum's muffled voice coming from deep in the bowels of the man's house.

"Coming, Mum," I called back, trying to keep DOG from slipping out of my hoodie. She had fallen back asleep.

Abdel Raouf looked concerned, following behind me. "I believe your mother needs help in the toilet."

I opened my mouth to say something, but realized I didn't want to say anything. What could I say? "Yes, let's all go help Mum in the toilet?" I could feel my cheeks burning again.

Following the sound of Mum's voice, we pushed through the narrow corridor.

"Here it is!" Mum's voice was getting louder.

The man groaned behind us.

"Abdel Raouf!" came Mum's voice, echoing from down the hall. "Willem! Amun Raaaa! Yes, yes . . . indeed! Oh, come quickly!" She sounded very excited. It's weird that someone could be so excited about a toilet, but remember it's my Mum we're talking about.

The roof over the back of the house wasn't fully built. There were only a couple of planks and a dried palm leaf. But there was certainly another bathroom back there. This one had even more horrid tiles. They were a hideous mustard yellow, and covered all four walls and the floor.

"Here!" echoed Mum's voice from a hole in the middle of the floor.

The hole wasn't that wide, but it was *very, very* deep. I peered down into it. There, where the homeowner had been planning to build his toilet, in the mud and smelly gunk of the Delta, was the shoulder and crowned head of a stone statue. Yup, there was a king in the toilet. Presumably, when the king had the statue built, being in a mustard-yellow toilet had not been on his agenda:

> 1. **RULE THE KNOWN WORLD.**
> 2. **BUILD A GIANT STATUE OF MYSELF.**
> 3. **WIND UP INSIDE SOME GUY'S TOILET.**

Yeah, not likely.

"I think I know who this is," Mum said, looking up at Willem and Abdel Raouf.

Willem crouched down and Abdel Raouf leaned over. Suddenly, DOG started to wiggle. I took her outside for a pee. By the time I came back, there seemed to be a general agreement among the three experts on the origin of the toilet king.

They were fairly certain that the statue was one of four, since there are usually four statues that guard the front of temples. From what they knew about the area, Mum, Willem, and Abdel Raouf concluded that there must have been a temple down there, on the site of this guy's toilet. Mustafa looked very guilty. He knew there was something important down there and he had tried to put a lid on it, so to speak. The last thing he wanted was a woman crawling around his loo. The guy must have figured that if he just didn't tell anyone and filled his toilet (ha ha, with dirt), no one would be the wiser. If no antiquities were found in the ground, then the Ministry of Antiquities had no real reason to stop him from building. Sorry, Mustafa, this was one toilet that would have no privacy.

Our short trip ended up being a lot longer than I'd thought.

The Minister of Antiquities arrived, armed with documents and official papers, within hours of Abdel Raouf reporting the find. It became clear that the Ministry had already purchased all the land in the neighborhood, including Mustafa's plot. The poor man wasn't happy about that, but he had no choice. By the next day, they had started digging up gardens and floors in and around all the houses in the area. Abdel Raouf headed this new dig and began hunting for the front of the buried temple. On the outskirts of the village area, there were abandoned houses. These were not interesting to Willem, Abdel Raouf, or anyone. They were out of the area where the temple could have been. Unfortunately for Mustafa and the other homeowners, the temple was right under their houses.

If Mum hadn't been so pushy, that temple might have been buried forever under . . . you know what. As it was, this discovery turned out to be one of the largest and most important temples in the Delta, dating from about 1400 BC.

But our fun with toilets wasn't over yet.

Once the find was secured and the workers began removing the muck, Mum suggested that Abdel Raouf offer Mustafa one of the abandoned houses outside the perimeter of the dig—it was bigger, nicer, and had a pre-dug, pre-piped latrine already in it. Mustafa tried to hide his excitement. Apparently, his wife's grandmother had given them the bathroom tiles. He'd found them as distasteful as we had, but hadn't figured out how to get rid of them. Perhaps this was a bit drastic, but Mustafa found a way for it to work in his favor. He agreed to take the abandoned house as long as Abdel Raouf would tell his wife that the tiles couldn't be saved. It was a deal.

Mum, Willem, and the rest of the gang had gone back to work on Willem's dig while things were being sorted by the Ministry. There was a lot of identifying, cataloguing, and listing. Mum identified a bunch of bones—hippo, pig, and cow—before focusing on the mud-, dirt-, and salt-caked statues, which were the main reason we were there. Mum hunkered down with the conservator. I found some rice and leftover chicken to feed DOG, and took her for a long walk around the dig. When we were as far as we were going to go, she lay down and fell asleep. I had to carry her all the way back.

Mum didn't even look up from her work when I arrived carrying DOG. She just handed me a wooden tool. With a sleeping puppy in my lap, I started gently chipping away at the dirt and salt encrusted on some cylinders or thick sticks made of something hard and white. Understand this: Egyptology isn't glamorous. In fact, it often involves making innocent people do a lot of boring work that frequently leads to nothing. If you were wondering, I was the chump with the piece of wood, oh-so-carefully chipping away at crusty dirt that covered who-knows-what. Hours and hours of scraping, and flicking, and chipping away. It was about as fun as rubbing pieces of rock with a toothpick. Oh, wait, that's exactly what I was doing.

I was glad to have DOG for regular distraction. That is, when she wasn't trying to chew my pieces of wood or the artifact I was trying to uncover with them.

If, after several days (that seemed like months), I ever looked around and wondered where all the dust, dirt, and salt from the artifacts had gone, I had only to blow my nose to get an answer. It's hard not to inhale that sort of stuff while doing this kind of work, even with those paper masks that are often already filled with someone else's dust by the time I get them. After all those days and all those tissues, it felt kind of good to know the work was not for nothing. It turned out that we were cleaning statuettes of ivory. Mystery solved. And they looked pretty cool once the dirt and salt had been removed.

"We can date them by their nipples," I heard Mother say to Abdel Raouf. Did everything in Egyptology come down to anal holes, toilets, and body parts?

I could actually see what she meant—some of the male statuettes had pointy nipples, while others had tiny lumps, and still others had tiny holes. Of course, if you try to quote me on this, I shall deny knowing what you mean.

"Look at those sharp, pointy ones," Mum added, picking up one of the oldest statuettes.

"Indeed, Amilas," Willem said, joining in with the nipple conversation. "Apparently, these earlier ones were sculpted to be more prominent, and later they became depressed." Depressed? Now that is something I could understand.

They sat there nodding, staring at various body parts. Honestly, these scientists.

Other statuettes were of women. Some had chips of blue lapis lazuli stones for eyes. "Those stones come all the way from Afghanistan," Mum explained to me. "And look at these."

She picked up a smaller statue. There were three like it.

"Children?" I asked.

"Dwarfs," said Mum. "As you know, dwarfs were considered blessed and magical people by the Egyptians. Note how these were sculpted with a loving hand."

There were also animal statuettes: several lions and baboons. I got to use the microscope to see the patterns on the ivory. Mum showed me how to tell the difference between elephant and hippopotamus ivory, since there were some of each.

"See there," she said, pulling out a photograph of an elephant tusk from Willem's notes. You could see the striations, the patterns in the ivory.

"The elephant ivory has these diamond-shaped patterns in it, formed by the lines of Retzius or Schreger. These fine intersecting lines are visible in cross-section. See? Hippo tusks are narrower than elephant tusks, and have some wavy lines, but no diamonds or triangles." I could totally see that through the microscope.

It was kind of weird and even cool to think of the people of the Delta going out to hunt huge hippos. They used the ivory and ate the hippo meat. At some sites, huge hippo leg bones were used as steps leading into houses. There had been elephants, but most of them had probably migrated south by 2800 BC, so the elephant tusks Mum found must have been traded through what is now Sudan. It was significantly less cool to think of elephants being hunted and killed only for their ivory. Sadly, that is still part of life on this planet. The wise and wonderful elephant continues to suffer at the hands of man.

"No!" I cried, as DOG tried to snag the statuette out of my own hand. I guess I couldn't blame her. It was a bone, and she was a dog.

"Well, that's the last of them," said Mum, standing up from the table of artifacts for the first time in what seemed like days.

"Does that mean we can go back to Cairo?" I asked, imagining calling Sadia and telling her all about single-handedly saving little DOG and giving the sweet, lost puppy a home. "Maybe we should think about leaving tomorrow? I mean, why wait when we're already done, right? It is the Delta, after all." I knew this wasn't Mum's favorite place to dig, so I suspected she'd want to go soon.

Mum looked over at DOG, who was scratching her back by rubbing it in the dirt. "*Someone* will have to get DOG cleaned up," she said, as if there was 'someone' other than me to do it. I raised my hand as if to volunteer.

"Better not use a bathroom, Amun Ra," she said. "It'll be too messy." I wasn't sure if she meant the dog would be too messy or the bathroom.

I looked at DOG. Her light brown fur was covered with Delta mud, and her back fur stuck up from the dirt she was using as a back scratcher. Her tail looked like it was sprouting plants, and on her nose was a little flower that she was trying to catch with her tongue. She was not a pretty sight. I wondered how the neighbors in Cairo—who were weirdly flexible about the myriad dead things that often came to stay in our apartment— would feel about a living dog. I knew our *bawwab* (literally 'doorman') didn't mind piles of dead creatures, but he had an unreasonable dislike of live animals unless they were clean, nicely brushed, and wore a ribbon. Most Egyptians aren't big fans of dogs unless the dogs are small, white, and fluffy. They call these dogs 'griffons,' as if they were all part of one breed. I suspect this Egyptian 'griffon' is really any small, white, fluffy dog. While DOG was not white or extremely fluffy, she was small and cute, and might just pass as acceptable . . . if she was clean. And then Sadia would swoon. My lovely thoughts of Sadia and the salvaging of my social life were interrupted by Willem shouting from the far edge of the site.

"Amilas! Amilas! Come over here and look at this!"

While I rolled my eyes and hoped beyond hope that some new discovery wouldn't slow down our return to Cairo, I wondered what he had found. I walked over, DOG at my heels. Willem was pointing down at something, not as deep as the original find.

"This is at a much higher level, Willem. It must be more recent—most likely 300 BC, judging by the pottery. Practically new!" Mum was rather dismissive of such 'modern' discoveries, but she started looking closely at whatever it was. With Willem in the way, I couldn't see what they were staring at. I moved forward and nearly fell over when DOG grabbed my shoelace.

"Yes, we haven't been digging over here much yet," said Willem.

"This layer is certainly the most recent. It might well be from the last moment that the site was occupied." Mum was getting excited, I could tell. Uh-oh.

"Mum . . . ," I started, trying to think of ways to talk her out of her excitement.

"There seems to be a line of pots here," she said, pointing to the line of pots. And even I knew this was important. But couldn't Willem and his crew deal with what was left without her?

Willem cleared his throat. I tried to telepathically beg him not to ask. He ignored me. "I know that you have finished the work, Amilas, but maybe you and Amun Ra . . . perhaps, if it's not too much to ask . . . ."

I was about to say "Yes, it is too much to ask," when Mum cut in.

"Of course we will stay, Willem," she said. "Amun Ra, since they're short-handed, you can help clean and catalogue the remaining artifacts. I assume, Willem, you would like me to oversee this part of the dig, as you have your hands full."

Mum's dislike of the Delta had failed to triumph over her archaeological enthusiasm. "That said, Willem," Mum considered, "you know that this really isn't my period." That was music to my ears. This meant there was a small ray of hope that we would leave sooner rather than later. With less to draw Mum's attention and interest, we just might be out of here in a few hours. This stuff that Willem was excavating was all made yesterday, as far as she was concerned. 300 BC? Bah! After cataloguing what was left, there was no reason to stay. There were only a few pieces left to catalogue and that took me all of an hour. Mum was almost finished, too. I could feel it in my non-mummified guts . . . soon we would be heading back to Cairo. I looked down and watched as DOG tried to chew on something sticky that was stuck in her tail.

"Come on, DOG," I said, feeling better by the second. "Let's have a bath." I figured I could probably use one, too.

Instead of following me, DOG jumped into the excavation trench. She started whining, growling, and digging like she'd gone nuts.

"Hey, DOG!" I shouted. "Come on, girl! Stop!"

But DOG did not stop. She didn't even look up at me. She just kept digging as fast as her wee paws would let her, utterly ignoring me. Mum shot me a this-is-why-we-frown-upon-bringing-puppies-to-excavations look. I shrugged my shoulders, helpless.

"DOG, stop!" said Mum. And not very loudly, either. Amazingly, DOG immediately stopped digging and looked up at Mum.

"Sit!" Mum said. DOG sat.

"Bad digging!" Mum said. DOG looked down and whined, as if she was apologizing for her moment of digging insanity. Did Mother expect DOG to use a trowel and record her finds in a notebook?

"I'm so sorry, Willem," said Mother. "I can only say that . . . um, she seems to have uncovered something." DOG had gently picked something up in her mouth and deposited it at Mum's feet. Mother took DOG's gift and let out a "hmm." The puppy had uncovered two pots, broken at the neck. I didn't think much of them until Mum held one in each hand, and . . . they seemed to fit together.

Mum let out another "hmm." I let out a tiny groan. This, unfortunately, looked interesting.

"Maybe I *can* be of some help here," Mum said with renewed interest. "Amun Ra, please take your brilliant furry little archaeologist and give her a nice big bone—from the kitchens, not the artifact table. And please get me my excavation tools so I can get to work on these. Make sure DOG is safely tucked away in your room and come back to help me."

"But . . . but I need to give her a bath before we head back, and—"

"Oh, you'll have time," Mum said, ominously. "We've got a couple of hours of work here first."

I took DOG off to get her treat.

"Traitor," I whispered. "Thanks a lot."

When I came back, Mum was on her hands and knees next to a line of big tubes made of clay that were partially exposed in the muck. It was like some weird pottery pipeline. I'd never seen anything like that before.

"Mum, what are those things? They kind of look like a pipe system."

"Well done, Amun Ra!" Mum beamed at me, a big smudge of dirt on her nose. "They're actually the necks of large amphorae, you know, jars that were used for storage of oil and wine. Except these weren't broken by accident. They've been broken off for another use. See? They've been fitted into one another to create a pipe. Now, grab that trowel and those bags that have already been labeled for this area, and start scraping. I want to see where this pipe system leads."

Okay, so we were still in the Delta, the dog was still a mess and so was I . . . but come on, this was like being a detective. While I'd rather have been on my way back to Cairo, I could handle another hour or two to solve this mystery. No problem.

The problem was that the digging and scraping took three more days. The farther we got, the weirder it smelled, particularly in the area next to the pipes. It was worse where the amphorae were broken or joined. The mud was a greeny-yellow color there, and extra sticky. Really sticky and totally disgusting. The smell reminded me of public toilets that I would rather have forgotten. I was, I admit, slightly less enthusiastic now about continuing the detective work.

Eventually we could see that the pipes led to a room with a finished floor made of black and white pebbles laid in a wavy design. The room was mostly cleared, and we could see that the floor sloped into the center from all sides. The walls had a weird solid ledge that went around the whole room. It was about 45 centimeters (about a foot and a half) higher than the floor. The whole ledge was covered in gunk.

"What is it?" I asked. Mother seemed much too excited, and I was worried.

"It's a surprise," she said. Now I was really worried.

"But . . . ."

"Amun Ra, today we can clear the ledges—I think we'll have a lovely surprise for Willem, too!" She kissed me on the cheek and went back to examine the ledges.

Fine, I thought to myself. *It's a great big surprise.*

Mum and the workers started removing dirt from the ledges. I was helping, too. It was strange, though, because the ledges weren't ledges. This was some kind of viewing room or something, I guessed, because it looked like a row of seats. But I couldn't figure out why the seats had holes in them. And there was some sort of gutter that ran along the bottom edge of the floor.

Mum pulled out her phone. "Amun Ra, quick, take a seat on that and let me take a picture!"

I sat on one of the seats. She started snapping photos. As I sat there, I could feel the seat and the hole in the middle. All too late, the realization of where we were hit me like a giant stone sarcophagus, and I knew what we had found.

"Mum?"

"Lovely," she said, snapping more photos. "Perfect."

"Mum?"

"Yes, dear," she said from behind her phone.

"Mum, please don't tell me this is a loo," I begged.

"Very good, Amun Ra," Mum said. "We've uncovered an ancient toilet dating from the Greco-Roman period! Your bum is sitting exactly where everyone back then sat down together to do their business."

"Mum, can you stop taking pictures of me on the toilet?" I asked, jumping off the ancient crapper. "Wait . . . the smell. That can't be . . . ."

"Oh, but it is! Isn't that amazing?" Mum was pleased as punch. "And they still stink! Imagine the work we can do on analyzing ancient diet by using the coprolite mass! What a wonderful source of information. Maybe we'll find evidence of parasites, too—how delicious!"

My head was spinning, and not only from the stench. And there *was* a stench. The amphorae pipes were filled with—you guessed it—all the crap that had gone down the toilet.

"Mum, the photos. Please tell me you won't—"

"You go up and have a shower. Clean DOG and get ready. We're heading back to Cairo!"

She snapped a few more photos.

~~ANCIENT TOILET SEAT~~
The weapon of my destruction

Needless to say, that was a very important find. The site was in the news. Willem was on the news. Mum was on the news. She was written up in the paper and interviewed for television in Egypt, the UK, the US, and all over Europe. She was most excited for the big issue of *Archaeology Today Magazine* to come out. I was completely absorbed with DOG and training her to come, sit, fetch, roll over, and dance on her hind legs.

Sadia came over to meet DOG.

"This is the cutest puppy I've ever seen!" she swooned. "She's so smart and . . . and so little and adorable!" Sadia had clearly fallen in love immediately. Unfortunately, it was with DOG. But it was my dog and that counted for something.

It was all too good to be true, of course.

What came next felt like an ancient curse upon me. Mum sent a copy of the magazine to Mr. Smithzerr's class, hot off the presses. He picked up the envelope and smiled. There was a note from my mother on the front.

"Class, we have a famous Egyptologist in our midst," he smiled, opening the envelope.

Without checking the cover for anything untoward or mortally wounding, he turned it toward the class. Like a muted explosion, there was a sudden ear-splitting silence. Then a huge burst of roaring laughter—cruel, cruel laughter—filled the classroom. It was a laughter that echoed out into the halls, into the streets, across the country, continent, and globe. It was a moment that—no matter how hard I bang my head against the wall—I will never forget. Ever. Never, ever, ever, ever, ever.

There, on the cover of the magazine, for the whole world to see, was a photograph of me. True, there was a close-up of Mum in the corner, but the main photo, the one that stretched across the whole front cover, was me and guess what I was doing. . . I was on the toilet! Yes, folks, I looked like I was having a poop on the ancient Greek crapper. From the expression on my face in the photo, I must have just realized what she was doing. It was a look of combined horror, agony, and shock. Unfortunately, that combination could easily be mistaken for constipation. I couldn't believe what I was seeing, though my vision was going wonky. My eyes had gone somewhat blurry, unwilling to focus on the horrifying image of me on the loo.

Rafiq leaned over. "Good thing you know about enemas." Et tu, Rafiq?

And then . . . The headlines. And the words like daggers in my heart. Right there, life was over; I knew it the moment I read the words. On the cover of the most popular archaeology magazine in the world, I was immortalized and would forever be remembered this way:

ANCIENT LATRINES UNCOVERED:
COMMUNAL TOILETS AS GOOD AS NEW

"As you see, they could be used today!" says Egyptologist Amilas Marquis. Her son, Amun Ra, is seen here demonstrating how to use the toilet.

The laughter in the classroom rang like clanging bells in my ears. My face felt hot, cold, tingly, and then totally numb. I barely remember what happened next. I only know that I managed to stand, somehow walk over to Mr. Smithzerr's desk, and open my mouth. I suppose something like "I'm going to be sick" or "I'll jump out of the window if I have to stay in the classroom" came out; because Mr. Smithzerr, trying not to laugh, escorted me to the door and let me go.

"I'm so sorry," he said. But the damage was done, and he knew it.

I don't think I picked up my backpack, or went to the office, or did anything but shuffle out of the building, walk down the street, cross various streets without dying in traffic, and get to my apartment building. I don't remember any of it. I either walked up several flights or took the elevator, I'm not sure. All I know is, I heard my mother's voice as I lay on my bed, contemplating the ways I could disappear, change my name, and live forever in anonymity.

"Did you see the cover of the magazine?" Her words slowly came into focus.

I tried but failed to block them out.

"Wasn't it wonderful? I'm so proud of you!" I think she then kissed my forehead. She really was proud.

"Amun Ra?" Mum put her cool hand on my face, feeling for a fever. "Are you okay?" She gently caressed my head, leaned over, and asked, "Are you feeling constipated?"

9
Murder by Papyrus

I f there's anything more tedious than an academic conference on modern ways of preserving papyrus, then it's . . . no, wait, there's *nothing* more boring than an academic conference on modern ways of preserving papyrus. Mum insisted I go, because she was delivering a paper on how x-rays and different kinds of imaging could help to orient damaged papyrus sheets and help line up and restore ancient papyrus rolls. Exciting, right? Mum wanted to know what I thought about it. I explained very clearly and with great confidence that I could easily share my opinions from my bedroom, in front of my computer, while watching Pewdiepie play video games on YouTube. Mum declined my proposal and insisted that I actually go to the most boring conference ever. Pleading and begging didn't work.

I was going to have to listen to Egyptologists talk for the entire weekend about papyrus restoration and there was nothing I could do about it. Mum's colleagues from Oxford and the Sorbonne were arriving at the hotel at the same time, and we were supposed to have tea with Bertram Heller-Roth, a colleague from her days at Cambridge. Great. An afternoon with a bunch of stuffy old airbags who'd get excited about the kind of brush they used for removing sand from pieces of rock. But wait, there's more!

"Bertram has a daughter about your age," said Mum, like she thought that would make me want to go instead of want, more than ever, to run away from home and join the circus.

"'About my age?' You mean under thirty-five? Mum, please don't make me spend the day with 'someone about my age' again."

While I know I'm not alone (so many kids have to suffer through this), the dreaded 'someone about your age' thing has followed me forever. In my mother's eyes, the 'someone about my age' could be anyone from age five to thirty. There was the 'boy about your age' last year at a conference in South Africa. He turned out to be the five-year-old monster son of an Ancient Studies professor. I had to babysit the little menace while his mother and mine talked shop. He bit me, and I still have the scar. And then there was the 'girl about my age' who turned out to be in her last year of graduate school at Yale. She was as thrilled as me to be stuck together for nine hours at a dig site. Believe me, she had a lot to talk about with a (then) twelve-year-old boy. And let's not forget the misadventures of seventeen-year-old Elvis Aaron Presley Floosbaganov, who was also supposed to be 'about my age'. . . Mum doesn't have a clue.

Oh, and did I mention that this conference would be over the summer break?

"Where's the conference?" I asked, realizing that I must face my fate.

"Not far," she said. "London."

"London? Not far?" I was trying to look as mortified as possible.

"You like London!" she said. "There's loads to do. I think there are two hours free on Friday and maybe three on Sunday during which you can do whatever you'd like. We'll be at University College in central London, near the British Museum and all sorts of fun things to do."

This was coming from a woman who thought it was fun to count dog skulls and brush dirt off pieces of pottery.

"Mum, it's my holiday," I said, trying a new tactic. "It's going to be a challenging year coming up—eighth grade is going to be hard. I really need this break. Can I please stay here with . . . a friend? I don't want to be a bother to you—"

"That's very sweet, Amun Ra," she said. "Of course I want you to come with me."

"But won't it be easier for you to—"

"Nonsense," she said. "I can use your help."

"But it's summer break, and—"

"It's only for four days. We'll be back on Tuesday. You'll still have the rest of the summer to play on the Facebook." It was like she knew my list of excuses before I got to use them, even if she had no clue about the internet.

And then a furry ball at my foot gave me an idea.

"But what about DOG?" I asked, pointing to our sweet sleeping doggie, who, as if on cue, put her little paw up to her wet nose and looked especially adorable. Aww, poor little lonely DOG. We couldn't leave her alone. . . .

"No problem," said Mother. "Mr. Smithzerr is going to take her for the duration. He's staying in Cairo for the break. She loves him."

Drat. Curse you, helpful teachers!

"But . . . what about . . . ." But I couldn't think of any other excuses.

"Don't worry," said Mum. "I already bought your ticket."

Don't get me wrong. London is great. But the bulk of the four days would be filled with hot air from old bags of wind. Imagine literal windbags, blowing sand, dirt, and pieces of papyrus at me. That's what a conference of Egyptologists is like. For real.

"You can't bring all that!" Mum said, pointing at my suitcase. "We're going for four days. Bring a book."

"Look, Mum," I said, also pointing at my suitcase, "I need this stuff to keep me from going crazy."

The suitcase was big enough for me and Mum to climb inside and use as a tent. In it, I had armed myself with my PS4, a set of carpet *boules*, my cozy blanket (London is cold), the entire collection of Rick Riordan's *Percy Jackson* books and Garth Nix's *Keys to the Kingdom* books, and everything by Terry Pratchett (what if we get fogged in?), as well as some board games (Avalon, Settlers of Catan, and Hanabi) to play if I did get stuck with kids and those kids are actually kids also stuck at the conference. Maybe it was a little overkill.

"And where are your clothes?" she asked.

"We're only going for four days," I said. "I'll grab four pairs of underwear."

"Get a nice pair of trousers and a button-down shirt," Mum insisted. "And a pullover, something non-hoodie. And a pair of sweats and T-shirts, in case there's a gym at our hotel."

We finally agreed that I could pick two books, one board game, and the carpet *boules*, which I could play alone in the halls of the hotel. And the ridiculous amount of clothes that Mum insisted I pack. She assured me that the hotel had heating, and I reluctantly left my blanket behind. We each ended up with a single piece of carry-on luggage, and brought them outside just as the car arrived to collect us.

"I said, I don't know how old Bertram's daughter is," Mum answered me, again. "I did find out her name. It's Gertrude."

Gertrude? Really? "Are you sure it's his daughter and not his grandmother?" I asked.

"I'm sure she's very nice," said Mum.

Right. I turned and faced her.

"Mum, I want you to promise that you won't push me to do embarrassing and/or lame things, or force me to partake in activities that are wholly and exclusively interesting to Egyptologists and not their children."

"What do you mean?" Mum really didn't know what I meant.

"Please don't force me to hang out with Gertrude." I was trying not to be blatant, but there it was.

Mum's eyebrows went up. "Force you? I *never* force you—I believe in free choice!" She took a look at my face. "Okay. I won't force you to—"

"And if someone else tries to rope me into something, you will defend me and allow me to go to our hotel room or do something else." I actually held my breath waiting for her to answer.

"Of course, dear," she said.

I had my doubts.

It's only about a five-hour flight from Cairo to London. Believe me, that's nothing compared to flying to the US or even to Casablanca, Morocco (yes, it's a longer flight from Cairo to Casablanca than from Cairo to London. People don't realize it, but it's true. North Africa is huge). I tried to sleep on the plane, but all I could think of was me and Gertrude, stuck in a room together for the whole conference. Gertrude. The name kept bringing up images that just got weirder and weirder, scarier and scarier. Gertrude. I imagined that she was really tall, then really short, then skinny, fat, with braces, buck teeth, glasses, pencils up her nose, fangs, antennae, three eyes, forked tongue. Would she want to play carpet *boules*? Or eat them?

The lobby of the hotel was massive and super fancy, with enormous chandeliers, and tapestries and bowls of apples everywhere. There were lots of people milling around. We were led to the registration desk by an over-enthusiastic porter.

"It's terribly, terribly exciting. I'm really, really excited to meet so many people who've truly, truly been mummy-hunting," he double-gushed effusively, about thirty times.

I began mentally separating the people into two categories—Egyptologists and non-Egyptologists. This is more or less how I generally categorize the world. There sat a man with hiking boots, a forehead torch (or lamp), and a notepad: Egyptologist. There walked a woman wearing an elegant dress and laughing with a guy in a tuxedo: non-Egyptologists. There were two rather round, straw hat–wearing people on their hands and knees, noses to the carpet, magnifying glasses at the ready: Egyptologists.

By the potted palm tree, there was a young woman—maybe 'girl' still applied, since she was not much older than me—with long blonde hair. And no, she wasn't an Egyptologist. Obviously. She turned slowly in my direction and . . . and . . . I had to look away. I don't know why, but I did. I could feel my cheeks burning. What an idiot! I tried to sneak another peek, but she had disappeared. In this mess of ridiculous Bermuda shorts–wearing silly academics, she was like a golden light . . . now gone.

I almost tripped over a clump of Egyptologists before we got to the registration desk. Still no sign of the girl. The porter kept smiling at us until Mum gave him a tip. We both jumped at the booming voice from behind the registration desk. It was a smarmy desk clerk.

"Dr. Marquis," he said. "It's so lovely to have you with us again."

I looked at Mum. *When were you here before?* I asked with my eyes.

I don't remember ever being here before, but this smarmy desk clerk seems to think I was, Mum answered with a shrug of her shoulders.

"In fact . . . ." A bead of sweat had formed on his moustache. "Well, how interesting that we seem to be . . . this is impossible . . . one moment, please." He grumbled out the last few words, clearly unhappy about something.

"I'm terribly sorry, but another clerk seems to have mistakenly given away your room," he said finally. "But, happy accident, the bridal suite is available, if you and your . . . brother . . . would like to stay at no extra charge." He grinned ear-to-ear. It was creepy.

Mum didn't fall for that stupid fake 'Oh, I thought he was your brother' flattery. In fact, it went right over her head and she ignored him.

"Is there a fireplace?" I asked.

"In the bridal suite, there are three," said the clerk.

"We'll take it," I said.

"Splendid," said the clerk, wiping his brow with relief. Clearly, the mess-up would have been on his shoulders. "The porter will bring your bags right up. Would you like to stay and join us here in the tea room for afternoon tea?"

"I think we'll see the room and freshen up first," said Mother. "Then we can come back down for—"

"Amilas!" came a cry from behind us.

We turned around. There was a man about Mother's age, medium height, with light hair just starting to gray.

"Bertram!" Mum cried, and they moved in for a big hug.

Next to him was a girl who was about a foot taller than me and three times my weight, with an angry expression on her face. She could have been a kid or an adult, her face was so squished with a scowl. Gertrude Heller-Roth. *Okay*, I thought, *it's just for four days . . . .*

"Hi, I'm Amun Ra," I said, about to reach my hand out to shake hers.

"Very funny," said the girl. "Do you think I care?" She shoved me aside, pushing past us all toward the desk.

"Gertrude?" I said, confused. Was this going to be even worse than I'd imagined?

"Ah yes, this must be Amun Ra," said Bertram, taking my hand and shaking my entire arm. "This is Tru, my daughter," he said, pointing to the empty spot next to him. "Oh dear . . . ." He looked around.

"Is that her?" I asked, pointing to the grumbling grump who was now at the registration desk, shouting about a reservation.

"What?" Bertram Heller-Roth looked at the grump. "Goodness, no!" he said. "But I seem to have misplaced my . . . oh, there she is." His daughter walked up and smiled.

I froze. Could it be? Gertrude Heller-Roth wasn't the grump—she was the beautiful girl who had been standing by the palm tree.

"Hi, I'm Tru," she said, shaking the hand that I'd left floating in the air in the wake of the grump, who was now stomping her feet and shaking her finger at the desk clerk.

I made a few grunts and swallowed hard, attempting to find my voice, then said, "Hi, Tru. I . . . I'm Amun Ra."

Her hand was warm, but not clammy. My hand was instantly clammy, and I had no time to wipe it. What about my breath? Was my hair sticking out? Did I use deodorant? Was I wearing pants?

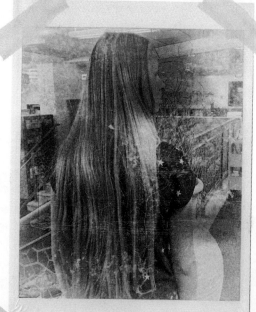

Tru

"Yes, I got that," she said, smiling. "What do you like to go by?"

"Excuse me?" My ears were still ringing from the shock of this being the girl I'd have to, or rather *get* to, spend four days with.

"Amun? Ra? Are you going with the New Kingdom god, or the king of gods, or what?" she asked. I was still unable to answer. "What do you prefer to be called?"

"Phil?" I offered, then realized this just sounded weird. "I mean, I'm not so crazy about either half of my name."

"Yeah, I understand," said Tru. "But at least it's a cool name. I mean, you're named after Egyptian gods. 'Gertrude' doesn't have any redeeming qualities I can think of."

"Tru is great, though," I said, maybe too quickly. "Amun Ra doesn't really present any nicknames that work."

"Yeah, Tru's good," she said, thinking about it. "My dad felt guilty for naming me after my grandmother. Gertrude really is a grandmotherly name. So he started calling me Tru. Tru's good."

"True," I said, then pretended I had meant to be punny. "True indeed."

"I can call you 'Ray' if you want," suggested Tru.

That was the kindest gesture anyone had ever made toward me. And it was made by the most beautiful girl I'd ever seen. At that moment, I was thinking that Tru might be the most amazing human being on earth.

"I like it," I said.

"But will you know I mean *you* if I call you Ray?" she asked.

"Ah, hmm . . . likely not," I had to admit. I'd probably need time to learn to answer to Ray, but the mere thought of her calling me, from across a room or on the phone, was heaven. She could call me whatever she liked. "It's worth a try, though."

"Okay, Ray," said Tru, reaching her hand out again to shake mine.

I quickly wiped mine on my trouser leg before I held it out.

"What are you *doing* in there?" Mum yelled through the door to our hotel bathroom. "We were just dropping off our bags. Everyone is waiting for us down in the tea room."

"Just a minute," I called back in that fake sing-song voice we all use when we are pretending things are not going horribly wrong. I had a large wet splotch across the crotch of my trousers. I had simply washed my face, and then turned the faucet the wrong way so it sprayed water right at my crotch. I now looked like I'd peed my pants. Not only that, but I had rose petals stuck to my socks. Yes, the hotel had scattered rose petals all over the flipping bathroom floor of the bridal suite. Those petals were now ground into my socks. I was a mess. My trousers were soaked and would not be dry for hours. Thanks to Mum, I did have a change of trousers. And a pair of sweats. The other trousers were the way to go, since we were going down for tea. I didn't want to look like a total slob. For the sake of the hotel, that is.

The tea room was like something out of an old oil painting. The ceilings were really high and covered in angels, fairies, and cherubs. While the ceiling looked like something from Buckingham Palace, the rest of the room was strictly Egyptian. There were large urns, and statues, and chairs, and just about everything was copied from ancient Egyptian designs. Most people think of pyramids and sphinxes when they think of ancient Egyptian designs. But ancient Egyptians also made wooden chairs with lion's feet and nicely built seats, curved for comfort, thousands of years ago. What we see nowadays are copies from ancient Egypt. There was a whole big change in interior design that happened after the discovery of King Tut's tomb late in 1922. Suddenly, everything was all about Egyptian stuff. It inspired all of the Art Deco designs, and the 1920s haircuts with those bangs like Cleopatra. It was so funny. This place had all sorts of things that you might call Deco, but which were really from designs created over three thousand years before.

We were brought over to a table that was laid with loads of forks, spoons, and knives in descending size. There were a couple of other people at the table. I looked around for Tru and her father.

"Um, aren't Tru and Bertram Heller-Roth coming to meet us?" I asked, trying to be casual.

"Oh, you like Tru, do you?" Mother said, much too loudly. "I'm so glad you have a friend to play with at the conference."

"Play? Mum, I'm thirteen," I said, trying not to look mortified.

"Yes, you are," she said. "And Bertram tells me that Tru is fourteen. She an older woman, Amun Ra!" Mum actually winked at me.

That was when I bent over to see if I'd fit under the table. But no, I had to buck up and brush it off. Mum was going to be Mum. I stood back up, pretending I had just dropped something, and the top of my head hit hard against the bottom of someone's chin.

It was Tru.

"I'm so sorry," I said, catching her before she fell over backwards.

"Ouch," she said, rubbing her chin. She dabbed at her lip, which was bleeding slightly. "I'm okay, really. It'll be fine. What were you doing down there?"

I obviously couldn't tell her that I'd been planning to hide. "I thought I dropped my . . . ," and I mumbled something inaudible since I couldn't think of anything I could have dropped at that moment. I hoped she'd ignore it, or at least that it would buy me time to think.

"Your what?" she asked.

No time to think. Luckily, her father interrupted.

"Do you kids want to sit on your own?" he asked. "The table's filling up and it's all Egyptologists."

We both spoke at once. She said "No," and I said "Yes."

Awkward. We looked at each other.

"Only I came to hear about Egyptology, didn't you?" Tru said, looking at me.

"Of course," I said. "I just meant that if they *need* us to sit at a different table, I'd be willing. My life is all about Egyptology. I join my Mum on digs and help with excavations all the time." This was, for the most part, true. Joining my mother of my own free will might be stretching it, but the joining was the important part right then.

"Oh, how lucky," she said. "That's right, you live most of the time in Cairo."

"Yes, we do," I said, casually adding, "You should visit some time."

"You hear that, Dad?" Tru said. "We've got an invitation to Egypt."

By then, the main table was full, except for two seats.

"Sorry, kids," said Bertram. "You two will have to sit on your own. I promise we'll all sit together for supper. Amilas and I are both on the panel tomorrow, and we need to chat with these folks who are running it."

Mum looked concerned.

"Perhaps it's best if I sit with Amun Ra, Bertram, and we can go over things after—"

"Don't be silly, Mum," I said, cheerfully patting her on the back. She was clearly trying to protect me. She had let me suffer with all of the other 'kids my age' over the years and now, at the totally wrong moment, she was going to prevent me from having alone time with Tru.

"They'll be fine on their own," Bertram said, fortunately.

Mum looked really sorry. I tried to say *Don't worry, I'm totally psyched* with just my eyes (obviously I couldn't say it aloud), and mouthed *It's okay*.

Then I tried to look disappointed. Tru actually was disappointed. I tried to look at it as her interest in Egyptology and not her lack of interest in me. I could work with that.

"You know, I was with Mum when she discovered the dog mummies," I said casually as we sat down. Tru's face lit up. Yes!

"Really? I didn't know," she said, leaning closer. I started telling her about our excavations, Mum's discovery of the dog mummies, and the stuff that we'd found in Sudan. To my infinite pleasure, Tru didn't mention the cover of the previous month's *Archaeology Today*.

The waiter brought out a three-tiered serving tray of finger sandwiches. There were cucumber and butter, salmon and butter, and ham and butter. Also tomato and cheese, with butter, and more that seemed to be just plain butter. And they brought tea. The tea in London is awesome! I really like tea. It's comfort food at its best. Whenever I'd scrape my knee, or get a cut, or bump my head, Mum would clean me up and say, "Shall we have a cup of tea?," and everything would be fine. So, tea had always been my go-to comfort drink. Sitting across from Tru Heller-Roth, I could use all the comfort I could get.

I tried not to stare at her, though it was hard. Unlike Sadia, who knew she was beautiful, Tru didn't seem to care, one way or another. She didn't pretend not to be hungry or eat her finger sandwiches with her pinkies out. Instead, she nibbled around the outside of each sandwich section and then popped the rest in her mouth. Between the two of us, we ate all three tiers of sandwiches, and then, by mutual agreement, we sauntered over to the grown-ups' table and stole the sandwiches still on their trays while they were all deep in conversation.

"The cucumber ones are my favorite," she said, stuffing two in her mouth at once. "You know they ate cucumbers in ancient Egypt?"

"Of course," I said, stuffing three of the ham sandwiches in my mouth. "They didn't have ham like this, the poor sods."

We laughed as the waiters brought another tiered tray with scones, brioche, jams, honey, pots of butter, and clotted cream. And fruit.

"They had lots of melons, though," I said, picking up a piece. I ate it, but only to get it out of the way of the scone I wanted.

"They ate well," said Tru. "There are lots of things still eaten in Egypt that have been eaten for thousands of years."

"Like fava beans, *kos* lettuce, onions, garlic, and beer," I said. "Though people had to be careful with that *kos* lettuce . . . ," I continued, before realizing what I was saying. I couldn't believe I was going there with the lettuce. The long heads of *kos* lettuce that ooze a whitish liquid when the leaves are cut were sacred to the ithyphallic fertility god, Min. In ancient Egypt, eating lettuce was supposed to . . . um, well, help enlarge certain body parts . . . .

Why on Earth was I going there? Apparently, I didn't need my mother to embarrass me in front of girls. I was well on my way all by myself.

Tru looked up from her clotted cream–covered scone. "What was that? Why would people have to be careful about eating lettuce?"

I quickly stuffed a whole scone into my mouth to buy myself some time. I grabbed the brioche and stuffed that in, too, in case the scone wasn't enough.

"Are you okay?" Tru asked. "Your face is turning bright red."

"Mmm," I said, handing her another scone. "Try this, yum."

She took the scone and sliced it, smothered it in clotted cream and strawberry jam, and took a bite. "Yum indeed. Now what about those people, and that long lettuce?"

My stomach moved at lightning speed. It cramped, then turned upside-down, then went numb, then did another flip. And then Tru started laughing.

"I already know about the lettuce, Ray, and how it was useful for . . . sexy reasons." She laughed so hard that I had to laugh, too.

"You should have seen your face," she said, though with some sympathy and without cruelty.

"You could have saved me," I said. "Instead, you made me gobble all the brioche."

"Let's steal some from the grown-ups," Tru said, winking.

We went over to the adults' table and pilfered their pastry basket.

"Hey, kids, we're going to need someone to run the papyrus table," said Bertram.

"The what?" I asked, trying to sound unconcerned, but worried that we were about to get roped into something stupid.

"We've set up a table for the personalized papyrus art, pre-sold to some of the audience members—mostly non-Egyptologists, that is," he said.

"Personalized papyrus art?" I asked. Uh-oh.

"We have papyrus, but we need a couple of young experts to write people's names in hieroglyphs. The donations go toward funding the renewal of the Khartoum Museum and buying cases for the Cairo Museum."

"Are the inks all authentic?" asked Tru.

"Of course, silly girl," Bertram said, beaming.

Mum stepped in, presumably trying to save me, again. "Oh, I don't think Amun Ra—"

"Sure, that sounds fun!" I said.

Mum looked at me, surprised. The second time she'd ever actually tried to get me out of being stuck with a strange kid or having to do some stupid activity, and she'd totally blown it. I couldn't imagine a worse time for Mother to discover an awareness of my general social misery. Or to completely miss the obvious fact that I was totally psyched to be near Tru and would do absolutely anything she wanted.

Tru smiled at me, and I returned the favor. Still smiling, I looked at Mum. Her eyebrows were raised so high that they had nearly disappeared into her hairline.

"*Lots* of fun," I said, before Mum could say something to wreck everything.

"Lovely," said Bertram. "Amilas, let's leave them to it, shall we?"

"Indeed," said Mum, checking my face again to see if I might be breaking out in a rash or something. Bertram took her arm and led her away.

"Let's go and make hieroglyphs!" said Tru, enthusiastically.

I know it sounds weird, but I was looking forward to it. Truly. Ha ha, yes, truly. I get it.

The table was set up in the corridor next to the conference room. Turning the corner, we hit a road block. We had to push through a crowd of people who were gathered right where we needed to go. And then I realized exactly why they were gathered there: they were waiting for us.

We quickly started unpacking the ink and the reed pens that Bertram had provided. The reeds needed a bit of trimming, and the ink needed some preparation. Tru took the red ochre and rubbed it on a stone, making it into a powder, while I mashed up some charcoal for the black ink. We put small amounts of the powder in shells from the Nile, added a bit of water, and mixed them together. The ink was ready. I smiled as Tru looked at my work and nodded with satisfaction. Yes, I did know what I was doing. So did Tru. We were good to go, and not a moment too soon. The line was crazily long and getting longer. There was a huge stack of neatly cut sheets of papyrus in a box under the table. There must have been a thousand sheets. I hoped there was enough.

"What's your name?" Tru asked a little girl wearing her hair like Cleopatra.

"Nefret," said the little girl.

"Ah, a fan of ancient Egypt, are we?" asked Tru as she began to draw the *nefer* sign.

"Yes, I am," said the little girl.

"I've read her all of the Elizabeth Peters books," said her father. "We're big fans of Egyptology." Elizabeth Peters (the pen name of Egyptologist Barbara Mertz) was the author of the Amelia Peabody books. Amelia is an Egyptologist who finds herself having to solve various murder mysteries with her husband, Radcliffe Emerson, and their son, Ramses. In the later books, they adopt a young woman named Nefret. And yes, I knew all the books—Mum had read them to me when I was younger. She loved them mostly because the author was an Egyptologist. I loved them mostly because the Emersons' son was called Ramses (well, his real name was Walter, but no one ever called him that) and I could relate. Ramses never seemed to mind—in fact, he quite liked it. Clearly, this little Nefret didn't mind *her* name, either.

"I was named for—"

"Yes, of course, we know Nefret and Ramses," said Tru, much to the girl's pleasure.

Nefret is the shining one.

Tru was somehow able to speak and draw at the same time, and did a beautiful job of creating a very authentic-looking piece of papyrus.

"Thank you, Miss . . . ."

"Tru," said Tru. "And this is Amun Ra."

"Are you both Egyptologists?" asked the little girl.

"We are," said Tru, with a wink to the father, who clearly could tell that we weren't adults. "My father is Bertram Heller-Roth."

"Of course," said the father. "I read his article on papyrus in the February/March issue of *Ancient Egypt Magazine*." Then the father looked at me, and smiled a smile that brought fear to my heart. "And, of course, you're the son of Amilas Marquis." He turned to his daughter. "Remember, dear, the pictures of Amun Ra—"

"ON THE TOILET!" shouted the rotten little whistleblower. Suddenly, little Nefret was no longer cute. "Oh, Daddy! He's the boy ON THE TOILET on the cover of the magazine!" She shouted so loud that my ears were ringing.

"Toilet . . . toilet . . . toilet" echoed in my ears like it was being shouted across the Grand Canyon. Everyone in line seemed to lean forward. That is, everyone who wasn't too busy laughing and pointing leaned forward to get a better look. Rather, everyone who wasn't too busy Googling 'boy magazine toilet Egyptology' and then bursting into laughter as they saw me sitting on an ancient latrine.

I wanted to die. I couldn't even look at Tru. I was waiting for her to join in, and point, and laugh. But she didn't.

"Next!" she called, urging the monstrous child and her father out of the way.

"Is he the famous toilet boy?" asked the next child in line, sneering at me and squinting his beady little eyes. Children really suck lemons. This one looked to be about twelve, and had a cowering little brother behind him. There was something nasty about the bigger boy, though I might have been a tad biased.

"He is *not* the famous toilet boy," said Tru. "Though every *intelligent* person knows that it's an honor to be featured on the cover of a magazine. Every *intelligent* person knows that being part of an excavation is only for truly talented people . . . ."

The boy frowned, trying to get what she was saying. Clearly, thinking wasn't his forte. "Yeah, but he's just a—"

"He's an Egyptologist and will make your name into lovely hieroglyphs—"

"But they said—"

The smaller boy pulled his brother's arm. "Bradley, maybe he doesn't want—"

Bradley punched his little brother. "Shut up, Bryce! I'm only here because Mum made me take you because of your stupid Egyptology obsession. I get to have fun." He rounded on me. "Now, they said—"

Tru leaned very close to the boy. "If you aren't polite and kind to both Amun Ra and me, as well as your little brother, you shall be cursed. Oh, yes. We know all about ancient curses and the power they wield. Not only will we write something that you'll never be able to read or understand, but you will be forced to carry that curse with you, for the rest of your life. That curse may prevent you from growing or give you crocodile skin or make you stink like a hippopotamus. Why will you have to carry it around? Because we will place that ancient curse that will come true if you ever destroy the papyrus . . . ." I was already drawing, moving my hands around, pretending I was making a curse. "And, as everyone knows, these curses come true. So you'd better learn to be a human being instead of a coprolite of a pig."

I did, in fact, write "Bradley is . . . ," but then I opted for "crocodile dung" instead of "a coprolite of a pig," since 'dung' and 'coprolite' mean the same thing, and I'm really good at drawing crocodiles. I added ". . . who will forever be better to his little brother instead of being a douche," though there's no hieroglyph for 'douche.'

Bradley was suddenly silent. He took the papyrus and held it like it was made of something dangerous. Tru gave Bradley the evil eye, tilting her head toward me.

Bryce is the sun in the horizon
His brother is the excrement of a crocodile

"Thank you, Mr. Amun Ra," he said, looking scared.

I pointed at my eyes and then at him, suggesting that I'd be watching.

Bryce, the little brother, was beaming when he took his papyrus. On his, I added ". . . who is a better man than his dung-like brother Bradley." When he looked at the hieroglyphs on his papyrus, he beamed all the more. I guess the kid could read it, because he smiled and nodded knowingly. It was going to be a great day at the Egyptology conference for that little archaeologist.

I looked over at Tru. She smiled at me and winked. She knew! I could see it! She knew about that magazine cover, and me on the ancient toilet, and my utter and eternal shame. And she hadn't mentioned it when we'd met. She hadn't teased me or used it against me. I couldn't help but shiver as warm feelings ran down my spine. Tru was more amazing than I could have imagined.

The next people in line were very friendly and didn't once mention the word 'toilet.' They thanked us more than was necessary. And so it went. Tru had nipped the toilet episode in the bud. And she made the whole papyrus event a total blast. Without saying anything aloud, but grinning at one another, we silently made a pact to include special messages on each papyrus—curses or blessings, depending on who was on the receiving end. Nice people, who were grateful and enthusiastic and enjoyed the work we were doing on their behalf, received little benedictions like "and thus shall have all things good and pure forever after" or "will have friends in high places" or "will never want for friends during the harvest." Grumpy or mean-spirited papyrus-getters were presented with extra comments like "shall eat excrement" (a special horror mentioned in the Book of the Dead, to be avoided at all costs) or "will suffer from tangled nose hairs during the inundation season" or a simple "suck dead bunnies."

You suck dead bunnies

"Amun Ra!" came a voice at my elbow as a very whiny girl with braces, who was complaining to her mother that she wanted two Bastet statues instead of one, was being handed her papyrus, on which I'd written "Felicity will always smell of goat hair until she learns not to be greedy."

"Mum!" I nearly jumped out of my skin. I was busted. "Mum, I . . . we . . . ."

"Do you know what—" but she stopped mid-sentence as Felicity punched her mother in the arm, folded her own arms, and refused to let the three small children behind her have their turns.

"Ah," said Mother, understanding. "Excellent job, children." She smiled benignly at us, and left us to our work.

"Come meet us for lunch when you're done," called Bertram.

Tru and I headed over to the café when the last of our papyrus was handed out. We'd gone through the entire pile! I couldn't believe it.

"Thank you," I said to Tru, before we got to the table where Bertram and Mum were waving.

Tru looked at me, first confused, then understanding. She smiled kindly, but said not a word. That was the best answer she could have given me. She knew exactly what I was thanking her for.

"We ordered a bread basket," said Bertram, "but there are lots of, well, special options that the chefs have created for the conference."

The 'special options' included Cleopatra Kebob, Cleopatra Curry, Tut Wellington with Tut Tatties, Fish and Chips à la Nile, Ramses Roast, and something called Pyramid Potatoes with Pharaoh Pie. For dessert, they offered Cleopatra Clafoutis and Tut's Trifle.

"Really?" I said, looking at Tru, who was equally aghast. They seemed to have used the only Egyptian names they could think of to spice up old standards.

The waiter came up and asked for the order.

"Where's Seti's Spotted Dick?" I asked, earnestly.

"Or Khafre's Knickerbocker Glory?" asked Tru, pretending to search the menu. "That was a favorite back in the day, wasn't it, Ray?"

"I fancy a Hotep Hog's Pudding myself," said Bertram.

"Or a Shepseskaf Shepherd's Pie," said Mum.

We all laughed as the waiter hunted through the menu for our requests, before he joined in laughing with us at the silliness of it all.

We settled on sandwiches and chips that didn't have shameful names attached. Tru and I got mango milkshakes. Mum and Bertram ordered ale. One thing the ancient Egyptians had in common with the Brits was their love of all things ale. Beer was big in Egypt, and everyone—children and adults, gods and humans alike—drank beer. Yuck.

As we ate, Tru and I heard about Mum's and Bertram's presentations on the papyrus panel, and we came clean about our decision to exercise our own expertise in papyrus art.

"But we said really nice things when people were nice," said Tru. "Only unkind, rude, or creepy people got warnings to be nicer, less rude, and less creepy."

"Absolutely," I said. "We put hexes on all the hex-worthy patrons and charms on all the charming patrons."

"Well, that's very ancient Egyptian of you, and I'm sure that the grammar in your sentences was correct, so who can complain?" said Mum.

"Speaking of charming patrons," said Bertram, checking his watch, "we need to get over to the Q & A in the salon."

"Oh yes," said Mum, taking the last bite of the Treacle Tut Tart. "I wanted to ask Dr. Vossman about the Apis embalming ritual—I really think that some experimental work would have been handy!"

"Do you have any more papyrus?" I ventured.

"I think you've had quite enough for one day, young man," said Mum, with a wink.

"We can go to the talk," said Tru. "There's a lecture at 4:00 on the comparison of New and Middle Kingdom techniques of mummy wrapping."

"Or we could go for a walk," I suggested. "There's a park not far away, or we could take the Tube down to the Eye."

"You mean leave the conference?" Tru looked surprised. "You'd want to walk away from the opportunity to learn more about Egyptology?"

"Never," I lied. "I only wanted to make sure that you didn't need a break."

"You think I need a break?" Tru asked, less chummy than before.

"No, I—" I was thinking fast. "I just rarely meet people as into Egyptology as me, so I didn't want you to feel stuck."

Tru smiled.

"Don't be silly," she said.

What fun, I silently lied to myself as we entered a seminar on verbal structures in King Seti I's Nauri Decree. Not a thrill a minute, but the decree was cool.

"I've seen it," I said, trying to brag without making it sound like I was.

"You have?" Tru was impressed.

The decree was carved high up on a cliff that we had to clamber up to from the edge of the Nile, because it talked about the holdings of King Seti's different temples in Nubia. But the grammar?? Give me a break. Even I could do better.

"Yeah, it was really impressive, but the grammar . . . ." I shook my head.

"I know!" Tru laughed.

I could handle another hour of sitting in a lecture. Maybe after that Tru and I could go for tea together.

"We've got the rest of the day to attend the conference," Tru said as we took our seats. "Why, there are six hours of lectures today alone." She smiled at me, and I managed to smile back.

"What luck," I lied.

Six hours? Good grief. At least I'd be sitting next to Tru.

10
Violating the Dress Code

E very Halloween, Mum has helped me with my costume. Sorry, did I say 'helped'? 'Helped' is definitely not the word I'm looking for. 'Coerced,' 'imposed her will,' tortured'—maybe one of those words? And all out of love. She put in some seriously hard work, spending days, even weeks, making my costumes for me. The problem was that the costumes were all, shall we say, of a theme. A singular theme. I'll give you three guesses what that theme has been since my very first Halloween. Don't need three guesses?

For my entire life, if I wasn't a mummy, then I was an Egyptian god or a pharaoh, or sometimes a famous dead Egyptologist. Surprised? Hardly. But that Halloween, everything was going to change.

It was October of eighth grade. Mum was working at the Smithsonian for a month, and I got to be in DC for Halloween. The previous year, I'd been in Egypt, where Halloween is just a shadow of what it is in America. In fact, the only thing that really translated from America was the creepy habit of throwing eggs, dressing up, and having a party. In Cairo, they threw eggs at cars, houses, and each other. It was really a bummer. Mum made me trick-or-treat in our apartment building, since going outside was treacherous. All of the kids who lived in the building would get into costume and run up and down the stairs, knocking on apartment doors, pretending it was like the real thing in America.

I can tell you from experience, everyone in the world dreams of a real American Halloween. In elementary school—in both the half-term I spent in London and my years in Cairo—we got to have a little costume parade in the days leading up to Halloween. In the US, there was a massive parade around the whole neighborhood and we got to trick-or-treat, too. Middle school was different. Teachers must all think that the minute you go from fifth to sixth grade, you no longer like fun. No one ever let us have a costume parade like we'd had in elementary school. But we all still wanted to do something to celebrate Halloween. It's not like we suddenly didn't want to dress up and eat insane amounts of chocolate and other sweets just because we were in middle school. After much petitioning, Haddful Arms gave in, and we got to have a costume party. The administration suggested a themed Halloween party—like Halloween isn't enough of a theme. We didn't care as long as we still got to dress up and eat candy.

That said, dressing up was going to be an issue. Having had years of Egyptian costumes thrust upon me, I had been thinking of ways to approach the subject with Mum. Actually, I'd been thinking about it since the previous Halloween. And I had a plan.

"You want to *what*??" Mum was not happy.

"I've been the same thing for the last . . . every year of my life." I tried to reason with her.

"That's not true," insisted Mother, who had already been planning my costume. "Every year's been totally different! Last year you were Ramses II. The year before, you were Amenhotep III."

"Exactly," I said. "And how did the costumes differ?"

"They were nothing alike! For Ramses, you wore the blue crown—you know, like the one he wore in all those battle scenes. And you carried a mace to smite your enemies, and you wore that long poofy kilt . . . ."

Oh, yikes, the poofy kilt. That was a nightmare on so many levels.

"And for Amenhotep, you wore a long poofy kilt . . . ."

Oh, gods, the long poofy kilt again. I'd tried so hard to forget!

". . . the nemes headdress, and you carried the crook and flail to discipline and care for your people. See? They were nothing like one another!" My mother truly believed she was enumerating the many fine differences between the poofy kilts and headdresses of two pharaohs. Instead, she was proving my point. Unfortunately, she didn't see it that way.

"Mum, I want to choose my own costume," I said, trying to be gentle. It was like she was taking this personally.

"But everyone loves your costumes!" she said, clearly taking it personally. "I've made your costumes every year since you were born. That year, you were a little Bes, the lion-dwarf god who protects children—you were adorable, especially when you stuck your tongue out like the god himself."

"Mum, I know," I said. "Maybe you can help me make the costume this year, too. I was thinking . . . maybe Batman."

"But Bat was a goddess," said Mum, completely missing my declaration. "But I guess we could work on a cow head for you, and—"

"No, Mum, I mean *Batman*," I whined. I admit, I was whining.

"Right, only that's a bit of a stretch, don't you think? We could check for Bat in the Narmer Palette, but she *is* a goddess, and—"

"Please, nothing from the Narmer Palette!" I begged. "Mum, I don't mean Bat, as in Hathor, as in the cow-headed goddess! I mean Batman, the world-famous superhero."

Mum mouthed the word 'Batman.'

I nodded.

Mum's mouth fell open.

"Mum?" I touched her arm, but she just sat there, her mouth open, silently mouthing 'Batman.' "Mum?"

It was several seconds before she said anything.

"Batman? Why Batman?" She could hardly get the word out of her mouth. "He doesn't even have magical superpowers . . . ." She trailed off.

"Well, Batman's cool, and it would be nice not to have to explain who I am to everyone . . . and I'd get to be something . . . something like everyone else."

"Who wants to be like everyone else?" asked Mum.

"For once, me," I said. "Nothing about me is ever like everyone else. Can't I just have a single Halloween dressed up as Batman?"

Mum nodded and left the room. I wasn't sure if I should follow. I waited a few minutes and then went to her room. She was folding up what was clearly the costume she had made me. I felt really bad.

"What's that?" I asked.

"Nothing." She kept folding, trying to tuck in the poofy kilt that was clearly part of the costume.

"Mum, is it something you made?" I asked. I really was curious.

"Well, if you must know . . . it's Seth, Lord of the Desert, Controller of Chaos, Protector of Egypt's frontiers," she said. "Now, before you say anything, I want you to know that this is completely different from anything you have ever worn before. I just thought . . . well, it's such a handsome costume and . . . well, I thought you might want to . . . ."

". . . be Batman?" I asked, faking innocence. "If that's what you thought, then you'd be right."

Mum was hurt. She just gave me a sad, sad look. Even DOG whined, putting her fuzzy face next to Mum for comfort. I felt awful, but I was determined.

"How about saving Seth for next Halloween?" I suggested.

She nodded, maybe a touch less sad.

I could tell she'd put a lot into the poofy kilt and this huge headdress of Seth, with his weird droopy nose and upstanding ears. But I wasn't going to let that change my mind. This year, I would be my own man. I would get my own costume and be like other kids who dressed like superheroes, or villains, or monsters. And this year, Marybeth Fauntleroy would think I was cool, and recognize what my costume was, and dance with me at the party. Or at least stand next to me without cringing. While I still had a thing for Tru Heller-Roth, she'd made it clear that our friendship was all about Egyptology. That was fine (sort of). But at the moment my focus was on Marybeth Fauntleroy and the Halloween party.

I had a week to get ready. I made a cool cape from a big black cloth that Mum used as a background for photographing artifacts (objects always look better on black). Yes, I was making my own costume. Mostly. Mum didn't believe in buying Halloween costumes. It had always been a point of pride for us, so it felt like cheating to just buy one, even if was Batman. That said, Target doesn't have Seti I or Ramses II or Anubis costume packs. And I doubt they'd be historically accurate if they did. So I made my cape, but I secretly went to the costume store and bought a Batman mask. There was no way I could make the bat ears, given my rather weak artistic ability. I didn't want to look like I was wearing black bunny ears or something, which was about all I could make on my own. I wanted to go as the cool Dark Knight version of Batman, so I watched the Dark Knight films for research. I was aiming for more of a ninja look.

"Do you want to borrow my tights?" Mum asked.

"No, thanks," I said, trying to smile. I knew she was just trying to help. She checked the pictures of Batman I had up on my laptop screen.

"Is that yellow belt holding up the black diaper?" she asked. "Do you want to get an extra-large diaper and spray paint it black?"

"It's *not* a diaper," I said, my voice cracking in frustration. I wanted to argue further but, looking at the photos, I could see how one might make the mistake.

"Sorry, the black panties look like—"

"I got it, Mum." I moved the computer so she could no longer peruse the screen.

She was really ruining everything. I looked at the screen and blinked a few times. No way! Now Batman just looked like he was wearing a diaper. *Think ninja,* I kept saying to myself. But I just saw diaper.

I finished my costume the day before the party. I got these really cool black boots from the thrift store near school. They fit me perfectly and looked amazing with my black suit and cape. I went to the hardware store and bought a yellow utility belt. I attached a flashlight, a rope, a laser gun (real laser, toy gun), and a water bottle in case Batman needed water while he was saving the middle school.

Haddful Arms had a great assembly room where the party was being held. I never checked about the theme for the decorations, but you can't go wrong with superheroes. No matter what, I was ready to *not* be the guy in the poofy skirt. For once, I would be in a cool costume. For once, I would not stand out among my classmates in a ridiculous—though historically accurate—pharaoh suit.

"I can't wait to see your costume," Marybeth Fauntleroy said to me the morning before the party.

"I'm making it myself," I said, trying to hide the fact that my face was turning red. Marybeth Fauntleroy was looking forward to seeing *my* costume? Did she mean it? Or was she anticipating another embarrassing Egyptian poofy skirt thing? The truth is, she hadn't talked to me since my seventh birthday back in second grade. No, wait, that's not true. She did talk to me shortly after that. She said, "Don't talk to me." After that, we only had one or two interactions that didn't include her making faces of disgust and running away.

In fourth grade, she was in my presentation group in science class. We did an experiment using litmus paper and cabbage. Or we made litmus paper out of cabbage, or something. In fifth grade, we were on the same badminton team, and she passed the birdie to me, once. I actually hit it over the net in surprise. I really looked good that time, and she smiled when we won. She didn't give me a high five like she did the other kids on our team, but I figured she just forgot. In sixth grade, we were in the same homeroom, but she never said anything to me. She once said "Pass the beaker" in science class. That felt like a big breakthrough. I did, in fact, pass the beaker. This elicited a quick "Thanks," which really made my day.

But this was different. Marybeth was actively talking to me, not talking at me, or near me, or over me, or around me. I was trying to figure out why she was suddenly being nice.

"I'm making mine, too," she said, with what I think was honest enthusiasm.

In fifth grade, she was Wonder Woman, and in sixth grade she was Catwoman. I was hoping we'd be superheroes together. Odds were in my favor.

"That's great," I said, not knowing what else to say. I almost told her about my Batman costume, but decided to let it be a surprise.

"I think you'll like it," she said, then flipped her hair, closed her locker, wiggled her fingers at me, and walked away.

I really wasn't sure what the heck had just happened. I tried to return her wiggling finger salute, but she'd already gone. Suddenly my eyes focused on Clay Koenig, who was wiggling his fingers at me, heading my way.

"Hey, b'Ra," he said. It was his new nickname for me. No begging or pleading could get him to stop.

"Hey, Clay," I said. No nickname.

"The party tonight is going to rock, yeah?" he said, flipping his hair.

What had I just seen? Clay Koenig just flipped his hair. Actually, his blonde hair had gotten longish in the months I'd been in Cairo and . . . did he have product in it?

"What was that?" I asked.

"What?" he said, checking his zipper.

"The hair-flip thing," I said. It was as if Clay Koenig, the pickles-dipped-in-chocolate-milk guy, was suddenly the hey-I-have-cool-hair guy. Was I Rip Van Winkle? Had I disappeared, only to land in an alternate reality?

"So what, dude? My hair's getting long," said Clay Koenig, flipping it again.

I looked carefully at his face. Was he joking? Was he intending to be cool? Or was he really totally unaware of the hair-flipping/cool guy connection?

"Hey, Clay," Kara Place and Arabella Paddington both said.

"Hey, guys," said Clay Koenig, and then—wait for it—he flipped his frigging hair again.

The girls giggled. They must—oh, please gods—they must have been laughing at him. Clay Koenig ate bugs. Clay Koenig picked his nose in the lunch line. Clay Koenig ate the entrails off my birthday cake!

"Hey, Amun Ra," said Katie Bertrand, who also had barely spoken to me since Mum eviscerated the class bunny. "Looking forward to seeing you tonight."

I tried to act casual. I tried to say something. When I opened my mouth, nothing came out. I quickly wiggled my fingers at her. It worked. She wiggled back.

"Dude, I said thanks for letting me borrow that stuff," said Clay, for what must have been the second time (I hoped only the second time). I was still geeking out and wiggling my fingers.

"Stuff?" I asked.

"Yeah, your stuff," said Clay, picking his nose.

"What stuff?" I really didn't know what he was talking about.

"My mother asked your mother if I could borrow stuff for my costume since I forgot to get one," said Clay.

"No problem," I said, secretly hoping he was borrowing some poofy skirt and other pharaoh-related costume stuff. I know that it wasn't nice to wish that upon my friend, but Clay could be such a pain—and, to be honest, the idea of girls liking Clay Koenig made my stomach turn. I felt a tiny bit bad that I felt pleasure imagining Clay Koenig at the party dressed as a pharaoh, but not as much as I actually felt pleasure about imagining Clay Koenig at the party dressed as a pharaoh. What do they call it? *Schadenfreude*? The happiness you get from the bad luck of someone else? "Really, no problem at all, Clay."

So I had my whole Batman costume laid out on my bed—the mask, the suit, the cape, the belt, the headdress. Wait, did I just say headdress? I meant cap.

Then came the dilemma. Do I put it on now? Or change at the party? What to do? I was really questioning the wisdom of wearing the costume in the street. It was five blocks to the school. That's not far, but dressed like Batman, it could be forever. I'd been in Egypt for the months leading up to (and first month of) eighth grade, so I'd missed the whole American transition from being a little kid to being a near-teen. Well, I guess it happens everywhere, but there was more pressure about the transition and being cool in the US, and I was worried I would do the wrong thing now that I was back in DC.

I couldn't believe I was going to call Clay Koenig and ask him for advice.

"Clay?" I got him on the phone. "Are you wearing your costume?"

"Uh, yeah, b'Ra," he said, though his voice sounded muffled.

"Where are you?" I asked.

"In the costume," he said.

"I got that part," I said. "The headdress slipped over your face, didn't it?"

"Yep," said Clay. "But I got it on now, b'Ra, plus the mask thing."

"I'm very happy for you, Clay," I said, rolling my eyes to myself. "Are you going to take it off, put it in a bag, and get dressed at school? Or are you going to walk across town, in front of the neighbors and random people, in your poofy kilt and headdress, looking like a freak?"

"Yep," said Clay.

"Yep, what?"

"I'm already in my costume, b'Ra," he said, muffled again by the mask and the fallen headdress. "Gonna wear it to the party."

This still didn't inspire me to wear my Batman suit.

"Do you know if everyone's doing that?" I asked.

"Yeah, I think so," he said, clearly messing with the headdress. "Marybeth called, and—"

Marybeth Fauntleroy called Clay Koenig?

"Marybeth called you?" Wow, just over a year away and everything really had changed.

"Yeah," said Clay. "She's been bugging me about her costume."

"Is she a superhero?" I asked.

"Yeah, b'Ra," said Clay. "She's always a superhero. A lady superhero."

Perfect! I was so psyched!

Happy, but feeling like an idiot, I walked down the street to Clay's house. After he'd knocked off his pretty realistic Seth mask and headdress twice while trying to walk out his front door—yes, twice, don't ask—Clay and I headed to the school.

"Nice one, Amun Ra," said Andy Landers, who was dressed as what looked like a banana. He came around the corner behind us as we turned up the street to Haddful Arms.

"I'm over here," I said, hidden behind my awesome mask. Understandably, he thought Clay was me.

"What?" He did a double-take. "Why?"

"What do you mean, 'why'?" I asked.

"Well, you always dress like an Egyptian guy," he said. "Why are you Batman now?"

Was he so dense? "I finally I told my mother I didn't want to be a friggin' Egyptian pharaoh or Old Kingdom god or something."

"Yeah, but why *now*?" he asked, nearly slipping. Yeah, it was funny: a banana slipping. Never mind.

"Hey, guys!" called Roland Seymour. He was dressed in a long white robe and some kind of scarf.

"Hey, are you a ghost?' I asked.

Roland gave me a cross look. "Are you kidding? Of course not! I'm a guy from Egypt. Isn't this right?" He suddenly looked worried.

I recognized the *gallabiya* (traditional Middle Eastern robe) I'd given him for his birthday. But the scarf, which just sat on his head, was all wrong. "Here, let me fix that," I offered, reworking the scarf so it looked like a legitimate *keffiyah*, an Arab head scarf.

As we got closer to the school, I noticed that there were a few princesses, a scarecrow, and a couple of mummies ahead of us. Actually, there were several mummies. Funny. I guessed there must have been a sale on mummy costumes. And then I saw it. There was a giant pyramid made of cardboard at the top of the school steps. I immediately wondered what poor idiot had thought of being a pyramid for Halloween, only to find that he couldn't fit through the front door.

"Poor guy, I wonder who that is," I said under my breath to Andy.

"What do you mean?" he asked.

"The pyramid," I said. "Do you really not see it? Someone's costume didn't fit through the door."

"That's not someone's costume," said Andy, looking at me like I was crazy.

He kept talking, but by then I was totally ignoring him. Slowly, with each step into the school, reality hit me like a giant stone block falling from the top of the Great Pyramid. Hanging on the wall were large panels of hieroglyphs (absolutely nothing coherent, but fairly accurate images), and drawings of sphinxes, and big paper statues of the different Egyptian gods, and—

"Guess who, Amun Ra!" cried Marybeth, putting her hands over Clay's eyes.

"I'm over here," I said, starting to shrink in my Batman costume.

"Um . . . Marybeth?" Clay guessed.

"What?!" Marybeth gasped when she saw me. "No! It can't be!"

That was exactly what I was thinking. There was Marybeth, looking totally amazing. She was wearing a long white gown that draped around her, leaving her shoulders bare. She had a headband that held horns and a solar disc on her head. She was obviously Hathor.

"What are you wearing?" she asked, a look of horror on her face.

"I'm . . . ," I said, and then felt really stupid, "Batman."

"Why?" she asked.

"Because I didn't . . . I don't . . ." I looked around. It couldn't be. This couldn't be happening.

"The theme . . . ." My throat was seizing up.

"Duh," said Marybeth. "Are you such an idiot that you really came to the ancient Egyptian–themed Halloween party dressed as Batman? You? The guy with the most awesome Egyptian costumes ever?"

Then she looked at Clay in his (or rather *my*) costume.

"Wow, Clay, you look amazing." Was she batting her eyelids? Suddenly, I was invisible, and she no longer cared if I existed. Clay Koenig, in my poofy skirt and the ridiculous headdress of a bad-ass god, was all she saw.

"Come on, let's dance," she said, grabbing him by the arm and pulling him into the gym and onto the dance floor.

"Yeah, Amun Ra," said Andy, dragging his banana butt, "that's what I was wondering. Where's your Egyptian costume?"

"It's heading for the dance floor," I said, feeling like an idiot.

And it only got worse.

"The Queen and King of the Nile and the Halloween party this evening will be . . . Marybeth Fauntleroy and Amun Ra Marquis!" I heard Vice Principal Kramer announce about an hour into the evening. I'd spent most of the party with Andy, since he couldn't dance dressed like a banana and I didn't want to. We sort of leaned against the wall and were mostly invisible, except for when someone would come up, point at me, and walk away laughing.

Someone ran up to Vice Principal Kramer and whispered in her ear. "No, that can't be," she said into her microphone, not realizing that the entire school could hear her. "Are you sure? Goodness, you would have thought Amun Ra would have been the one . . . oh well . . . ." She cleared her throat. "Sorry, that's Marybeth Fauntleroy and Clay Koenig, the Queen and King! Come on up here, kids!"

And that's when I got to watch Clay and Marybeth walk on stage holding hands, get crowned king and queen, and bow to enormous applause.

Hurray.

"How was the party?" asked Mum when I got home. "Aren't you back early?"

I grunted grumpily, pulling off my Batman belt.

"Tru Heller-Roth called," she said. "She tried to get you on your phone."

My heart fell through the bottom of my stomach. "You didn't tell her about the Batman costume, did you?" If so, I didn't think I could ever face Tru again.

"No, I didn't," Mum said, tilting her head to get a better look at me. "Is everything okay?"

"You gave Clay my costume," I said.

"Oh, that old thing?" Mum said, hardly able to contain her glee. "I thought you didn't want it."

"Did you know?" I asked.

"Know what?" She looked up from the table, where she was examining a piece of a statue.

"The theme of the Halloween party," I said, trying to keep the agony from my voice. "It was ancient Egypt."

Mum honestly looked mortified on my behalf. She stood up and hugged me.

"Come on," she said. "Help me put this old pharaoh back together."

And that's what we did.

11
The Mummy Vanishes

All things considered—and I really mean all things—it was the worst day of my life. I don't mean 'worst' like 'most embarrassing' or even 'really crappy'—Mum pointing out all of the severed penises at the Egyptian museum, or Mum putting the dead mice in my birthday goody bags, or Mum sharing Mr. Tickety-Boo's entrails with the entire class. Or me as Batman. Even the scorpion adventure, which might have ended my life, or Mum getting arrested in Sudan . . . they don't come close. No. This was the *worst* day of my life.

Why? Because my mother disappeared. And it happened in the middle of the desert.

The whole thing started like one of a thousand expeditions we'd been on together. Well, not exactly. Mum had been mapping some ancient tombs near Kharga Oasis and theorized that there must be another group of tombs further into the desert where she'd noticed a hill that, from certain angles, looked like the head of the god Seth, ruler of the desert. As always, we expected Emad, a driver who we'd known forever, to pick us up at 5 a.m. But it wasn't Emad waiting for us outside the house that morning; it was a different guy neither of us knew. He was dressed in the traditional Bedouin *gallabiya* and *keffiyah* head scarf. He looked surly and didn't even get out to help us carry our gear.

Mum asked where Emad was.

"Fayn Emad?"

The driver shrugged, but said nothing. Mum knocked on the back door of the jeep for him to open the trunk. He grumpily got out and opened it, still not offering to pick up the obviously heavy packs that held our tools, tents, sleeping bags, and other supplies.

"What a jerk," I murmured to Mum.

"Hmm," said Mum, her eyebrow raised.

At that point, I was guessing that this guy had heard about the trip and had somehow taken the job from Emad.

"Should we call Emad?" I asked Mum, but she was already dialing. She waited. The phone rang. I mean, it rang in the jeep. The driver picked it up.

"Aywa?" he said, Arabic for 'yes.'

"This is Emad's phone," Mother said, speaking directly to the driver through the closed window.

He waved his finger, making a clicking sound with his tongue that signified denial.

"I am cousin," the driver claimed. "Emad sick." He did an impression of barfing.

There was something weird about all this. I suppose if Emad was really sick, he may very well have given his cousin the job. And his phone, in case we needed to call. Still. He would have told us himself.

I went to get DOG. She started growling at the driver as soon as she was near the car. Not good. She's never like this. I tried to calm her down, while Mum tried to calm the driver down as he was panicking about the dog. Finally, we packed up and got into the jeep. Sitting in the back with the pup, I rolled down the window. That was enough to calm DOG. She immediately assumed her favorite position—head hanging out of the window, tongue hanging out of her mouth. Questions aside, we were on the way to the desert.

It was a long drive through lots of sand—what's new?—and a rather bumpier than normal ride. As I've said, most people think of the Sahara as nothing but sand dunes. Not so. We drove through the Black Desert, for example, which is covered in black dolerite. There are parts of the desert around Bahariya and the Fayoum that are littered with shells and the fossils of sea creatures. There's the White Desert, which is (wait for it . . .) white, with amazing rock formations, and makes you feel like you're on the moon. We drove through the small oasis of Farafra, and then shot off on a shortcut through the dunes (yes, there are *some* dunes, but they only make up a part of the massive variety of terrain in the desert). DOG loved it. She got to run around every time we stopped, and got to hang her head out of the window when we were cruising. The sun was getting low in the sky as we were getting close to the campsite. It just is not smart to be driving around in the dark—the really, really dark—of the desert. Mum said they had set up camp a short drive from the excavation because it was rather rocky by the site.

As we passed through a village, Mum asked if we were stopping for supplies. The driver just drove through, so we assumed everything had already been purchased.

Then came the thing that was really odd and unlike any desert excavation I had ever experienced. We arrived at the campsite, and, normally, food would have been prepared and the tents would have been pitched and tables for artifacts would have been set up before we got there. But when we reached the campsite this time, nothing had been done. The Bedouin workers hadn't prepared the space, at all, and they were nowhere to be found. There is always a fire burning, and food, and a wind tent (a long colorful wall made of fabric that protects the campsite from blowing wind and sand), and a small tent for Mum to work in. Nothing was there. No supplies, nothing. Luckily, we still had a few sandwiches that we ate for dinner. We offered one to the driver, but he refused. And Mum had brought our own big tent that she likes to use for the finds from the dig. It looked like we'd have to sleep in it that night.

Odd as it was, we did not have time to worry about it. It was getting dark and we had to set everything up ourselves before the sun was totally gone and it was freezing.

And it was cold. We were wearing all of our clothes, in layers, since we did not have blankets. The ground was soft, so that was good. But throughout the night, DOG barked and growled. She gets excited whenever there are creatures outside the tent, so I didn't pay much attention. When I got up to pee, I took her with me. She howled and barked. I tried to keep her quiet, but something was bothering her.

In the morning, the camp was still ominously empty, except for the driver, who reluctantly stoked the fire and put on water for tea, and some other guy we didn't know. They must have gone for food, at least. I assumed that breakfast was going to be the usual. We always shared traditional *baladi* bread and honey, lentil soup, and, of course, tea. Most of the time—like, fifty times a day—tea is served sweet and black, except for breakfast when it's served sweet with milk. In the desert, we used powdered milk, since it was too hard to keep fresh milk from spoiling. Sometimes we had hard-boiled eggs for breakfast, using eggs bought from villages on the way out. That morning, though, we had to fend for ourselves. There was nothing cooked and no supplies that Emad and crew usually organized. There were no cans of *fuul*, or eggs, or anything, except a couple of half-eaten pieces of *baladi* bread that were hard as a rock and full of sand. Luckily, we'd brought a couple of apples and bananas and some *baladi* bread of our own. I couldn't figure out what was happening. The workers were nowhere in sight. The camp helpers weren't there, either. Only the driver and the other guy were just hanging around, smoking and drinking tea. We offered them bread from our bag, but they refused.

"Mum, this is weird," I said.

In the distance, barely visible in the early dawn light, we could see a jeep coming toward us. As it approached, we saw that it was Willem, our Egyptologist friend from the toilet adventure. He climbed out of his car and huffed over. A small fellow in jeans and a loose shirt followed him. I couldn't remember his name, but I had seen him on digs before. Behind them came a pick-up truck driven by two Bedouins, with four camels (looking bored, like always, and barely tolerant of their humans' shenanigans) sitting in the back. This was a common way of transporting camels long distances over asphalt without tiring them out, so that they were fresh when they reached the desert, where it was harder for the cars to travel but easier on camels' feet.

"Amilas," Willem said, catching his breath. "What are you doing here already?"

"What do you mean?" Mum asked, brushing crumbs from her shirt.

"We had word you wanted to start tomorrow, but we came today to view the site and campground." He was still panting.

"I never sent word to change our plans," Mum said, indignantly. "Who gave you that information?"

"It was in a note," said Willem. "Never mind, we have the gear and can start now, if you'd like."

"Yes, I'd like that." But Mother wasn't happy. "Is that why Emad wasn't there to fetch us? But why did that other driver have Emad's phone?"

"His phone? I don't know. Emad has packed his truck and is coming today," Willem said. "And the rest of the crew, too."

The driver from the day before came running over. He pointed behind him at six other Bedouins who were coming our way. DOG started growling and barking. I should have listened to her magical doggie sense when there is someone who shouldn't be trusted.

"I suppose he's brought a crew," said Mother, unhappy about this mix-up.

The guy with Willem muttered something to a Bedouin who was standing nearby. The Bedouin responded, nodding emphatically. He pointed over to the camels, which were being packed for the ride to the excavation site. There were two jeeps filled with gear, and the rest would be packed onto the camels.

"He's saying that these six men are the hired workers and that they are prepared," said Willem, doubt in his voice. "We can get started prepping now. When Emad and the other workers arrive, we can get the real work done, yes?"

"I suppose," Mother said. She was over at the other side of the camp. The group of Bedouins huddled together. They kept looking over at us, too, then huddling closer. It was very uncomfortable. "Did you hire those fellows, Willem?"

Willem looked over at the group of surly men. "I thought you did."

"Not me," said Mum. "Well, let's make the most of it. We should contact Emad. I hope he knows what happened." She began packing tools for the excavation.

I stood up and reached for a trowel.

"Honey, you stay here," she said quickly, taking the trowel out of my hand. I knew something had to be seriously wrong if Mum was stopping me from digging.

"What do you mean?" I asked. "I'm here to help you."

"Yes," she said. Then, turning her back to the surly Bedouins, she added softly, "And I need you to stay here and keep an eye on the rest of the tools."

"You think they're thieves?" I asked, throwing a glance over at the huddled group.

"I think they're up to mischief," she said. "I don't want to leave our things unguarded. Until we know who they are, who hired them, and the reason for all of these shenanigans, I want to keep an eye on them. I don't know what they're after. This isn't a dig that promises gold and jewels. The only value of these artifacts will be to the worlds of Egyptology and science. So what's their game?"

Indeed, what was their game?

"What should I do?" I asked, wondering if I should carry the trowel for protection instead of digging.

"Willem will be back in a couple of hours," she said, grabbing two of the GPS units from the table. "You stay here and keep an eye out. Don't approach them if they look like they're up to no good. I don't know if they'd be so stupid as to steal from the table, but they might try. Who knows?"

"I'll send Magdy with you, Amilas," said Willem, nodding to the fellow he'd brought. Magdy nodded, moving to stand near Mum.

"Okay, I'll keep a lookout," I said, patting DOG on the scruff. "DOG will keep guard, too. I'll do some homework with one eye on the page and one on them."

"And I'll take my phone," said Mum, grabbing her phone and sticking it in her sock.

"Mum, you're in the desert," I reminded her. "There's no reception. And why are you sticking it in your sock?"

"You never know, my boy," she said. "Remember, I have that electronic tracking thingy on the phone that will help find it in case it goes missing, and it's the special phone I got from the generous Floosbaganov grant. It should work in the desert."

She smiled, pulled me down to her height, and kissed me on the forehead. Then, very deftly, she climbed up on the back of her camel, which had been unloaded from the pick-up truck.

Camels are definitely from another planet. If you've never seen one, you cannot imagine how strange they really are. Big feet, weird neck and hump, and weird backward-bending space-alien-like legs are all part of the package. Although she didn't technically own the camel, he thought he was hers. Since he was old enough to ride, Mum rode him. She called him Khufu, after the pharaoh who commissioned the Great Pyramid of Giza. Khufu, like all camels, displayed a bad attitude toward anyone who tried to boss him around, but never toward Mum. We were there when he was born, and he'd been a constant companion whenever we were out in these parts. He always remembered us when we arrived, and would raise a stink, sometimes literally, if someone offered Mum another camel to ride.

Mum rubbed Khufu's nose and smiled at me, but I was suddenly strangely worried. On the kneeling camel, she was closer to my height, and I hugged her

Khufu

so hard that she almost fell off. She hugged me back. Something in my gut turned.

"I love you, Mum."

"I love you, Amun Ra." She smiled at me as the giant beast stood up in that awkward way camels do—front knees, and then back legs, all the way up, so you feel like you're going to do a flip over their heads and fall on yours. She hummed a few bars from "You Are My Sunshine," and Khufu hummed back. Yes, camels love music. In fact, it helps to relax them. What my mother was doing was arguably not music, but clearly the camel didn't mind her humming completely out of tune.

"Mum, I . . . I'm worried . . . I . . ."

She reached down—or, to be more accurate, dangled by her knees—and took my hand. I looked up at her in the glare of the desert sun. I so rarely looked *up* at her any more. Suddenly, it felt like when I was small, watching her work her magic, giving new life to the ancient dead. She squeezed my hand. "It'll be all right."

But she was very, very wrong.

I woke up because the sun was in my face. I'd been sitting in the shade of the tent wall, but the sun had crept over it at midday. Mum must have been gone for hours. I didn't know how it had happened, but I'd fallen asleep in my chair shortly after she left, my head on the table of tools. It was hot in the midday sun, even though the air was relatively cool. My face was stuck to a trowel and my neck was sore. My head felt thick and throbbed like crazy. It took me a second to remember what was going on: the weird circumstances of this dig, and the creepy guy who'd brought us here. The last thing I remembered was drinking some tea that one of the Bedouins had given me. It had tasted a bit weird.

I rubbed my eyes and tried to clear my head. I needed to check stuff. There were a few trowels and some brushes, but the other tools were gone. Maybe Mum had taken them. I couldn't remember. I got up to check out the campsite and ask someone where Mum was.

But there wasn't anybody to ask. I was alone. Impossible! No one leaves a campsite empty, and no one leaves a kid alone in the camp. But no one was there, not even the creepy guys. Not even . . . .

"Deee-Ohh-Geee!" I called.

I ran around the camp calling for her.

"Deee-Ohh-Geee!" I yelled.

"Deee-Ohh-Geee!" I cried, wiping the hot tears from my eyes. "Deee-Ohh-Geee!"

And then I heard it: a tiny whimper. There were three other tents besides ours. I threw open the first two, and they were empty. The third contained only a big wooden trunk.

"Deee-Ohh-Geee!" I shouted, and heard frantic scratching coming from inside.

I tried to open it, but it was locked! I grabbed a rock—a readily available tool in the desert—and smashed the padlock. I pulled open the lid. DOG was cowering inside. Her feet were bloody, and there were scratches and wood chips from where she had been trying to dig her way out of her prison. As soon as she realized that it was me, she howled and jumped up, but then fell back down. Her leg was hurt, and there was a gash on her neck. I picked her up and she yelped, a mixture of joy and pain. I held her, and she covered my face with kisses. Her nose was dry and her body felt hot. It was boiling in that trunk, and there was a small puddle of pee in the corner. The poor thing must have been in there for hours. I took her out of the tent so she could get some air. I put her down and she limped back toward me, whining and sniffing the air.

"DOG, I'm so sorry," I said, pouring water into a tin soup bowl. She guzzled it gratefully, looking up at me, asking for more. I gave her another full bowl, which was lapped up in two seconds. "Something is seriously wrong here, DOG." I wiped the blood from her paws. It wasn't as bad as I'd thought, though she'd nearly torn out one of her nails. The cut on her scruff wasn't deep, but it clearly hurt. I was furious.

I went to the kitchen area. Everything was gone. I ran back to our tent. Someone had torn through our stuff. Luckily, I always keep my passport with me, and it was still in my pocket. But my wallet and my clothes were gone. Mum's stuff, too. I hoped she had her passport on her.

And then I saw it. There was a jeep driving fast toward the camp. I ran over to the table and grabbed a trowel. It was the only thing I had to use as a weapon. I scooped up DOG and ran into our tent. I crouched down and waited. There was nowhere else I could hide. I didn't know who was coming. Was it help? Or was it someone who meant us harm?

I waited. It was probably a few minutes, but it felt like forever.

Peeking out, I saw the jeep skidding to a stop. I pulled my head back in and closed my eyes. I heard two doors opening and closing. There were voices, but I couldn't hear what was being said.

"Amun Ra!" came a shout. "Amun Ra, are you here? Are you okay?"

It was Willem!

I ran out of the tent. There he stood, looking pale and anxious. He had Emad, our friend and driver, with him.

"Here!" I cried, waving and running. DOG limped behind me, barking.

Willem turned and ran toward me. He grabbed me and hugged me. He was crying!

"What has happened to you?" he asked.

I explained to him about falling asleep, the tea, the dog.

He asked me to take him over to the teacup. He sniffed it.

"Lemon balm and valerian," he said to Emad.

"What's that?" I asked, suspecting it wasn't good.

"Those are sedatives," said Willem. "The herbs aren't harmful or poisonous, but they were clearly used to put you to sleep."

Willem's eyes filled with tears again. He wiped them and blew his nose. Then he sat down and insisted that I sit, too. Then Emad sat down, his hand on my shoulder.

"Those men, as we suspected, were not asked to join the dig. One of the Bedouins called Emad and the crew, and told them that the dates had been changed. Needless to say, the strange driver and the other Bedouins who showed up were not his cousins."

"Just to get paid for the dig?" I asked. "There has to be more to it than that. What's going on?"

"Son, we have just received word," he continued. "When I returned to the office, I had a message. They are claiming . . . ."

"What's going on? Please, tell me now!"

"I am so sorry. I do not want to say," he said, wiping his eyes again. "Amun Ra, they have kidnapped your mother."

I just stared at him. The words felt like they were fighting their way to my ear, but trying to keep from getting there at the same time. They reached me like some garbled message in a strange language.

"I don't understand," was all I could say.

"The men were pretending to be workers but were part of a band of kidnappers." Willem looked to Emad for help, but Emad was struggling with tears, too. "Amilas is missing."

"No!" I shouted, standing up. DOG jumped up, too. "She's out on the dig! She . . . it's not possible! We have to go to her! Now!"

In seconds, we were in Willem's jeep, driving out toward the excavation site. As we approached, I saw a camel galloping toward us. It was Khufu.

"Stop!" I shouted, jumping out of the jeep as Emad slammed on the brakes.

I ran to Khufu as he sped up and ran to me. As we met, he wrapped his long neck around me like an elephant's trunk. He squeezed, and I squeezed back. Then he rubbed his face against mine and nudged me with his big soft nose, grunting like he was trying to tell me something. He didn't have to tell me that Mum would never have just abandoned him and left him to wander alone in the desert.

He had a rope hanging from his neck. Deep scratches showed that he had been tied up and had tugged until he snapped the rope. I rubbed his nose and tried to calm him with a little song, but I was more worried than ever. Khufu would never have pulled himself free and run away if everything was okay . . . and Mum would never have allowed him to be tied up like that.

"Khufu must have escaped!" I shouted to the others, trying to keep my voice from cracking.

"Khufu, where's Mum?" I asked.

Before you think I must have gone nuts to be talking to a camel, you should know that camels are smart. Really, really smart. They remember everything, so you'd better be nice or they'll take revenge. I'm serious. That said, I did not expect Khufu to actually say anything back, but I would not have been surprised if he understood me.

Khufu let out a groan and hugged me again, whining like a baby. I could feel the blood rush from my face. He was telling me that something was very, very wrong. "It's gonna be okay," I lied to both the camel and myself. I rubbed his cheek.

We were near the site, so I rode Khufu the rest of the way there. The guys followed in the jeep.

At first, Khufu didn't want to go back. I had to urge him and tell him we were getting Mum. He reluctantly turned and headed toward the excavation site. As we approached, I turned back to look at Willem and Emad. They saw it, too. The prep area and equipment stores were a total mess. There had clearly been some kind of struggle—chairs upturned or broken, picks and trowels lying on the ground, all of the equipment scattered and broken or missing, and two of the new GPS units smashed to pieces—and the jeeps were gone. So were the other camels.

"Mother!" I shouted, running toward the site.

"Amun Ra!" I heard Willem and Emad shouting to me, but DOG and I ran to the site anyway.

I followed DOG down into the tomb entrance through the narrow opening.

"Mum!" I called.

I heard a groan. Someone was there! I felt around in the dark, found a torch, and flicked it on. Magdy, the guy who had come with Willem, was on the ground. He had a deep gash on his forehead, and his hands were tied behind his back. I had propped up the torch and was untying him when Emad came down through the opening. Willem followed, but had to struggle to get through the narrow space.

"Magdy!" he cried, and bent down to help me untie the poor man. We gently pulled Magdy up to stand, and then we all climbed out into the light.

"Bad men," Magdy kept saying. "Bad men."

Emad grabbed a water bottle from the jeep, and Magdy drank the whole thing.

"What happened?" asked Willem.

Magdy kept shaking his head. "*Mish kwayiis, mish kwayiis.* Not good, not good." We gave him a minute to catch his breath and adjust to the light. "We arrive, but they know nothing. They take *Doctura* Amilas—she fight, but they are big and many. They hit me, and *ana mish araf* . . . I do not know. *Ana asif*, I am sorry. I am sorry, I am so sorry."

"It's not your fault, my friend," I said, putting my hand on his arm.

"*Ana asif*," he kept apologizing.

Of course, there was nothing he could have done. I was sure he'd tried to stop them and received a thrashing for his efforts.

But whatever the case, the only sure thing was that my mother had been kidnapped. What if they hurt her . . . or worse?

With DOG at our heels, I rode Khufu back to the campsite and left the rest of them to the jeep. I needed a little time on my own. I had to think . . . or stop thinking. Gods, where was Mum?

Khufu was clearly thinking the same thing since he kept whining unless I sang. So I did. I sang "You Are My Sunshine" to Khufu for the entire ride back. It was his favorite song, and it was the only way to keep him moving. Every time I stopped to catch my breath, he'd stop walking and start whining at me. As I said, camels like music. By the time we got back to the campsite, there were five jeeps, and loads of men, some in uniform, some not, running around, setting up satellite equipment and looking very busy. There were clearly security forces and police, taking notes and shouting.

"I contacted the police before we left," said Willem. "We will find her, Amun Ra. I am sure we will find her." He tried to look like he meant it.

"I know we will," I said, trying to look like I meant it, too.

DOG was whining a lot—sniffing and whining. I had to put her on the leash, because she kept running off toward the hills, then running back and barking, then running off again. I couldn't risk her getting too far away and not being able to find her way back.

That said, she was a dog, and dogs usually find their way. In fact, dogs find a lot of things. As I sat there, watching her whine and tug on her leash, I suddenly realized: *She's a dog!*

"Willem!" I cried, "DOG is a dog!"

"Yes, she is," Willem said, sympathetically patting me on the head. He probably thought I'd totally lost it.

"No, I mean, she's a dog and has been running off in that direction." I pointed in that direction. "And . . . what if she's smelling Mum? What if she can find—"

"Son, these men are doing their job," he said, pointing at the policemen, who, at that moment, accidentally shorted out the satellite connection. They would have to send someone back to town for another.

"Right, I can see that," I said. "It's going to be another five hours before they can hook the satellite thing up again. What if we let DOG lead us? She's got an excellent nose and is very good at tracking things. It couldn't hurt to try." It seemed really obvious to me.

"These men won't follow that puppy to—"

"She's not a puppy any more," I said, defending her honor.

"They will not follow the dog," said Willem.

"Then *we* can follow her," I said. "It's probably a bad idea for a bunch of bumbling policemen to charge into some kidnapper's camp and attack, anyway. We can go, find the location, and get Mum out."

"I don't know," said Willem, scratching his big balding head. "I think you're right about the police charging in, though. It could go very wrong and someone might get hurt."

"Can we just follow DOG up there, over that crest?" I pointed up there, over that crest, in the direction DOG really wanted to go. "From up there we should be able to see if there's a camp or something?"

Willem looked around. One of the policemen accidentally spilled very hot tea on another policeman's walkie-talkie, which was now sputtering. The two were arguing about it. I think it really dawned on him, right then, that we if we didn't do something, we were otherwise leaving Mum in the hands of these guys who clearly had no idea what they were doing.

"We'll just go up to that crest of the dunes," he said, pointing over that crest of the dunes. "No farther, yes? It could be foolish and dangerous." Obviously, we could not chase the dog into the camp of the kidnappers.

We grabbed some bottles of water, since you never go anywhere in the desert without water. Ever. You can get dehydrated really fast in the dry desert air without even realizing it. I ran over to DOG and untied her leash from the post. She immediately started tugging hard in the direction of the dune. Willem and I followed. He stopped to say something to one of the policemen, then decided not to. They were clearly busy trying to deal with the equipment they kept breaking.

Whether we were doing the right thing or not, it felt good to be doing something. DOG still had a limp from being locked in that trunk, but she was moving fast. I was running and Willem was having trouble keeping up with us. I can tell you, running in the sand isn't easy. Only camels and horses seem to move fast in sand. And the farther we went, the farther away the crest of the dunes seemed to get. But we were moving. Our campsite was just a dot behind us by the time we got to the bottom of the hills.

"It's farther than I thought," said Willem, sitting on a boulder, panting and sharing one of our water bottles with me.

"I know," I agreed, handing back the bottle. "But it's not that far now."

The only thing harder than running in sand is running uphill in sand. Willem was sweating so much that the sand was sticking to his hands and arms. He was wheezing and had gone all pink. I felt a little guilty for making him do this. I should have gone on my own.

"I should have gone on my own," I said, handing him water as we sat on the side of the dune for another moment of rest. "I'm sorry, Willem."

Willem waved his hand to say 'no'—he couldn't quite catch his breath to speak. He drank and seemed to recover, and we set off again, as DOG was really tugging and whining.

After an hour or more, we reached the crest. Out in front of us was a vast field of dunes. But there was no visible camp or anything. My throat was dry, and now it just got drier. My heart was beating in my ears and I could feel a sob trying to get out. I'm sure tears would have come down if I'd had any moisture left in my eyes.

Now what?

"It's impossible," said Willem, finally able to talk. He looked up at the sky, and I knew he was thinking the same thing as me: if we took too long, it would be dark.

"But we know she must be in this direction," I said. It was a feeble attempt to sound hopeful.

"I hope so," he said. "But we don't know for certain." He shook his head. "If only her GPS hadn't been smashed, you know?"

"Wait! She has something better!" I couldn't believe I hadn't thought of this before. "She grabbed her phone before leaving this morning, which she usually never takes into the desert. It has that Find My Phone app on it. We didn't see the phone at the dig site, and she had tucked it into her sock when she left, so maybe she still has it with her!"

"That is very good news," said Willem, furiously doing something to his GPS. "I can't do any tracking from here. We must get back to the camp!"

Getting down a sand dune is significantly easier than getting up. We ran back down the dune (okay, we fell, stumbled, slid, rolled, and engaged in other undignified measures of self-transport down, but we got down). DOG wasn't happy about turning around and giving up, but she followed after us, occasionally tugging to go back up.

As we approached the campsite, we heard a lot of shouting and general kerfuffling. We walked into camp, and into a sudden silence as we passed the anxious men. Emad ran up to us, throwing himself at Willem.

"Sir, we had thought the worst!" he said, face buried in Willem's large chest.

"*Fayn?! Intu kaan fayn?!*" shouted a policeman who seemed to be in charge. He wanted to know where we had been.

"Us?" said Willem. "We . . . we were just walking the dog."

"Walking the dog?" Emad looked at us. We were covered in sand and sweat.

"Yes, well . . . ." Willem looked at me. "It was a long walk, and . . . ." He mumbled something. Emad was still looking at us oddly, clearly expecting more of an explanation later.

"It's important to let DOG get exercise. My mother is always insistent about that," I said, with whatever false authority I could muster.

After covering our tracks, so to speak, Willem took Emad aside to explain what we needed to do. Emad, besides being a driver, was an expert with technology and general tinkering. He had synced Mum's phone with his, as she'd kept losing it on the digs that they'd worked on together. He assured us that he would be able to find Mum as long as her phone was still with her and was powered on.

As my mother's tuneless humming was to Khufu, this was music to my ears.

Now he just had to get online and start looking.

We waited until the policemen and guards were having lunch, and then snuck into the tent with the satellite and internet equipment. Emad immediately started doing something that I will not even begin to try to explain.

And then, Emad's phone started beeping.

"I see it!" I said, totally excited. I could see the little dot. Then I was totally confused. "Wait, isn't that here, where we are now?" The GPS was beeping, indicating a location on the screen, but it showed where we were sitting in camp.

"That's your phone, Amun Ra," said Emad. "Your mother asked me to activate the same tracking system on your phone as well."

I could live with that. But where was Mum?

We waited for what felt like ages as Emad fiddled with his phone and with other things on the screen of the satellite system. Everything was silent. Then . . . his phone beeped again.

"Is that still me?" I asked.

"I think no," said Emad, without too much conviction. Was it too much to hope for?

Emad, Willem, and I all leaned in to look at the screen, but the cursed loading symbol was all I could recognize. It spun around and around for what felt like an eternity. The space was getting stuffy with my face so close to the others, so I leaned back for air. Then Willem made a sound like a tiny squealing mouse. I looked at him.

He smiled, nodding. "We got her."

The screen had finished loading and we could see her bleeping in the desert. We knew where she was. I watched. And watched. The blinking dot on the screen didn't move. Not at all. I started getting really worried again.

"It just means she's sitting in one place," Willem said, unable to mask his concern.

And then, at last, the dot moved. It moved in a zigzag, then in circles.

"Is she trying to escape?" I asked.

Mumkin," said Emad. "Perhaps."

"But it seems more likely," said Willem, now scratching his head, "that she's just walking around or—since it seems that she's moving at some speed—riding a camel in circles."

What was going on?

We had to have a plan.

"We have to have a plan," I said.

"I suppose that should not include our resident policemen," said Willem, looking at the crew of men standing around smoking, drinking tea, and eating whatever of our supplies they could get their hands on.

"Absolutely not. I can't imagine we'll do her any good by letting *them* know," I said. "And they might just put her in danger if they do get involved."

"Unfortunately, I agree," said Willem, with a sigh. I am sure he would rather have had a team of police on our side, having our backs as we headed into the unknown danger. But not this lot. "How far is she from here?"

"I am seeing it is perhaps ten or fifteen kilometers south. More southwest," said Emad.

"Do we take camels or cars?" I asked.

"We would make noise with the cars," said Emad. "I say camels. But we must be careful. These people could have guns."

Oh yeah, guns. I hadn't thought of that. Right. We would definitely need to be careful, but we had to go and had to go now. Or as soon as we could. Anything besides going in there on our own, and trying to free my mother and get out of there alive, would take too long! Every second we waited felt like a second too long. Getting help, organizing some raid or plan of attack, would just waste time, and put her and us in worse danger. If we could sneak in and free her . . . . But if they had guns . . . . yeah, I was worried.

"Thank you," I said to the guy dumping a spoonful of something grayish and gloppy onto my plate. Not that I would have eaten even if it had been something edible. All I could think of was Mum.

"It's some kind of porridge," said Willem. "I think we're running out of options for meals."

I offered the glop to DOG, who wasn't that excited, but she took a couple of nibbles from it. Khufu had untied himself and wouldn't let me out of his sight. I offered him some glop and, after sniffing it, he ate it. I sniffed the glop and opted not to eat it. Willem didn't bother sniffing and just tucked into his.

"The sooner we go, the better," I said, quietly. None of the other fellows there spoke English, but I spoke softly, just in case. "I know it might be safer going out in the dark, but . . . ."

"Depends on what you mean by 'safe,'" said Willem. "Wandering around the desert in the dark is never safe." He accepted a second bowl of gruel.

"What do you suggest?" I asked, refusing the offer of seconds from the fellow with the gruel pot. "Can we go now?" I looked up at the sky. It was still early, and we could definitely make it to Mum before dark. "Maybe now is the best plan."

Willem choked on his mouthful. "Now?"

"Well, when you're done with your meal," I said. "The longer we wait . . . ."

I didn't need to finish.

Willem nodded, swallowing hard. He looked at Emad, who was pushing the gruel around his bowl. He was as excited about this meal as I was. "Emad, we should go after lunch," said Willem, eyeing the gruel.

"I am with you," said Emad, pushing the gruel to Willem, who gladly ate it.

We were going to go, finally. All things considered, I was so glad we had Emad. He was the best navigator. The chances of not getting lost in the desert and not dying were significantly higher with Emad leading us.

"I will need a few minutes to gather equipment," said Emad. "Then, we go."

I'm not exactly sure what the policemen were doing. A couple of jeeps full of officers left. There were a few guys milling about, but I didn't see them actually doing anything other than snooze, walk around, smoke, and snooze again. If anyone was going to find Mum, it was us.

I had a great plan of stealth and cunning, to sneak out of the camp, find the camels, and head out to get Mum. But, to be honest, no one noticed us go. The camels were kept out behind the big tent. I don't know if the police even knew they were there. Taking the camels was safer, we all agreed. They weren't as noisy as jeeps and we could maneuver better if the terrain got too rough. Except for an occasional grunt, or fart, or snorfle, camels are silent.

Emad went over to ask the policemen if there had been any word. There hadn't. At least, not that these guys knew. We brought our dishes to the washing-up pile as the policemen settled in for an afternoon nap.

Was no ransom request a good thing or not?

"I'll ride Khufu," I said. Not only had he been over there before, but he would be like a bloodhound and sniff Mum from a mile away. Plus, he would have followed us anyway, and I knew he was worried. Yes, camels can worry. Khufu would be happier with something to do instead of sitting there, anxious, and wishing someone was singing to him. "We're going to find Mum," I told him. He understood.

We packed water, ropes, and tools. We had a wrench, wire cutters, and various pliers and trowels. There were only two pairs of binoculars. One of them belonged to a policeman who was asleep in my tent. I had no problem taking them from him—I'd borrow his binoculars while he was borrowing my tent. Fair trade. Willem, Emad, and I had each slipped into a *gallabiya* and had put *keffiyahs* (scarfs) on our heads. We decided that it would be better to be dressed like everyone else out in the desert; we'd seem less out of place if any locals saw us riding around in the sand. Willem and Emad mounted two other camels, and we headed out with Emad and his GPS in the lead. No one stopped us. No one asked us where we were going. To be honest, I don't think anyone at the camp even noticed.

As we rode along, I quietly hummed "You Are My Sunshine" as thoughts raced through my head. What would we find when we got there? How would we be able to sneak into their camp? Why had they taken my mother? Would our tools be enough to break her out of whatever shackles they had her in? Worst of all, I kept wondering if they would really have guns . . . and how we'd manage to avoid getting killed.

We headed further east, past the excavation site. It was then a rather long trek to the next ridge, which we made our way down slowly and carefully. Within the next half hour, we rode over one dune and around another. It was then that the oasis came into view. The sun was still high enough in the sky that we knew we had about four hours of real daylight before the shadows of dusk would begin to lengthen. Depending on how the kidnappers had set up their lookouts, we could easily be sitting ducks for anyone with a gun. Yep, sitting ducks. Or walking camels, more accurately. However you put it, we were going to be obvious to anyone keeping guard over that camp. I stopped humming. I was too busy worrying.

Emad was occupied with his tracking system. He'd brought along instruments that allowed him to use satellites to track Mum's phone. Or something.

Willem was sweating and in a general quiet panic.

"How are we going to approach the camp?" I asked him. "They might have guards surrounding the entire oasis, or . . . ." My mind was filled with a thousand awful possibilities.

"Indeed," said Willem, mopping his brow with his scarf. "We might have considered some other gear, something for protection, something like—"

"Bulletproof vests?" I suggested. I tried to crack a smile as if I was joking. I wasn't. Since we didn't know whether they had guns, bulletproof vests might have really helped. We should have taken them from the policemen. We should have brought the policemen. Maybe armored vehicles. My heart was pounding.

"This way," said Emad, pointing to the left. "There is a hill that will help us stay hidden."

We took the camels around the hill and came out slowly on the other side. Luckily, we were near the oasis, and there were a couple of scraggly trees and bushes that helped keep us out of sight. From there, we could check the oasis and scan the area with our binoculars. Emad and Willem each grabbed a pair before I could. I was about to say something, but decided they should have a look first in case there was something so awful it would traumatize me for life. That did not make me feel better. They scanned the area for a couple of minutes before I demanded to have a look. There were no guards that we could see. And then the wind shifted in our direction. That's when I heard it.

"Do you hear music?" I asked. I could hear music—*tablas* (traditional drums) and an *oud* (a traditional stringed instrument with a rounded body and a bent top). Both have very distinct sounds, and I could hear them coming from the camp at the oasis.

I focused the binoculars on the campsite, among the trees that surrounded the oasis. Something was definitely going on there, but it didn't seem like there were armed bandits guarding the camp. Just musicians and dancers having a serious party.

Willem sniffed the air. "I smell roasted goat," he said, licking his lips. Hungry at a time like this? Figures he'd be the one to spot the food. The wind wafted smells of roast meat and spices right at us. Even my tummy began to rumble.

"Are we sure this is the spot?" I asked. I was worried that Emad had gotten the GPS stuff wrong. It would be the first time ever.

He checked his phone. "No, this says the phone is there." He pointed at the oasis.

"Do you think it's safe for us to go?" I asked.

"Perhaps they'll feed us instead of killing us," suggested Willem.

"Maybe they find the phone," said Emad. "I do not know."

"But what if . . . ." And then I heard it.

I heard it, and my heart nearly pounded its way out of my chest. Khufu also heard it. He started groaning and whining, like he was singing. In fact, Khufu's whining didn't sound that different from what I was hearing from the camp. Off-tune and ridiculously loud, there was no doubt.

"It's Mum!" I cried.

"Yes, I can hear her . . . um . . . singing," said Willem tactfully.

We jumped on the camels and rode like the wind toward the camp.

We approached and slowed down. It was all I could do to keep Khufu from running into the middle of the campsite. We still needed to be careful. But as we entered the camp, things were not as we expected.

What we found there was pretty weird. A bunch of people were sitting around the campfire. There were three *tabla* players and an *oud* player and a few whirling dervishes, who were dancing around the middle. There were women with platters of food and . . . there was Mum. She was singing at the top of her lungs. At least, I think that's what she was doing. She was dressed in traditional Bedouin robes and a head scarf, but the noise was definitely Mum's version of singing. A woman was placing a big plate of food next to Mum, offering her meats, breads, and fruits.

"Mum?" I called, climbing down from Khufu, but the camel didn't stop and I tumbled right into the middle of everything.

The men jumped up. Mum stopped singing. The men and women yelled and someone grabbed my arm.

"Amun Ra!" she cried. "*Da ibni! Da ibni!*" she yelled, telling them I was her son. The men backed off and smiled.

"*Itfadalu,*" one said, welcoming us.

One of the veiled women immediately led Willem over to the food. He was clearly relieved, grateful, and hungry, though not necessarily in that order. He sat down and gladly took a handful of meat from the large platter he was offered. The women were making a fuss over him. Emad, too, was urged to sit. I was too busy hugging Mum.

"What's happening?" I asked Mum. After all the terror and worry, I felt flushed with relief. But what on earth was going on? Was she still kidnapped?

"I was kidnapped," she said, smiling up at me.

"What?" I gulped.

"Oh, don't worry," said Mum. "We've worked everything out."

I spluttered, and then words came out. "You've what?"

"Oh, yes, they kidnapped me at first," said Mum, as if she was sharing the story of afternoon tea with old friends, "but that's ridiculous, just stuff and nonsense. Would you like some goat?" She nibbled from a plate that was being passed around.

"Mum," I said, not wanting to eat any goat, since my appetite was at zero and, well, I don't like eating goats, "we were terrified. We were running around the desert, thinking you were in terrible danger and injured or . . . or something worse. We came to save you!"

"Save me? Pish-posh. You think I'd need saving from these fine people?" Mum handed me a piece of goat meat. It only fed my nausea, and I put it back down on the platter. She smiled and took it back. "Darling, it's true, they did take me. But you'll be so pleased to see what I've discovered. One of the sheikh's children was sick—and once I was able to heal his stomachache, they offered to show me their secret cave. Now, wipe that look off your face. I've never been in any danger, love."

The look stayed on my face. She popped a date into my mouth. I spat it out.

"Mum, we had no idea—"

"Well, of course you did," Mum said, nibbling around the stone of another date. "I sent word with Khufu."

"You *what?*" I was in an alternate universe. I was in Crazy Town. I was losing it.

"Khufu," said Mum, tearing off a piece of Bedouin flat bread. "I sent word with the camel."

"What are you *talking* about?" I said, loudly. Everyone turned.

"Now, don't upset them," said Mother reprovingly. "They've been very hospitable."

"Mother." I tried to collect myself. "You disappeared from camp, Magdy was tied up, I was drugged, DOG was beaten and locked in a box, and you're telling me that the people who did this were being hospitable and that you sent word with a *camel*? Are you *crazy*? How was Khufu supposed to tell us what was going on? By singing 'You Are My Sunshine'?"

"Don't be ridiculous," said Mum. "I sent a note."

I opened my mouth to say . . . I don't know what, but Mum had jumped up and gone over to Khufu. She reached under his saddle and pulled out a scrap of papyrus. She brought it back and handed it to me as she sat down to continue grazing on dates and figs. I unrolled the scroll. Emad and Willem both moved closer, so I read it aloud.

Dear Amun Ra,

I know it will be distressing when you find me gone. I seem to be in a spot of bother, and am finding myself apparently kidnapped by a clan of Bedouins. But fear not. These are good people. Word came to them that a doctor would be coming to the desert. In their confusion, they thought I was a doctor of the physical kind. Rumor had it that I was not allowed to leave our camp, so they devised an unnecessarily complex plan to spirit me away.

They're asking for nothing more than medicine for a sick child, the son of the sheikh, their leader. As it turns out, I have some tummy tablets with me, as I always come prepared, and I was able to help the child. I opted to forgo scolding them and reprimanding them for the kidnapping. As you know, I would have been happy to come and see the boy without all of this foolishness.

They kindly offered me a goat, which I graciously declined. It was then that they asked another favor of me. They've been haunted by spirits for as long as anyone knows. Apparently, their clan has grown and they need more space. There's a cave here, but it's off limits, guarded by the spirits of their forefathers. It's a long story I shall explain later. They let me have a look at this cave. You won't believe what's here! After much ado, which I shall explain when I see you, they've offered to present me with the items that are inside it, in lieu of the goat.

Darling boy, please let Willem and the others know I'm fine and shall be returning to camp the day after tomorrow. We shall come back to this oasis, bringing only a small team of Willem, you, and Emad to help retrieve the artifacts. They've assured me that they're thrilled to free their cave from these things.

Your loving mother, *Mum*

Willem, Emad, and I all stared at Mum.

"See, I told you I sent a note; I'm a bit surprised that you didn't think to check," she said, unfazed by our bewilderment. "Here, have this lovely dried fig."

"Mum, I don't want the fig," I said, feeling fury, anxiety, joy, and misery, all fighting a horrid battle in my heart and mind. "I still don't get this whole insanity."

"Amilas," said Willem, wiping his brow. "We set out into the desert to save you. Khufu, sadly, did not tell us that he was carrying a secret message from you and, since he speaks neither Arabic nor English, we had no way of knowing you weren't kidnapped. This all could have gone terribly wrong. We could have brought armed police with us!"

"But it didn't," said Mum. "And you didn't. And what's the use of all of this concern now that everything's fine? Wait until you see this cave, Willem. Wait until you see!"

"But Mum, you don't understand the truly awful state we were in." I looked to Emad and Willem to back me up. But they were already getting up and stumbling behind her, trying to keep up, as she led them off into the cave. I couldn't believe it! They'd dumped me for a cave full of artifacts! Utterly frustrated, I got up to follow. DOG, too. Could a bunch of broken stuff be worth the suffering we'd been through?

When we looked into the cave, the answer was a resounding YES!

The cave wasn't just a cave—it was a temple to the god Seth, Lord of the Desert. There were hundreds of statuettes of him, sitting or standing, some of clay, some of faience (a quartz or glass ceramic), some of stone, some with bits of gold on them. There was even one statue that had been inscribed and turned out to be dedicated to King Khufu, who built the Great Pyramid! There were tons of small stelae left by ancient travelers (who had hoped that the god would protect them on their trip through the desert) and several larger ones left by royal expeditions. I saw inscriptions with the names of King Djedefre (Khufu's son), of King Pepi (who had sent the explorer Harkhuf via the oases to the land of Yam; he had returned with a pygmy for the king), and of King Tuthmosis III. There were generations and generations of these offerings.

It was incredible. Nothing like this—so perfectly preserved and just sitting there in a cave—had ever been seen before by modern archaeologists in this region. This was really a remarkable find.

"And no one ever touched any of this?" I asked.

"You have to remember that these people, their families, have been here for hundreds, if not thousands, of years. Word would have been passed down from father to son," said Willem.

"Oh, yes," said Mum, "likely there were warnings from the elders to the young."

"But why not get the stuff out, if they thought it was cursed or something?" I asked. How awful to live next to a cursed cave of stuff!

"They feared that the spirits might cause them harm," said Mum. "The curse wasn't only upon these items, but there was also a curse upon anyone who ever tried to move them. This is the story that came down through the generations, but the origins of the curse and the reasons for it have been lost in the sands of time. It's like a game of telephone where the message gets garbled in the end."

"But why are they letting *us* in here?" I asked. "Why can we take stuff?"

"Because I removed the curse," said Mum.

"You what?" Again, Mum had given us pause.

"Well," Mum winked, "I removed that awful curse." She smiled, as if she was talking about picking a splinter out of someone's toe. "And I promised to send medicine for the whole clan."

I had to sit for a moment and try to get my head around all of this. Mum had been kidnapped, but had somehow flipped the whole thing into curing the clan of curses and illness. And we can't forget the unbelievable find! Ridiculous! Mum got kidnapped and we somehow got the ransom! Was that for real?

Of course, it was. Amilas 'Miracle Mum' Marquis! Would you expect anything less?

12
Love in the Time of Eggheads

I know I haven't spoken about my father. That's because I don't have one. I never have. No, I'm not getting all spiritual and talking about divine intervention or anything like that. It's just that it's always only been Mother and me.

Yes, there was a biological father, but he died before I was born. Mum doesn't talk about him much, but she has told me the story. His name was Bastiaan Thijs Luuk Janssen, and he was Dutch. And no, I can't pronounce Thijs, either. But this explains why I was taller than Mum by the time I was ten. It explains why I'm taller than average, redheaded, and fair of skin. Mum is a mixture of English, Portuguese, Indian, Pakistani, Egyptian, and a smidgeon of Ethiopian (Mum's great-great-great-grandmother was an Ethiopian princess, so I hear), and has olive skin, and dark hair and eyes. If you know anything about the Dutch, then you know that they're the tallest people on the planet (okay, maybe the second tallest people in the world, if you consider the Bosnians. Depends on who is asked). And the Dutch are generally fair-haired, fair-skinned, and, let's face it, look nothing like Mum. But the Dutch thing explains a lot when it comes to me.

Mum was in graduate school at Cambridge, and met Bastiaan Thijs Luuk Janssen, a brilliant Dutch graduate student who was also there studying Egyptology. Tall, dark-redheaded, brilliant, handsome, you say? That's where I got it? Indeed. They fell madly in love and were engaged to be married. The wedding was set. Actually, two weddings were set. One wedding was to be in London, for her family and friends of theirs from graduate school. One wedding was to be in The Hague for his family. The week before they were heading to The Hague, Bastiaan set off on a two-day trip to a newly discovered Paleolithic painted cave in the south of France. Mum had been feeling poorly (vomiting in the mornings, apparently, and craving pickles, chocolate, and peanut-butter sandwiches), so she didn't go.

The events that followed are still painful for Mum to recall. Friends of hers, colleagues who knew her from Cambridge, and other people from that time in her life have all told me pieces of the story. After two days, Bastiaan still hadn't returned. Mum called another friend who had planned to go. No answer. She waited. But after four days and still no

Bastiaan Thijs Luuk Janssen
and his friends at Cambridge

word, Mum went out to the excavation to find out what was happening. She arrived and found emergency crews digging, an ambulance nearby. She knew then that something very bad had happened. There had been a cave-in. Three graduate students and a professor were trapped. It was another three days before they found them. None of them made it out alive.

Instead of their wedding in The Hague they had a funeral. At Cambridge, they had a memorial for Bastiaan Thijs Luuk Janssen. Mum devoted the rest of the academic year to finishing her dissertation and defending it. And having me. What she'd thought was the flu was me. I was born the day after she was awarded her PhD. She and Bastiaan had already decided they would name their first son Amun Ra. She kept that promise. Technically, my name is Amun Ra Bastiaan Thijs Luuk Janssen Marquis. Thanks, Dad.

Mum never really dated or even looked for another man. She just was not interested. She had me and her work and that was enough. Oh, there were loads of creepy men—Egyptologists and non-Egyptologists— who tried to woo her. What a bunch of boobs. There was one fellow she met at a conference in Switzerland who sent her flowers and chocolates every day for a month. She wanted to send them back, but I ate the chocolates, so he kept sending them. Finally, he stopped. It was hard on me, I can tell you. They were good chocolates.

To be honest, I never much missed having a dad. Sure, there were times when I'd imagine what life would have been like if Bastiaan Thijs Luuk Janssen had been around. When I was small, I'd play games, like I was at a dig with Dad, or we would be cuddling in bed and he would tell me stories about Egyptian gods and I'd say "Dad" this and "Dad" that, pretending he was there. But that was rare. Mostly, it was Mum and me—just the two of us.

So you can imagine my horror when I came home from school one day after a meeting with the high-school counselors (a requirement for all eighth-graders), only to find Mum blushing into the phone and talking to some mystery man. Mum's voice was weird and soft. It was different from the way she generally talks when she's chatting about mummies and other work stuff. She was making little noises. She was saying things like, "I miss you, too," and "Oh, that would be truly lovely."

"Who's that?" I asked.

She jumped, and accidentally hung up on whoever it was. Then her phone rang. She giggled and grabbed for it before I could see the name of the caller.

"Hello?" she said, and her cheeks turned red. Mum was blushing! Then she turned her back and spoke softly into the phone, before walking into the other room.

I was totally irked. What was going on? I assumed that she was not merely excited because someone had found a baboon mummy in Saqqara.

"Who was that?" I asked, trying to sound casual when she came back, still blushing.

"No one," she said.

"It was a man, Mum," I said. "And you were blushing."

"It was not," said Mum, touching her cheeks. "I mean, it was a colleague. And I most certainly was *not* blushing." She was blushing.

And that was just the beginning.

I found out later that Sir Egghead von Douchenheimer was the mysterious caller. Fine, so that isn't his real name. Sir Edgar Makepeace DesChamps *is* his real name and it's almost as douchey. What I didn't understand was why she'd blush. She'd known old Egghead—okay, fine, he's not that old—since her days as an undergraduate at Cambridge. They'd lectured there together after receiving their doctorates. They'd even collaborated on a paper that traced a series of letters exchanged between a young princess in the royal house of the Thirteenth Dynasty (very late Middle Kingdom Egypt) and a suitor who was of slightly lesser royalty. It was actually pretty interesting to read about the intrigue, see the secret notes, and learn about the angry parents who eventually relented and let the two marry. Mum and Sir Egghead—I mean, Sir Edgar—had done all of the translations. Those translations were published as a book called *Love in the Time of Sekhemresewadjtawy Sobekhotep III*. Nubkhaes was the queen at the time, and was buried in a pyramid near Dahshur. The ancient lovers mention her in the letters.

The book was a big seller (that is, for a translation of ancient Egyptian), and Mum and Sir Egghead did a book tour around the UK. There was even talk of a film, but no one could pronounce *Sekhemresewadjtawy Sobekhotep*, or even Senebhenas Nen, the protagonist princess. Both Mum and Sir Egghead refused to allow the film folks to change the name to *Love in the Time of Cleopatra* or *Love in the Time of Tut*. So the whole thing kind of fell through.

I was too small to know what was happening, but Mum read me the letters and I thought they were cool. There was a lot of sneaking around, and dramatic statements about passion, and swimming across crocodile-infested waters to be with one's beloved, fighting with lions, and so on.

Anyway, it was really confusing that out of the blue, after however many years, all of a sudden, Mum was blushing when she and Sir Edgar started working on another project together. To be honest, it was embarrassing. And I got dragged into the middle of it. Okay, that might have been my doing, at least partly.

About three weeks after that phone call incident, Sir Edgar came over to take us out to dinner. At that time, there wasn't much worrisome activity, other than the phone call, to raise my hackles, and I was not yet suspicious. Well, maybe a bit. Sir Edgar arrived, and he and Mum did a nose-bumping attempt at a double-cheeked kiss. They both giggled. I just assumed this was no more than two friends, albeit close friends, having an accidental nose encounter. Did one of my eyebrows inadvertently rise up in protest? Yes, it did. But I coaxed it down. Mum wouldn't possibly be interested in her old pal.

"Great to see you, lad," said Sir Edgar, giving me a hug. Very un-English of him, but he spends a lot of time hanging out with Americans, Egyptians, and the odd Italian, so a hug and a double-cheek kiss were no big thing. "It's great to see you, much too long. I hear you're in year seven—"

"We call it eighth grade at the American school," I said.

"Of course you do," he said, laughing. "And I hear you've been an incredible help to your Mum. Saved her life with that scorpion? Rescued her from kidnappers? And cataloguing all those dog skulls. I'm sure that wasn't an easy task. Amilas, you're lucky Amun Ra was generous enough to put in all those long hours!"

Mum honestly looked surprised. It was like she thought of those long hours as a gift to me rather than a chore. "Well, you're right, Edgar. Amun Ra, did I ever thank you for—"

"No," I said, looking at Edgar, who looked back with empathy and a wink.

"Well, I thank you, my dear boy," she said, tiptoeing up to give me a kiss. I'm not one of those teenagers who gets embarrassed when his mother kisses him in public. Plus, this wasn't so public.

"For saving your life, or for scraping dirt out of eight million dead dogs' eye sockets?" I asked, folding my arms. I was sort of kidding, but it felt good. To be honest, I'd never really thought about me being the one who should get thanked. It's been my entire life, so getting a 'thank you' was never on my mind.

"I think she owes you thanks for both," said Sir Edgar, patting me on the back. "Maybe she can lead us to that fabulous Lebanese restaurant down the street and start counting up the thanks she owes you." He gave me another wink.

And I was buying it. I felt really good as I was getting my hoodie on. He helped Mum on with her jacket and scarf. But as we walked out of the flat, he placed his hand on Mum's back. Now, this wouldn't be a big thing if he hadn't then rubbed her back with that hand. Definitely suspicious. That said, the guy had just defended my honor, so I once again rejected my own instincts and pretended he was just being friendly.

And then Mum turned and looked up at him, beaming. Was she beaming because he'd rubbed her back? Or for being nice to me? Or . . . what?

Again, I wasn't yet clear on the gravity of the situation, so I assumed it was because they were friends, that's all. Sir Edgar couldn't possibly have other nefarious intentions. Not that kind, jolly, friendly old fellow.

At dinner, he asked about school, and about sports, and other things I might be interested in doing.

"Do you have a girlfriend?" he asked, casually.

I almost choked on my halloumi cheese. "Excuse me?"

"Sorry, Amun Ra," he said softly. "I didn't mean to pry."

"No," I said. "Yes, I mean, no." Why was this so complicated? "It's not about prying, I just don't have a girlfriend." Flashes of Marybeth Fauntleroy, and Sadia, and Tru, and . . . no, I didn't have a girlfriend.

"Well, there's plenty of time," he said, giving me a wink.

What was that wink for? I must have somehow been looking at him with that question mistakenly written all over my face.

He cleared his throat and looked uncomfortable. "I mean, a handsome fellow like you will certainly—"

"I'd like a hot chocolate," I called out to the waiter. My face was burning hot and likely red as a tomato.

A handsome fellow like me? Was this guy for real? I suddenly got the feeling that he was trying extremely hard with this man-to-man thing. Maybe it was because he thought I needed some kind of guy talk since I didn't have a dad.

"I'm not worried, thanks," I said, focusing on my lemon cake, which was suddenly less appealing. Still, I stuffed a big piece in my mouth so I didn't have to say anything else.

Sir Edgar opened his mouth to say something, then didn't. Phew. Mum was looking from me to him, to me, to him. I could see her out of the corner of my eye, but I refused to look up at either of them. When my hot chocolate came, I focused on that. I took a big gulp and nearly died. It was hot. I spluttered and chocolate foam went all over my face.

"Let me help you, Amun—"

"I've got it, Mum," I said, instinctively rubbing my face with my sleeve. Both Mum and Sir Edgar were just frozen there, holding out napkins for me. I felt trapped between them, but kept examining my hot chocolate and stuffing the last bits of cake into my mouth. I couldn't wait to get home and lock myself in my room.

The next time Sir Egghead came up in conversation, I gagged. I had been doing an excellent job at pretending I didn't know he existed, but he was calling the house way too much and I wasn't happy. By then, I was definitely sure that the guy didn't mean to be my friend. I was just a means to an end, and that end was Mum.

"Sir Edgar's organized a dig near Dahshur," said Mother. "I know it's late in May and it'll be hotter than we'd like, but the weather has been clement and it's near the site where we discovered the cache of letters all those years ago. And, as he and I had hypothesized, there appears to be evidence of a significant settlement not far from Dahshur. The doorjambs of some of these houses have inscriptions that provide the names and titles of the people who lived there, and I—we—are fairly certain that our princess and the treasurer lived there after they were granted dispensation to be together. If this is the case, and we can prove that they lived there and find out more details about their life, we'll have to revise much of the work presented in *Love in the Time of Sekhemresewadjtawy Sobekhotep III*, though that isn't a problem, as we've always worked and continue to work very well together . . ." (here she giggled!) ". . . and this presents an entirely new perspective on such a fabulous find, and we're both thrilled to see if this new excavation will lead to a deeper understanding of this pair, the times in which they lived, and the timeline of events that led them to—"

"Mum!" My head was spinning. She was rambling on and on, and speaking faster and faster. I think I'd blocked out everything she'd said after "Sir Egghead's organized."

"Yes, dear?" she said, out of breath and, dare I say, flushed.

"What are you talking about?" I had a sinking feeling, but I wanted her to tell me to my face.

"We're going on a dig to find fabulous things," she said, beaming.

"We're always going on a dig to find fabulous things," I said.

"Well, tomorrow we're going on a dig," she said.

"Great," I said. "Have fun."

"We will," said Mum. "So pack your things. We leave in the morning."

"I'll help you pack your things," I said. "And I'll wave and wave until your jeep is out of sight."

"Dear," Mum said, smiling. "Don't for a moment think that I would leave you behind. You're going to be with me when we excavate this dwelling, or indeed group of structures," she said firmly.

"Mum, I'm old enough to be left alone, and—"

"It's not about being old enough," said Mother. "This is an important event, and I want you with me. Tomorrow is a school holiday."

Like I said, there are always mysterious school holidays in Egypt. Lots of feast days and war-related days give us extra days off—in this case, just when I didn't need one. It was a four-day weekend.

"We can camp out at the site!" Mum smiled in anticipation of my own enthusiasm at the prospect.

"I don't want to go out to Dahshur and spend the night, Mum," I said, more harshly than I meant to.

"What . . . what do you mean?" Mum looked shocked.

I felt bad. "Mum, I . . . I've been to Dahshur a million times. I've got homework. And—"

"You can do your work out there," she offered.

"You mean like the time the camel ate my homework?" I reminded her.

"Well, we won't use your notes to trap scorpions," she suggested. "What work do you have?"

The truth is, I didn't have any. I'd already finished my work for the following Sunday (in case I didn't mention it, we have school Sunday through Thursday in Egypt) so that I could play my PS4 and not feel guilty. Rafiq (in Cairo) and Clay (in America) both got *Destiny 2*, as well, and we were going to meet online and play. I couldn't explain this to Mum, because she didn't know what 'meet online' meant, or what a PS4 was, or why this was going to be fun.

So I settled for:

"I . . . I kind of have plans," which sounded so lame compared to her babble of excitement about the Dahshur excavation.

"Well, how about coming out tomorrow for the afternoon, and . . . and I can have Emad bring us home in the evening," she said, smiling.

I was going to protest, but what could I really say?

"Okay" was the only thing possible.

Mum reached up and hugged me.

"I'm so thrilled!" she said. "I can't wait for you to be forced to spend time with the completely ridiculous and annoying Sir Egghead von Douchenheimer."

Fine, that isn't what she said. But it felt like that to me.

"I can't wait for you spend time getting to know Edgar again. We had that nice dinner together, and we all hit it off. You loved him when you were small. He's very excited."

I'd loved him when I was small? This was her measure of the man? I also liked pulling poop out of my diaper when I was small, but that doesn't make it a worthwhile activity. And the dinner we'd had was more 'hit-and-run' than 'hit' from my point of view.

"The dinner *wasn't* a hit," I said, maybe a little louder than I wanted. "I burned my tongue and was miserable, and he embarrassed me, and . . . and . . . why are we going to spend time with him?"

"Because he . . . he's a very good friend, and . . . and . . . and it would be nice." Mum wouldn't meet my eye. She suddenly started rubbing a crease into the tablecloth.

I felt a glob of something hard and heavy growing in my stomach. I didn't want to ask, but I knew I was going to. "Mum, is Sir Edgar your boyfriend?"

Silence.

It was like someone had sucked all the noise out of my ears and replaced it with a deafening nothing. The words seemed to swell and swell, until they filled the room and there was no place to hide from them. Why had I asked that? Did I really want to know?

I looked at Mum, who seemed to be doing some rather remarkable facial acrobatics.

I got up and left the room. I didn't want to know.

No amount of kicking, screaming, or throwing myself out of windows would have prevented my mother from taking me on that horrible expedition. So I didn't even try. I thought about it, but I didn't kick, scream, or self-defenestrate (yes, that's the word for throwing yourself out of a window. BTW—the Thirty Years' War in Europe was started because some guy was defenestrated in Prague—Mum and I visited that window. It looked like, well, a window). Instead, I sulked. I sulked in the kitchen. I sulked at the dinner table. I super extra sulked when Mum giggled on the phone to Sir Egghead.

"It'll be great fun," Mum said on the drive out to Dahshur.

"Says who?" I said, as full of grump as I could muster.

"Says me," said Mum. She beamed up at me.

As was appropriate for the situation, I rolled my eyes.

"You know, next month when we go to Petra, you can—"

"What do you mean 'when WE go to Petra'?" I nearly hit my head on the ceiling of the car.

"Well," said Mum, smiling at me, "I thought it would be fun to go, the three of us, since Edgar will be—"

"Oh, Sir Edgar is going to do something, so we all have to go," I whined. This was really getting a bit much, but I had to stand my ground. Sir Egghead was going to complicate my life, so it was my job to fight it.

Mum gave up her gentle tone and looked me straight in the face.

"Amun Ra!" She spoke with such force that I jumped again. "I don't know what's gotten into you! You spent time with Edgar when you were small, and you thought the world of him. You haven't seen him in two years, and now this? What's gotten you on the warpath out of the blue?"

"Out of the *blue*?" I was really shocked that she'd say that. Well, no, I wasn't. Yes, I was. No. No, actually. Typical. "Oh, that's typical," I said.

"Typical of what?" she asked. Her face was cross, but there was worry in her eyes.

And then I blurted it all out before I could stop myself:

"You want me to suddenly love this man, who I hardly remember, and who you are suddenly in love with, and you want him to come into our lives after my whole life of being the only person in your family, and now you're asking me to accept Sir Egghead, just like that?"

Wow, I couldn't believe I'd said all that.

"I . . . ." Clearly, Mum couldn't believe I'd said all that, either. She made some spluttering noises as she tried to form words. "I . . . I'm not asking that you accept him as anything more than a friend. My dear boy—my son—no one's going to impose himself on our lives. Edgar is a dear friend, and yes, we've become closer than . . ." (here I struggled to keep my hands from covering my ears) ". . . just friends, I suppose. But—"

"Are you going to marry him?" I asked.

"Am I what?" Mum's turn to blush.

"You heard me, Mum," I said. "Are you planning to marry him?"

And at that moment, I did something that I hadn't done in a long time. I wasn't happy about it, but it happened. Tears—hot, wet traitors—came pouring down my face. I wanted to shove them back in and tough it out, but I couldn't. And I suppose one good tear deserves another. Mum started crying, too.

She touched my cheek, which made my already overly wet face even wetter. It sucked. Then she took my hand. "My most wonderful son," she said, between sniffs, "I know it's been you and me alone against the world forever. No one will ever, EVER change that, or get between us, or do anything to alter the fact that we're a team. You've been my best friend, my companion, my colleague, my comrade, my savior, and my child. You are my past and future, and you . . . you are *you*. You are your own man. I know that not everything I love is necessarily something you love. And I know that I've forced you to do lots of things—lots of smelly, embarrassing, challenging things. But having you with me, getting to share the desert and the ancient magical past with you, has been the best part of my life. In some ways, you've raised me as much as I've raised you, Amun Ra. I think that's the way it goes with parents and kids. Nothing will ever change that."

"But . . . B-but . . . ." That was about all I could get out for several minutes. Finally, through hiccups, snorts, and a rather large gob of snot, I managed: "But it will change. Sir Edgar is a colleague. I'm just a kid. Your passion is being out there, being a hero, rescuing the past, bringing it into the present, offering it to the future. You and Sir Edgar will . . . ."

"Are you really afraid he'd take me away from you?" she asked.

I opened my mouth to say, "No! Of course not!," but instead I said, "Yes."

"Never—totally absurd!" Mum shouted. She hugged me so hard. And, I have to say, I believed her.

By the time we arrived at the site, we were something of a mess. Lots of snot and tears had left both of our faces blotchy and red. Sir Edgar was waiting there, waving as we pulled up in the car. When he saw us, his arm came down and he looked worried.

"What happened?" he asked in a panic. "Are you all right?"

Neither of us could talk. He looked from Mum to me, and back. Then his cheeks turned red. He waited, but Mum and I didn't make a move to get out of the car. The driver said nothing and let us sit. Then Sir Edgar opened the door.

"Come on," he said . . . wait for it . . . "Let's have a cup of tea . . ." (of course, he's English) ". . . and talk."

Instead of being mortified, we followed, Mum and I still clinging to each other.

A tent was set up, and we sat down at a small table inside, Mum still holding my hand. Sir Edgar brought three cups of tea on a round tray. He added milk and sugar to mine without asking how much. I'll admit, he got it right.

"Now," he said, "I'm going to be brave here. I think there's something that we should talk about. Would you like to go first, Amun Ra?"

I shook my head and sipped my tea.

"Amun Ra is afraid you'll take me away from him," said Mum before I could stop her.

"I'm neither going to act surprised nor claim this is unfounded," said Sir Edgar. His face was serious. He wasn't trying to act with me, and I could see he was trying to be honest. "Your mother, as you know, is an amazing woman. You are the luckiest fellow in the world, because you get to spend every day with her. She never left you behind on any adventure, did she? Now, it might have felt like a pain at times, always being dragged along, but you know how lucky you are? My parents were rarely around when I was young. I had endless nannies and tutors. I see what you have, and I know how special it is."

I realized that he was right. So many kids I knew rarely saw their parents. Mum and me, we were together all the time. It was a pain sometimes, but on the whole we did tons of cool things together that no one else I knew ever did. I looked at her, and tears were flowing once again—on her face, not mine; I was keeping it together this time.

"I will never take your mother away from you, Amun Ra," said Sir Edgar. "But I do love her. Yes, I do. I love her, and I think she is the most amazing woman on the planet. Part of what makes her so amazing is that she's your mother and you are her son. All I ask is that you give me a chance. See if I'm worthy of acting as suitor and winning her heart . . . and yours. I ask that you get to know me, and see if I might possibly, with your permission, have a place—a small place, or even a part-time place—in your family. As an addition, but not as a replacement for anyone."

I was still not ready to suddenly roll over and let the man move in or anything. That said, he was being reasonable. I guess. But . . . I was still scared. I was almost as scared as I was when she disappeared. It felt a little bit like that. "Are you asking for her hand in marriage?" I asked, swallowing hard.

"I am asking that you give me some time and see how we all fit," he said. "Then we can take it from there. Does that sound fair?"

I looked at Mum, who still had tears running down her face and was uncharacteristically quiet.

"Mum? Do you love Sir Edgar?"

Sir Edgar cut in. "Please call me—"

"Don't say 'Dad,'" I warned.

He laughed. "I was going to say 'Edgar' or 'Ed.' The 'Sir' bit makes me sound so much older than I feel."

"Do you love him, Mum?" I asked again, since she hadn't answered.

"I . . . I do," said Mum, still sniffling, still holding my hand. She looked over at Sir Edgar.

"And you, Sir—I mean, Edgar—do you really, really, really love Mum?"

This was getting a little weird, but I really wanted to know, even if he'd already said it.

"Amun Ra, I have loved your mother for longer than you have been on this planet." He smiled and—wait for it—*he* started crying. This was getting ridiculous.

But through the silly tears, and running noses, and the occasional hiccup, I could see it in their faces. I knew, at that moment, that everything was in this weird balance, and I was the one who held the power. I could say, "Absolutely not! In no way will Mother ever marry you, you cad!," and Mum would take this to heart, and that would be the end of it. But who would I be if I said that? "Well, I'm willing to take things slow," I said.

"That's all I ask, son," he said. "And I use 'son' in the most general sense of the word. No imposition intended."

"None taken," I said. And this led to a very uncomfortable silence.

"Um . . . shall we say three years?" asked Mum finally.

"What?" I asked, not sure what she meant.

"Ah, yes," said Sir Edgar. "A three-year trial period. We can call it an engagement. Will that suit you, Amun Ra?"

I considered. Three years would get me to the end of my penultimate year in high school. I'd rather have said nine years, but I had to compromise. "That sounds reasonable," I said. "I could do three years."

"Excellent," said Sir Edgar, beaming. "It's settled, then."

I smiled.

"I guess that gives us time to decide where to go on our honeymoon."

~~Sir Egghead~~ and Mum
Edgar

Epilogue: Facing Facts ... and Artifacts

Well, there you have it. The long, sordid, crazy, often messy, sometimes smelly, wacky life I have shared—and continue to share—with my mother, Amilas Marquis. These events, as recounted and remembered, tell how my life looked in those days. While this is the story told from the perspective of my nearly-fourteen-year-old self, I have grown quite a bit since then. You might suppose that, as I grew, my interests would shift as far from Egyptology as possible—I certainly spent enough time pretending to want nothing to do with the subject. You might imagine that I grew up and became a particle physicist, or a circus clown, or a poet, or an acrobat, or even an accountant. Of course, considering the excitement of my young life, that assumes I actually did grow up and did not die of embarrassment. Funny thing about embarrassment. Apparently, it does not kill you.

I have wondered about growing up. I don't mean getting older, because I did. Growing up might be a different thing than getting older. I still love winning at Scrabble, playing Settlers of Catan, skiing, hanging out at the beach, eating chocolate and pizza, and playing with Legos. Don't think for a moment that I've grown up *that* much! But now I do those things with my wife and children. Crazy, I know. But it's true. I, Amun Ra Bastiaan Thijs (pronounced 'Tice'—yes, I eventually learned Dutch) Luuk Janssen Marquis, am now for all intents and purposes what is referred to in the vernacular as 'an adult.' Worse than that, I'm (wait for it . . .) an Egyptologist.

Yes, it is true. I am an Egyptologist. If you can't beat 'em, join 'em, I guess.

The truth is, as I discovered the hard way, there's no job better than this. I get to run around the desert, abseil down cliffs, crawl into tombs, play with skeletons, read hieroglyphs, and spend

Ramses sand surfing, White Desert

lots of time with Mum and Tru— yes, it's true (no pun intended), Gertrude Heller-Roth Marquis is my wife and colleague. We met again in graduate school at Cambridge. Needless to say, I didn't let her go on a dig before our wedding. Let's just say I'm superstitious.

So I now get to spend my days with Mum, Tru, the kids, and Edgar. Yes, as the story goes, Mum married Sir Edgar, the former Sir Egghead. For the record, the honeymoon in Rome was awesome! We had a blast! And you know what? Edgar is the best grandfather

Ramses and Imi in Saqqara

Ramses and his major find

my children could ever want. My children, Imi and her little brother Ramses, are huge fans of Egyptology. Imi loves it. She and Mum are thick as thieves. Ramses . . . well, he does a lot of eye-rolling, and prefers to play football with his friends (real football, not that American one that includes very little foot and a lot of ball), and does his best to avoid us whenever possible. And for some reason, he always pretends that his name is Ron, or Richard, or Rex. But when we go into the field, he always joins us—he's even made some rather important discoveries.

And I have a great idea for his next birthday party. I was thinking of building a cardboard tomb in the living room, and we could all dress like ancient Egyptians and act out a whole funerary sequence. If there's time, we could even reenact one of Ramses II's battles in the garden. Building the chariots would be a blast! We can serve barbecued liver, oxtails, beans, kidneys, radishes, cucumbers, and the other foods of ancient Egypt. Too bad we can't get our hands on some hyena meat. Mum and I also have a pretty amazing idea for a cake. What great fun! I'm sure he'll love it.

It is possible that he'd prefer something else. All he needs is a little time. I'm sure he'll come around.

Glossary

abseil   If Spiderman could not stick to walls, he would be abseiling down the side of buildings. Abseiling, or rappelling, means climbing down a sheer face of rock using a rope. You see rock climbers do it all the time. It helps if you hang your butt down and put your legs on the rock face at a 90° angle. Then you can bounce down the side of anything.

alhamdulillah   Praise be to Allah (God). Everyone in Egypt and Sudan always say it—there is a lot of gratitude to God, always, even when things aren't so great, as God's will is supposed to be perfect. I try to say it when Mummy is particularly difficult, so I use it often.

Amun Ra   Chief god of the ancient Egyptians from about 1550 BC onward and the totally coolest god ever, even with two feathers coming out of his head. Objectively speaking. He was often painted blue, which was expensive and hard to make, as far as colors go, and really did have two feathers coming out of his head. The big temple at Karnak near Luxor was dedicated to him, as was part of just about every temple made from about 1800 BC onward.

Anubis   Possibly Mother's favorite god? Chief of embalmers, who was shown as some kind of super canine, sometimes as a man with an animal head. He did have a dog head. Or jackal. Or wolf. Doggish. Definitely a friend to the dead.

baculum   I'd rather not do this but, since you asked . . . here it goes . . . The bone in the penis of dogs, cats, and some other animals. Yes, some animals have a bone in their penises. Ha ha, very funny.

basbousa   My favorite Egyptian dessert, a semolina cake soaked in sugary syrup, with hazelnuts or almonds stuck on top.

bawwab   Doorman (*bab* is 'door' in Arabic). But they do more than open doors—they run errands; sometimes fix things; help around; clean the hallways and water plants. Sometimes they don't do much.

bowel   No, this is not something you put your cereal in—that's a 'bowl'. This is b-o-w-e-l and everyone has bowels. Except mummies. Their bowels are in canopic jars. Bowels are your intestines. If you poo, it's called a BM or bowel movement. Had enough?

canopic jars   You remember that when you are mummified your lungs, liver, intestines, and stomach are taken out? Well, they get mummified individually and each one gets to be put in a jar. Until about 1550 BC the jars were not too exciting; then they started having human heads; and then, in about 650 BC, each had a different head, belonging to the god who was in charge of the body part. So, there is Imseti, who has a human head and is in charge of the liver (no clue as to why—liver is not my favorite food); Qebesenuef has a falcon head and looks after the intestines (raptors love to rip open the belly and pull out the intestines); Hapi the baboon watches over the lungs (ever heard a baboon? loud, because they have good lungs), and Duamutef with his dog/jackal head takes care of the stomach (and yes, if a jackal attacks a carcass, it goes for the soft belly first).

cursive   Seriously? Okay, joined-up handwriting. It used to be taught in school, Mum says, but you'd never know that from looking at her writing.

dervish   Really cool Muslim holy men who put themselves into trances so that they are closer to God. Many of them are known for whirling (as in 'whirling dervish'), and even though they do this for religious purposes, you can watch them dance.

elucidate   Literally, enlighten or make clearer or brighter. Lucid, you know? Light, clear.

enema   Really? You still don't get it? Or are you torturing me on purpose? This is a way to clean out your lower bowels or get medicine into your lower intestines. An enema is a procedure in which liquid is injected into the . . . up your . . . through the . . . oh, please. Read the book. Use a dictionary.

evisceration   All righty. To remove the viscera (internal organs). Literally, spill your guts.

excerebration   More fun. To remove the brain. Either through the nose, breaking the bone (called the ethmoid) that stops the snot from going into the skull, or by removing the head from the neck and using the hole at the bottom of the skull.

faience   Non-clay ceramics, made of glass or quartz, generally colored blue or green. Lots of those scarabs are made of this; so are small figures of gods. And bowls (not bowels).

feces   In one word . . . poop.

fuul   Egyptians' favorite dish. Fava beans are cooked slowly in water in special pots overnight. You eat it with oil and spices, tomatoes, chillies, and bread.

gallabiya   Traditional robe worn by men and women in the Middle East. No, it's not a dress. But, yes, it can look like one.

gauze   Thin cloth, often ripped into bandage lengths.

gebel   'Mountain' in Arabic.

Gebel Barkal   A site in Sudan where the god Amun came from. A mountain in the shape of a rearing cobra is at the center, with temples all around. Travelers used it as a landmark. Tombs (pyramids!) and houses are not far away. Local folks still think it's a sacred place.

habibi/habibti   Arabic for 'my love' or 'my dear.' Feminine forms end with 't', just like in ancient Egyptian.

halloumi   A kind of white cheese you can grill. Really good and chewy. Squeaks between your teeth.

inertia   The opposite of excitement or enthusiasm or action. Sloth, shlumpy, couch potato. Basically, the state of not moving or changing or doing anything. Same root as 'inert.' Not 'a nerd.' Like an inert gas. No, not that kind of . . . never mind.

intestine   It's the long twisting tube that takes stuff from your stomach to your . . . just see 'bowel.'

ithyphallic   Why is this here? Let's just say 'phallic' is related to . . . the part of the body pretty much only men have. Fine, it's the penis. 'Ithy' means, well, erect, from the ancient Greek. So, ithyphallic, well, that's when there's something standing at attention and I bet you know what that is. Don't tell anyone I told you.

Kharga   An oasis in the south of Egypt, probably the largest oasis in Egypt and one in which I have spent Far Too Much Time with scorpions.

Lower Egypt   Opposite of Upper Egypt—and this seems totally backwards. Since the Nile runs south to north, it all made sense back in the day. Lower Egypt is the northern part of Egypt, basically from Cairo to the end of the Delta, which is closer to sea level. In ancient Egypt the papyrus and the cobra goddess, Wadjet, were symbols for this part of the country.

Luxor   This would be the city that now stands upon the ground of ancient Thebes. Lots of awesomely cool ancient stuff, including sphinxes and the Karnak temple, Valley of the Kings, home of King Tut's tomb, and lots more.

mummy   Well, before we even address this, THEY DO NOT WALK! A mummy is the preserved body of a human or animal (and there are a lot of mummified animals, believe me). Many cultures traditionally mummify their dead (most notably Egypt, in case you haven't worked that out) and sometimes bodies can be naturally preserved, like in bogs or ice or really dry places. Those are also mummies.

mushkela   'Problem' in Arabic. This is used all the time, often in the phrase 'mifeesh mushkela' which means 'there's no problem' and that is often not true. *Mushkela kibira*: Big Problem . . . like Elvis Aaron Presley Floosbaganov and Shaker Babek.

Narmer Palette   An object of embarrassment and misery. And the first artifact that lays out all the rules for Egyptian art as well as (maybe) being a record of the victory of a king from the south of Egypt over the northerners. Some cool smiting going on, as long as you ignore the embarrassing stuff.

penis   Does this really need to be in here? Who put this in the glossary??

putrefy   Or, as I think of it, doing the big yuck. Okay, lots of things around here can be qualified as doing the big yuck. How about doing the big-rotting-mess-of-goo-that-used-to-be-living-matter-but-now-has-decayed-and-stinks yuck? Anyway, rotting away and being stinky should cover it.

pyramid   C'mon! The big pointy things (four triangles, leaning in on a square base) that pharaohs used to be buried in from about 2700 to 1700 BC. What people don't know is that some kings made a bunch of smaller pyramids all over Egypt to show their power and strength, but were not buried in them. There are more than eighty pyramids in Egypt, and a bunch more in what is now Sudan.

register   The first time we see one is on the Narmer Palette (where all the rules of Egyptian art first appear). It's a line that divides a space so you show different activities over time, and there is a line for people to stand on.

runnel   A narrow channel that things flow through. If you cut a straw in half lengthwise, you have a runnel.

Sahara   Really? The big desert all over North Africa. Cool thing, in Arabic, *sahara* means 'desert,' so when you say the Sahara Desert, you are really saying the desert desert . . . yup, king of all deserts, filled with snakes and scorpions. Oh, and sand.

Schreger lines   Lines (actually microscopic tubes) that create a pattern of cross-hatchings or elongated diamond shapes that are visible on elephant teeth when they are cut open. Experts use them to distinguish elephant ivory from hippopotamus ivory, bone, and plastic. Obviously, some German guy called Schreger noticed them first, so they are named after him. Similar lines/lozenges can also be seen on the outer, shiny part of the elephant ivory, and these are sometimes called the lines of Retzius after some Swedish guy—yes, it gets confusing. All one really needs to know is that elephant ivory has these and hippos, walruses, warthogs, whales, and plastic (I kid you not, there is some really good fake ivory!) do not.

Sekhemresewadjtawy Sobekhotep III Um . . . yeah, she was real! And, yep, it's pronounced the same as it's spelled. Good luck with that!

serpopard A cool mythical beast that is a combination of a leopard (body and head) and snake (neck). Get it? Serpent . . . leopard . . . very clever.

Seth God of the Desert, controller (and sometimes bringer) of chaos. The animal associated with him still has not been identified (combinations of aardvark, donkey, anteater, and bush pig have been suggested), but Mum is determined to figure out what he was, or what combination of animals he was. At least this means we get to go on safaris in Kenya and Tanzania.

Seti I King of Egypt. He ruled from about 1323 BC until 1279 BC and made some of the most beautiful temples in Egypt. His mummy is pretty cool too—he looks like he is napping and will open his eyes any moment. A bit creepy when you are stuck in a room with him at night by yourself (another story . . .).

shib-shib Arabic for 'slipper,' 'flip-flop' (kind of the same idea), or 'thong,' as in footwear, not underwear.

smite Getting whomped, hit with something hard, like a mace (stick with rock at the end). Usually we think of gods or pharaohs doing the smiting, but sometimes people get smitten (yep, that's the word!) when they fall in love.

stela (plural is **stelae**, but if you want to be Greek about it, it's **stele/steles**) One of those pieces of stone with carvings on them. They fill museums, temples, tombs, and sometimes our house. They generally have a picture in the top part showing whoever commissioned the stela, with a text underneath that explains what it is all about. Kings set them up in temples sometimes to commemorate victories in battle, or as gifts to the gods. In tombs they generally have prayers to the gods so that the dead guy has a guaranteed entry to the afterlife.

striations A series of lines or ridges.

Tut Better known as King Tutankhamun, who ruled Egypt from about 1332 to 1323 BC. He came to the throne when he was about nine years old, and died (no one is sure from what, but he probably had malaria, and might have injured his leg that got infected and caused his death) when he was about eighteen or nineteen. He might have fought a battle or two, but he is most famous because his tomb was found almost completely intact in 1922, by a guy called Howard Carter. This was pretty unique, and the gold, jewels, chariots, weapons, and other stuff in it (even his underwear!) are a clue to how kings lived.

Upper Egypt Opposite of Lower Egypt (duh!). The southern half of the country—remember, the Nile flows south to north because the land in the south is higher. Lots of high limestone cliffs here to cut tombs into.

Yalla! 'Come on' in Egyptian Arabic.

Acknowledgments

We are most grateful to Nigel Fletcher-Jones, Neil Hewison, Jody Baboukis, Cyrus Unger Bowditch, Lyric Unger Bowditch (for all her help on every page), Abdelrahman Orabi, Brandon Zerr-Smith, Steve Parke, Kazel the Camel, Laura and Olivia Ibrahim for being properly shocked and dismayed by entrails at the museum, and their mother, Nadine Ibrahim, who allowed them to participate, Francis Dzikowski for his devotion to dead bunnies, the AUC Bunny Mummy Gang, Ken Garrett for adventures throughout Egypt, Daan Jordaan, Anna-Marie Kellen, Anastasia Liakhnovich, Wendy Vissar, Sandra Guirguis, Fayzal Haikal for her handwriting, Kent Weeks for the cuffs, the staff and objects of the Egyptian Museum, and the spirits of Barbara Mertz and Joan Hess.

Photo credits

Francis Dzikowski: p. 18
Nigel Fletcher-Jones: p. 154
Kenneth Garrett: p. 23
Salima Ikram: pp. 45, 94, 116
Abdelrahman Orabi: pp. 39, 40, 47, 52, 56, 186
Leslie Warden: p. 185
Unger Bowditch family collection: pp. 8, 81, 126, 138, 174, 187, 188
Lyric Unger Bowditch: pp. 16, 124
Anonymous donor: p. 85
Photograph production by Nigel Fletcher-Jones and Lyric Unger Bowditch